Just a Girl in LA

"I WANT TO BE WITH YOU. IT IS AS SIMPLE AND AS COMPLICATED AS THAT." – CHARLES BUKOWSKI

LAURA MULLALLY

authorHOUSE®

AuthorHouse™ UK
1663 Liberty Drive
Bloomington, IN 47403 USA
www.authorhouse.co.uk
Phone: 0800.197.4150

Published by AuthorHouse 10/18/2018

ISBN: 978-1-5462-9554-9 (sc)
ISBN: 978-1-5462-9555-6 (hc)
ISBN: 978-1-5462-9553-2 (e)

Print information available on the last page.

Dedicated to all the girls with messy buns, red lipstick and wild hearts.

Prologue

Dear Universe, how did I end up here? How did this happen to me? I never believed in fate or miracles. I just believed that things happened the way they did, in no particular order and with no particular purpose. That life was just a series of unrelated events, all with no rhyme or reason. I believed that life gave us highs and dealt us lows, brought people into our lives, and took them out again. That was just the law of things, the natural order, right? Of course, some people get a better deal than others and my life had been pretty standard, at least up until now. A year ago, I would've never guessed things would be this way. After all, I was just a girl in LA.

—Ellie Gibson

Chapter 1

My computer dinged again, snapping me out of my daydreaming. Another email! God, it had been a long day. I'd had a feeling from the moment I stepped into the office this morning that it was going to be a tiring eight hours, and I had been right. I leaned my elbows on my desk, resting my head in my hands, rubbing my temples as a headache started to creep in. Shutting my eyes, I drew in a deep breath. What time was it? Not much longer to go now, surely? My eyes stung as I opened them and glanced down at my red high heels. The colour was starting to wear round the tips, and the leather was peeling away ever so slightly on the heel. I needed to invest in a new pair, but I also needed to pay a thousand bills this month. Besides, I'd never find a more comfortable pair, I thought, as I reached down and brushed the left toe, my long dark hair falling over my face. I always felt good when I had these shoes on, ready to face the world. Well, OK, maybe not quite that ready, but they were a bit like my armour, and I'd worn them through so many good times. Memories were ingrained in the very soles of them, and I wasn't quite ready to let them go.

George, my manager at the bank, where I'd been working a couple of years now, bounded into the room. He was smiling his usual cheeky grin, hands on his hips, his navy-blue tie dragging over to one side. He always walked with such a fluster about him, as if he had a million things to do and was racing around to do everything at once. "Sooooo, who's up for a drink after work tonight?" His eyes glittered mischievously.

I fiddled with my silver stud earring and bit my lip. I *really* needed to get out of this, but my brain couldn't think of an excuse quickly enough.

"Sure," I found myself saying. "I can't stay late though. Finn texted me earlier. He asked me to go straight home tonight. He wants to talk about our weekend plans." I shrugged and scrunched up my face. I had no idea why Finn, the boy I was currently seeing and also living with, wanted to speak with me so urgently about going up to his parents' home this weekend. It was something we did at least one a month and a trip that consisted of the same routine every time.

"Ooooh, what plans?" George's personal assistant, Carla, peeped her sparkling eyes from behind her computer, her mouth curved into a smile.

I shrugged. "I don't know. We're meant to be going to visit his parents this weekend, so nothing unusual there. I'm not sure why he wants to talk about it."

Carla pouted and started tapping her perfect French-manicured nails on the desk. "Well, you must come!" she said. "At least for one drink. It's nearly Friday. George is flashing the expenses card about, and I have had a shitty time of it with Tom, so I need a chat. I don't think George is too interested in my is-he-or-isn't-he-going-to-propose saga."

"Erm, no, I don't think he is." I looked at her plausibly. "Don't worry, I'll be there. I just can't stay too long, that's all."

Carla beamed at me as she stood up. Holding a handful of letters in one hand, she flicked her impossibly straight, long, blonde hair back with the other. She always looked so polished and glamourous. I often found myself watching her in complete wonderment, promising myself I'd book in for those long-overdue salon treatments. But, in truth, over the years I was no stranger to the salon. I'd had mani-pedis, facials, and all kinds of plucking, waxing, and tinting done to my eyebrows, but I'd somehow always felt it a waste of time, and I'd never felt much better about myself afterwards. Sure, my skin felt softer for a couple of days and my eyebrows looked as if they'd been sponsored by Nike for a week, but after a while, inevitably, I was back to feeling a bit of a mess. The commitment to stay preened to perfection was too much, and so I'd started telling myself the "au natural" look was much more in vogue anyway.

"Fabulous," Carla said. "I'm heading to the post office, and then I'll go straight over to Lounge Bar. See you guys soon, okay?"

I nodded and smiled as Carla turned and briskly headed out, quickly followed by George, who was muttering something to her about a client's loan-to-value ratio. I shook my head and sat hunched in my chair. I hadn't done the greatest job of getting out of that one, but Carla had been so persistent. I knew she wouldn't have given up until I had said yes, as usual. Most of the time I just saved myself the hassle and agreed from the start. She had been the first person I met two years ago when I started at the bank. She'd greeted me with a sassy smile the moment I walked into the office, and now we were firm friends. She'd been seeing a guy, Tom, for a year and was just desperate for him to propose. Like, psycho desperate. After two glasses of wine, the conversation always steered to one thing—Tom's lack of a proposal and her will-he-or-won't-he melodramas. But, I didn't mind. That's what friends were for, right? I listened and nodded and reiterated over and over that she was acting like a crazed bunny boiler and that she should slow down. But she never listened, of course, always replying to me that the heart wants what it wants, to which I would roll my eyes. I guessed though, in the end, she was probably right.

Pulling up the emails on my computer screen I searched through for any that looked like they couldn't wait till tomorrow. Nope, I was free to go. I pulled my black trench coat off the back of my chair and walked out of the office and into the bathroom. I looked in the mirror, pulling the skin around my eyes upwards. I pouted. I was only twenty-nine. Were those crow's feet already creeping in? Grimacing, I reached for my highlighter pen and placed a few dots of it under my eyes, trying and failing to cover the black shadows that gave away my tiredness. I'd been struggling to sleep recently, tossing and turning, first too hot and then too cold for hours. I didn't know why. There was nothing in particular on my mind, and so I assumed it was just a phase—hopefully a short one. I'd taken to leaving the TV on until I finally passed out, which I knew wasn't healthy and was probably making things worse, but I hated just lying there in the darkness with my thoughts. I dotted on some pillar-box-red lipstick and rubbed it across my cracked lips with my finger. I liked this shade but was never confident enough to apply it in a bold, thick layer. That would be way too "out there" for me. I preferred a much subtler, sink-into-the-background look.

My phone beeped, and I reached into my brown satchel to retrieve it. Looking down at the screen, I saw it was a text from Finn in all caps: "You on your way?"

3

What was going on? The plan for the weekend was the same as the plan for so many other weekends before it. Friday evening after work we'd take a road trip to Nottingham, stay with Finn's parents, have dinner, drink wine, and maybe go for a few drinks with Finn's friends. Then, more often than not, we'd end the weekend with Sunday lunch and a nice long walk around the park with his brother and two sisters. I couldn't think what would be different about this coming weekend. Maybe Finn was planning to surprise me with a romantic weekend away? We were well overdue for one of those, but the cynic in me, having known him for years, said this was not a talk about him whisking me off into the sunset.

Finn and I had met whilst studying for our degrees. I was in my second year of law, and he was in his final year of music production. He was a friend of a friend of a friend, and we'd hit it off almost straight away. He was funny, witty, and just my kind of handsome with long, brown shaggy hair, a well-groomed beard, and that "hipster" style. He loved music and had big dreams. Meanwhile, he was working for a small, independent music production company in Soho. His dream was to work in sound on TV or films, and I had complete faith in him that he'd make it one day.

As I stood at the lift doors waiting for them to open, I hugged myself with my arms and stared down at the sterile black-tiled floor. I couldn't believe I was nearing the age of thirty and still in a dead-end job. I envied people who loved what they did and had a passion for their careers. I needed something to change, but I had no idea where to start. The lift tinged, and the doors slowly opened. I stepped in, welcoming the relief from my over thinking. One drink, and then I would head home.

After swapping my red heels for comfy Converse trainers for the walk home, I hastily left Lounge Bar two and a half hours after promising to be home for Finn's urgent "chat". I had totally lost track of time. George had bought round after round of drinks, and everyone had been in a good mood. Finn would understand, surely! It was only just gone eight o'clock anyway.

I loved this walk, even though it was a short one. The street lights were just starting to come on overhead, casting shadows on the road and illuminating my pathway. I glanced over at North Bar, one of my favourite haunts as a student, and hurriedly made my way down the street. It was raining, but the soft raindrops on my face were cool and refreshing on my clammy skin after I'd been squeezed into the stuffy Lounge Bar for the last two hours. I missed my uni days. *Perhaps I'll suggest a visit to North Bar next weekend with Finn*, I thought, as I turned onto Melbourne Road and climbed the few steps up to the communal doorway of my block of flats.

As my key clicked in the lock and I opened the flat door, the smell of chicken Korma hit me. Oh, delicious! Finn had made dinner. The flat felt roasting hot as I took my coat off, hung it on the back of the door, and made my way into the kitchen. "Finn?"

"I'm in here," Finn called out from the bedroom.

As I walked in, I noticed that a large, brown leather overnight bag sat on Finn's side of the bed wide open. I peeked inside. His small grey toiletry bag was also open, and I saw toothpaste and shower gel. I raised my eyebrows. He was not usually so organized; I normally ended up packing for both of us. "Finn?" I said again, moving into the en suite bathroom.

Finn appeared in the doorway, looking red faced, his towel tied around his waist, water dripping down from his long hair onto his shoulders. He was so skinny. Despite eating whatever he wanted, he never seemed to put on a single pound of weight. Hollow legs I would always joke. "I'm here. Sorry, just finished showering." His expression hardened. "I thought you would've been here earlier. I asked you to come straight home after work tonight."

"I know, I know. I'm sorry. Carla has been stressed out and had the usual boyfriend problems, so I couldn't say no." I held up my hands in innocence. "What's up anyway?"

Finn lowered his head and walked over to the edge of the bed. He sat down and started rubbing his hands along his towel. "Look, Ellie ..." He drew in a long deep breath and folded his arms across his body.

I shook my head, bending down to untie my shoelaces. "Finn, what's up? Spit it out."

I kicked my trainers off and looked up. The colour had drained from his face. I stood glaring, waiting for him to speak.

He rubbed his eyes and kept his gaze on the floor. "I've been thinking about this weekend, and I'd like to go to my mum and dad's alone. I think we just need a break from each other, a bit of time to ... I don't know ..." His voice tailed off as his chest heaved up and down and he kept his eyes firmly on the floor.

I gaped at him, unable to speak. Eventually, though, after a long and awkward silence, my words came spewing out. "What? I don't understand. Why? What are you talking about?" My voice was high pitched, breaking as tears formed in my eyes

Finn was expressionless. He just sat there, calmly staring down at his feet, but I could see he was breathing hard. I folded my arms tightly across my chest and my eyes burned into him. "Seriously, what's going on?"

"I don't know, Ellie. I just feel like I want to go home, be on my own for a bit, just get some space."

I inched towards him. "Get some space? From me?"

Finn threw his arms in the air and stood up, pulling his towel tighter around his waist and walking to the other side of the bed, further away from me. "Oh, for God's sake, Ellie. I knew you would do this! I knew you would just ask me loads of questions and not listen. Why can't I just make a decision and do something? Why do you always have to ask questions? I don't have the answers right now, okay?"

I stood there, my whole body starting to shake. I couldn't think straight as my mind whirled with questions. Was this some cruel joke? I come home to my boyfriend who, out the blue, tells me he wants to go away for the weekend without me for no reason at all—or no reason that he is telling me—and I'm just meant to go, "OK. Sure. Go ahead! Have fun!" Why was he doing this? How could he not expect me to ask questions? "But there must be something, Finn? Something I've done or not done?" I sat down on the bed feeling my knees start to buckle. "Do you want to break up with me? Is that it? Is this your way of doing it? You can't behave like this and expect me to be OK with it. You can't just drive off for the weekend and not expect me to ask why."

Finn stood with his back to me, looking up at the ceiling. After a few moments, he started shaking his head. He turned to face me, his eyes making contact with mine. "Ellie, I'm sorry, okay? I'm not asking you to agree with it. I'm just telling you that this is what I am doing. I don't know what I want, or what I feel, and that's why I need some time. You need to let me go on my own. Okay?"

He was "just telling me"? Wow! I hadn't seen this side of Finn before. He was usually so laid back, so relaxed. I was stunned. My eyes started to swim with tears, but I couldn't let him see how upset I was. Instead, I drew in a sharp breath and stood up. I walked towards the en suite door, wiping my eyes. Then I turned back around to face him. "Okay, if this is what you want. For how long?" I looked intently at his handsome face as I waited for him to respond. I'd be lying if I said I hadn't known for a while that our relationship had lost its shimmer and sparkle. We didn't go out on date nights anymore, preferring to sit in with a film and a pizza. We didn't get dressed up for each other and, between the sheets, well ... let's just say we weren't all over each other. But all this, I had told myself, was normal, right? We had been together so long—over five years now—that we'd just got comfortable. But maybe things *had* got stale, and I was just kidding myself that I was happy. That *we* were happy.

Finn looked down at the floor again, combing his hair back from his face, his lips pursed together. "Just the weekend," he said. "I have work Monday, so I'll be back Sunday night. We can have another chat then, okay?"

I nodded in defeat and looked down at my fluffy pink socks. He had made his mind up, and nothing I could say was going to change it.

But none of it made any sense. Only this morning before I'd left for work we'd had a conversation over our coffee about a trip to IKEA next weekend for a new bath mat and some blinds, with no indication from him that anything was wrong. But all the while he was thinking about something else, plotting his next move? It just seemed so strange and out the blue.

Fidgeting with my earring—something I always seemed to find myself doing when I got nervous or felt awkward—I walked over to the bed and sat down. I felt weak and needed to lie down. This whole thing had been so exhausting.

Finn walked over to the chest of drawers and pulled out his pyjamas. "I'm going to get to bed, Ellie. I'll sleep on the couch for tonight." I watched him as he shuffled over to the bedroom door. "I'm sorry. I really am. I don't know what else to say. I'll see you in the morning."

I turned my head away and waited to hear the clunk of the door shutting. I drew in a deep breath and stood up. I walked into the bathroom and looked at myself in the mirror. Mascara was smudged under my eyes, and the red lipstick was sitting in the cracks of my dry lips. My skin felt tight as I rubbed my hands up and down across my face, trying to draw some energy from somewhere. I pulled off my cream shirt and black skirt and climbed into the shower, letting the hot water wash away the day.

Chapter 2

Cracks of daylight peeped through the bedroom curtains as I opened my sore eyes. The night had been a long one, and I hadn't slept much. My head was fuzzy as thoughts whirled around, once again stopping me from falling into the sanctuary of sleep. I found myself, as I had on other recent nights, just lying there, warm and secure under the duvet, staring at the cracks around the ceiling light. But this sleepless night had been different. I had a reason to be wide awake. All I could think about was Finn. What was he trying to tell me by leaving this weekend without me? Did he really just want space? And if that was the case, did people in happy relationships do that? Did they walk away from each other for a while? Was that normal? I always thought that, if you loved someone, it would only mean pain to be away from that person, but perhaps that was just the silly romantic in me.

I couldn't understand how things had got to this point. Was it my fault? Was it Finn's? Or maybe it was nobody's. It was just the natural order of things. I'd spent the last twelve months telling myself that at least my relationship was OK. I'd been in denial perhaps. I'd reassured myself that the lack of passion and excitement was normal. But, after what seemed like an endless night of darkness, I knew we both had to change things if we wanted to get back on track. One question was niggling me though—did I even want to?

My whole body ached, and my legs felt heavy as I shifted about in the bed. Dragging myself up, I stood and listened. Was Finn up? Silence. I picked up my phone from the bedside table. The time was 7.34, and he'd sent me a text message half an hour ago: "I've headed to work early this morning. Hope I haven't woken you. I'll go straight to my parents' after work. I'm so sorry. I hope you aren't too upset. See you Sunday."

He hoped I wasn't too upset? Taking a sharp breath in disbelief that he'd just got up and left, I heaved my small green overnight bag out from under the bed and started to pack. I hastily grabbed knickers and bras and concealer stick and threw them into the bag. My neck was getting hot as I felt myself getting more and more angry. How could he? Well, if he wasn't going to stick around to sort things out, I wasn't going to sit in the flat all weekend alone, wallowing in self-pity, drinking cheap Merlot, and eating takeout pizza!

In the bathroom, my clothes from yesterday were strewn all over the white floor tiles. I switched on the light and stared at my reflection in the mirror. Jesus. I looked a state. My hair was pinned up, still damp from my shower last night. My skin was sallow and grey, and my eyes looked red raw. I couldn't face work like this. I couldn't face anyone like this.

Taking a deep breath, I quickly threw on my blue jeans, a blue T-shirt, and battered Converse trainers. I grabbed my overnight bag and headed out the door. My stomach was in knots, and I felt cold, shuddering as I walked down the hallway and out into the cool, dewy morning.

George was in the office kitchen when I arrived at work, making his usual black coffee in a hopeless attempt to sober up from the night before and mask the smell of stale alcohol on his breath. As always, he looked like he'd been dragged through a hedge backwards. I could feel my cheeks turning rosy. "Hey, George, can we have a chat?"

He turned, looked me up and down and drew his brows together "What the …? What's happened?"

"George, I'm so sorry." My voice cracked as my eyes welled up.

He hastily grabbed his coffee off the kitchen counter, spilling a little of it over the side of the cup, and ushered me into his office, closing the door behind him. "Come on, Ellie, in here. Sit down. Are you okay? Do you want some coffee?" George motioned to the chair opposite his. I sat down and grabbed a tissue from the box on his desk.

"No, it's fine," I said, sniffling. George sat down on his black leather desk chair, looking baffled. *Poor guy*, I thought. *He didn't expected this over his morning coffee.* I took a deep breath in to compose myself, but I still felt my top lip trembling as the words tumbled out. "It's Finn," I began. "I think we've split up. I mean, I don't quite know what's happened, really. We were meant to go away this weekend but he …" I trailed away, unable to finish my sentence as the tears fell down my cheeks again. I needed to get a grip. This wasn't helping anything.

George frantically grabbed some more tissues from the box and handed them over to me. "Take your time," he said, nodding and sipping his coffee. He probably wished there was a shot of vodka in it right now.

"He decided to go alone to his parents this weekend. He says he needs space and time to think. But I think … oh, I don't bloody know what to think! I can't work today, George. I'm sorry, but I'd be no good to anyone!" I shook my head and then rested it in my hands.

"Right. Yes. Of course. We'll sort things here. You get home, and we'll just see you next week."

I nodded, grateful, still spluttering into my tissues. Picking myself up, I wiped my eyes and threw my travel bag across my shoulders. "Thank you so much for being so understanding. I'm so sorry to lay this on you today. I'll work extra hard next week to catch up. I promise!"

George motioned to the door. "Don't worry, Ellie. Just go. We'll see you Monday."

As I was standing on the platform ten minutes later waiting for my train to roll in, my phone beeped. Could this be Finn? I hadn't heard from him since the text message early this morning. Wasn't he thinking about me at all? Reaching into my bag, I pulled my iPhone out to see a message from Pete. "Hey, you. We need to link up. It's been weeks. When are you free? I have soooo much to tell you. Can we meet this week for a drink? Tuesday?"

Throwing my phone back in my bag, I reminded myself to reply later. I wasn't in the mood for speaking to anyone right now, not even good friends. My throat felt scratchy, and my legs ached as I boarded the train. Just over an hour later I was in Farnborough.

Mum greeted me warmly and guided me upstairs to my room where lavender candles were burning and a fresh pair of pink pyjamas lay on my bed. This was exactly what I needed right now.

"I just don't know, Mum, I really don't." My voice quivered as I sat hugging my mug at the kitchen table, fresh out of a nice hot, lavender-scented bubble bath. Mum had made us Earl Grey tea and opened a packet of my absolute favourite biscuits, chocolate Hobnobs. "We've been together such a long time—five years nearly! But when I think about it now, I realize we've never talked about our future, children, or even just getting engaged. It had never bothered me—never crossed my mind, until now." Mum fidgeted in her seat. "But every time I log onto Facebook, I see that someone else has just given birth or is announcing their engagement. I've already got four wedding invitations for next summer! The only big event in *my* life is which series I'm gonna start watching on Netflix." Mum fidgeted some more, and I took another chocolate Hobnob. "I can't help thinking that we both, in a subconscious way, didn't think we had a future. Why have we never talked seriously about all that stuff? Sure, we'd joked about it all, but there was never any sign of a ring. He didn't even seem to want to whisk me away on a mini break."

Mum scrunched up her face. "It's not the movies, darling. Men just aren't like that, not really. Especially once they get comfortable. Your dad never took me away. Every trip we've ever been on I've booked. He's hopeless."

I reached over to Mum and gave her shoulder a squeeze. Dad wasn't that bad. "You don't think it's the Universe sending me a sign?"

A sign of what?" she queried, knitting her brow.

"That he isn't my forever? That we aren't in each other's long-term plans?"

Mum let out a long sigh and sipped her tea. "Or, maybe, darling, he really does just want some space this weekend. We all need that from time to time. Look at your father—he buggers off all the time on his golfing weekends. He wouldn't dream of taking me anywhere. I don't even get a call from him anymore." Mum rolled her eyes, stood up, and walked over to the sink. But, it's healthy, you know? Maybe when Finn returns on Sunday things will be okay."

I put my mug down on the kitchen table and sat up straight in my chair. "I get what you're saying about Dad," I offered, "but this is totally different. I don't know if I want things to go back to the way they were. You think you're okay—happy even—until something changes. The Universe blindsides you with a low ball, you know?" I bit my lip, determined not to cry. "Maybe this is what we needed, and Finn was just the braver one

11

of us to do it. And now it's happened, I don't know if I want to go back. I mean, I'm still here, still breathing. I'm not gonna shrivel up and die without him."

Mum walked back over to her chair and sat down. Stroking the side of my face with the backs of her fingers, she nodded. "Well, Ellie, just wait till Sunday. Go back to London, speak to him, and see how you feel. Sleep on it, as they say." She leaned over and lightly kissed my forehead as I shut my eyes. "I worry about you. Even after twenty-nine years, I worry about you every day."

I pushed my hand into hers and kept my eyes closed, letting the comfort and familiarity wash over me. I stayed that way for a few minutes, taking some slow, deep breaths. When I opened my eyes, Mum was still looking at me, the skin between her eyebrows crimpled up. I smiled. "I know you do, Mum. But, honestly, I'll be okay."

Chapter 3

My keys clinked in the lock as I slowly opened the door and made my way into the flat. I could hear rustling in the kitchen as I pulled off my coat and kicked off my trainers, tossing them onto the hall floor.

I hadn't heard from Finn all weekend, and I hadn't bothered to text him either. He'd wanted space, and that's exactly what he'd got. I felt my mouth go dry as I walked into the kitchen and he turned to look at me. "Hey," I managed.

Finn forced a smile. "Hey, yourself. You're back later than I expected."

I folded my protectively around myself and cleared my throat. "How was your weekend?"

Finn turned back around to the chopping board and started rubbing the back of his neck with one hand while he fidgeted with the knife handle that lay on the countertop with the other.

Oh God, he's going to kill me. This is where he's going to chop me up, store my head and torso in bags at the back of the freezer, and boil the rest of me. Please, God, no! Oh, stop it Ellie! I scolded myself. Prone to irrational thoughts and melodrama on occasion, I forced my eyes away from the knife to the back of his head, trying to focus in on the conversation. "Erm, yeah. It was okay. Didn't do much." He shrugged.

"Oh, right." I tried to hide the relief and satisfaction from my voice, but it was tough. My mind, in typical dramatic style, had envisaged Finn up to all sorts of debauched single-life behaviour over the weekend. Amongst other similar scenarios, I had pictured him in Panther's Strip

Club, a bevy of scantily clad women ogling him, thrusting their vags in his face and pushing his head between their huge boobs.

"Did you not go into town with Ryan and Alex?" I asked casually, not wanting to seem too keen to know exactly what the hell he had been doing.

"Err, no. They weren't about." Walking over to the fridge, he pulled out a block of cheddar cheese and some milk. Then he trundled back over to the chopping board, his shoulders hunched forward. "You want some cheese on toast? I'm making some."

My eyes narrowed as I watched him shuffle the cheese packet about. "No, thanks. Ryan and Alex weren't about? That's odd. Ryan tagged himself on Facebook in The Green Room in Sheffield on Saturday night. He didn't tell you he was going?"

Finn started to cough and covered his mouth. He shrugged his shoulders. Clearing his throat, he spluttered. "Erm … no, he didn't. Maybe he was out with a girl or something? How was your weekend anyway?"

I perched myself on the edge of the couch, arms folded, continuing to watch him. I was hardly about to tell him I'd been sitting in my bedroom alone all weekend stuffing chocolate chip cookies into my mouth and watching reruns of *Sex and the City*. Instead I said, "And you care because …"

Finn rolled his eyes. "There's no need to be like that, Ellie. I'm only asking. This is hard for me too!" He kept his back to me as he pushed bread into the toaster. "I just don't know what to do," he said finally, leaning the palms of his hands on the worktop and hanging his head forward. "I feel like we're going in different directions at the moment. Like we're more friends than—you know—together."

I nodded my head and suddenly felt shivery. I pulled my grey cardigan across my chest. It was time to ask the question that had been hanging in the air like the sword of Damocles. I felt a lump in my throat as I gulped back tears. "Are we breaking up?"

Finn lowered his head and put his hands in his pockets. "I think we need a break, yes. We shouldn't have moved into this flat. It felt wrong. I mean, I was unsure of things when we were signing up for it, but I didn't have the heart to say anything. I'm just sorry that I didn't face things at the time."

My eyes narrowed, and my voice became harsh. I hardly recognized the sound I made as I spat the words out. "You're sorry you didn't face things at the time?" I sat staring at him. He'd had his back to me this whole time. I clenched my fists in anger. How dare he treat me like this? He was calling it quits after all these years, and he couldn't even bring himself to look at me? "We've been living here for nearly ten months," I said, "and all that time you've been feeling this way? Leading me on? Perhaps you could have shared a little of your knowledge with me, and we could have got on with our own lives a lot sooner. This last ten months have just been one big charade. You can't even bring yourself me in the eye!" I shouted.

Finn pulled his hands out his pockets, turned around, and threw his arms in the air. "Why are you being like this? I don't want to argue with you. I'm just trying to be honest."

I flew both of *my* arms in the air. My voice became screechy. "I don't want to argue either! I'm just trying to understand what's happening here."

Finn lowered his voice. "I don't know, Ellie. I'm sorry. I just don't know." His shoulders were hunched down as he looked at the floor. We faced each other in silence as the toast popped up from the toaster. "Look," he said. "I'll go and stay with a friend for a few days, give us some more space to think."

"It seems there's already a lot of space between us, Finn." I turned my face away from him, my stomach in knots. And there we both were, looking in different directions. I had nothing else to say as tears fell from my eyes onto the wooden floor.

Finn walked over to the kitchen door, and I could feel his eyes on me as I kept my head turned away from him. I didn't want him to see me crying like this. "Look, we need some milk. I'm gonna nip out. I'll be back in ten," he muttered quietly.

I nodded and sat motionless, waiting for him to leave. As the door banged shut behind him, I slowly sank back into the couch and let my shoulders relax. I stared at the blank TV screen, going over the conversation we'd just had. I shut my eyes and rubbed my temples. Something Finn had said was bothering me. If he'd gone home this weekend, why hadn't he gone out with Ryan to The Green Room? Finn had said that Ryan hadn't invited him and that maybe he was with a girl. OK. That made sense, but I'm sure I remembered Ryan tagging other lads in the photo on Facebook, and if that was the case, why hadn't Ryan at least asked Finn to go? Finn had said he knew nothing about it.

I grabbed my bag off the table, reached for my iPhone, logged into Facebook, and pulled up Ryan Kelly's profile. There it was—his last entry on Sunday. It was a photo of Ryan with Alex and a couple of other lads from Finn's hometown with the caption, "Catching up with the boys this weekend. Bit of a messy one." This didn't make any sense. Ryan hadn't been with a girl that weekend at all. He was with all of his and Finn's friends, and I would pretty much stake my life on it that, if Finn knew about the night out, he would have gone. So why hadn't he? They were all such good mates. There was no way Finn would go up to Sheffield and not go out with them, and there was no way Ryan wouldn't invite him. Even if Finn chose not to go, he should still have known about it.

My head was spinning as I stood up and walked over to the patio doors. As I glanced down, I saw Finn's brown overnight bag, half open, next to the couch. I could see Finn's grey toiletry bag buried inside. Suddenly, there I was, riffling through his bag. I wasn't sure what I was looking for, but I just had to do it. Something was telling me to look, and to keep looking in every pocket. I needed some clues to help me figure out what Finn had been up to. His trip "home" just didn't sit right with me.

And then, tucked inside a side pocket, I felt it—a small packet rustling between my fingers. I pulled it out, trying not to tear it. A pink-and-white-striped paper bag. On one side was a picture of a chocolate-box-perfect cottage with trees around it. Above the cottage were the words "Winchester House. North Yorkshire". I slowly peeled the bag open and peered inside. I pulled out a small card. It was a namesake card which read: "The name Finn is an Irish baby name. In Irish, Finn is fair. Finn is cool and creative. A lover of the arts."

I stared at the word; I hadn't seen this before. Where had it come from? I opened the bag again and saw a receipt crumpled at the bottom. I pulled it out and looked at the date: 09 July 2017 at 14.17 p.m. That was yesterday. I grabbed my phone again and googled Winchester House. Within seconds a site came up showing the same picture that was on the bag. Winchester House was a bed and breakfast. Why would Finn be in a bed and breakfast this weekend in North Yorkshire? I turned the card over, and then I saw it: "To the cool, creative one. Remember this weekend. I will. Love, L." Love L? *Love L? Love fucking L?*

Just then the door opened. "I'm back!"

I just stood there reading the words over and over. What the hell was this? I turned the card over, searching for more, something else, but I knew everything I needed to. Finn walked in, looked down at my hands, and froze in his tracks. His complexion turned pale. He gaped at me but said nothing.

I had no intention of keeping so quiet. Finally, I found myself able to speak. "What the hell is this? Winchester House? Only yesterday?" I thrust the bag with the receipt towards him. "And who the fuck is L? What is this, Finn?" He gulped and bit his lip but still said nothing. He looked like he could pass out. "Have you been at your parents this weekend?"

A flush crept up onto his cheeks. Caught! "No, I haven't."

"I guess I don't need to ask where you have been all weekend then?" I said, shaking the bag violently in the air. I felt tears roll fast down my cheeks as I glared at him, waiting for him to say something—anything. My hands were shaking in anger, and I closed them into fists, trying to calm myself.

"I've been with Louise. She's from work." Finn's eyes narrowed as he inched towards me. "I know I should've told you. I just … I didn't know how to. I'm so sorry, Ellie."

I pointed my finger at him, my hand still quivering. "Don't come any closer. Finn! Just get the fuck out of here. Get the fuck out of here right now!"

My breath deepened and came faster as my eyes filled with more tears. I didn't care that he saw them now. I wanted him to see the upset he had caused. How could he?

Finn rubbed his neck and his mouth twisted. "Ellie, I—"

"Don't even bother saying anything. I don't want to hear it!" My chest was heaving with rage. He wasn't used to seeing me like this. I wasn't used to seeing myself like this either, but I had never felt so angry and hurt. "I can't believe you've lied to me like this. Five years of my life wasted on you. I've given my all to you, and this is how you treat me?" I felt myself starting to choke back more tears. I turned away and wiped my face. Then I turned back. There was no stopping me now. I was on a roll and determined to say my piece. "You're a scumbag liar and a cheater. I've been at home, upset all weekend, and you've been off getting your end away with some whore from work!" I took a step towards him, thrusting my finger at

17

his face. The anger was raging inside me. He stepped back, his eyes wide. "When did *we* ever go on a weekend away? You never asked *me* to go to the bastard Winchester Bed and Breakfast, did you? Perhaps if you had done, we wouldn't be where we are now!" Finn hid his face with his hands and lowered his chin. If he thought for one minute he was going to get off lightly, he was very wrong. "Pack your shit and go!" I shouted. "Get the hell out of my sight!" I waved my arm towards the door and turned my back on him, my heart beating out my chest.

He said nothing as he moved slowly towards the door, his brown brogues clomping on the floorboards. He clearly wasn't going to fight for this—for us. Maybe he didn't have the energy or maybe he didn't have the will, but either way, his silence said it all. If our life—our relationship— was what Finn wanted, he would be in front of me, right now, fighting for us, saying something. But instead, only silence.

Just in time, I spun around, "Hey, Finn!" He turned to look at me, eyes widened and expectant. "Take your fucking cool and creative namesake with you," I said, throwing the card and paper bag at his feet.

He didn't attempt to pick them up. He just looked at me, pursed his lips together, and walked out, leaving the bag and its incriminating contents strewn on the floor. I stood, listening, waiting for the relief of the door opening and him leaving. After a few minutes, I heard the familiar clunk of the lock. He was gone.

The room fell silent, and I was alone. After standing in the same spot for a few moments, I drew in a long deep breath and exhaled. I picked up the bag and card from the floor, ripped them up, and threw the tiny pieces in the bin.

Chapter 4

"I literally have no words," Pete said, doing the diligent best friend thing of listening intently whilst nodding and frowning in all the relevant places. He took another sip of his gin and lemonade and, sitting back in his chair, he put his head in his hands. "I mean, fuck me!" he said. "Finn? I can't believe Finn would do this," he added, just to make sure I knew how shocking the whole thing was. I already knew.

I looked down at the red lipstick smeared around the side of my wine glass and shook my head. "I know, me neither."

Pete scrunched up his face. "I mean, who is she? What does she do? You ever met the bitch?"

I'd replied to Pete's text about a drink shortly after arriving back in London, and we'd arranged to meet the next day in Vincent's Wine Bar, a quirky and cosy little basement place close to Pete's work. He was full of questions. Naturally, he was deeply troubled, but he relished the drama at the same time. He'd been single for a couple of years, preferring one-night stands to overly "complicated" relationships. But I knew him well enough to know that, deep down, meeting a nice guy and settling down was something he wished for. He'd just never admit it.

"No, I don't know her. I haven't met her, and I don't want to. I just feel so angry!" I sipped my fourth glass of Merlot and reminded myself that the night wasn't going to end well if I kept knocking them back like this.

"I bet you do! I'd want to friggin' rip his dick off if he did that to me!" Pete thrust his hands towards his pants.

I laughed, placing a hand over my eyes. "Pete, I am aware of the location of the penis. You don't need to illustrate, thank you." We both giggled and took another sip of our drinks.

I'd known Pete for years, since university, and if there's one thing he was always guaranteed to do, it was make me laugh, even when the shit was hitting the fan, like it was tonight.

I let out a harsh breath as I slumped back in the wooden-and-not-particularly-comfy chair. "Believe me, I felt like that on Sunday night. I still do. But then part of me thinks, maybe he's done me a favour, you know? If he's capable of doing this, then maybe I'm best shot of him?"

Pete raised his eyebrows. "Wow, how very philosophical of you. But you sound way too healthy considering this has just happened. How many glasses of wine have you had?" I pouted. Way too many. "But yeah, I agree," he continued. "You're better than this. You deserve better than him. Kick him out and get on with your life. Take the opportunity to have a fresh start."

"You're right. I know you're right. Once a cheat always a cheat, hey?"

Pete took another sip of his drink. "Exactly. Use this time to change things, move on."

I nodded, but I felt like a drop in the ocean and had no idea where to begin in making changes to my life. I was stuck in a rut—cheating boyfriend, crap job, no money. Where would anyone begin? I was feeling sorry for myself, and I disliked it when I did that. There was always someone worse off, right? Taking another sip of wine, I gave a dismissive wave of the hand. "Anyway, enough about Finn. I'm sick of thinking about him. What's been going on with you?"

Pete's mouth curved into a smile and his eyes lit up. "Well, I do have some news, actually. You know I've always wanted to go to the US but never had the chance? Well, I'm off to California, baby!" Pete did a little dance in his chair, failing his arms in the air and bobbing his shoulders up and down.

"Wow, you serious? That's amazing! When?"

He ran his hands through his short spikey blonde hair and then clasped his hands together behind his head "Yep, I know. I fly out on Tuesday the twenty-eighth of July. I can't wait."

I gasped. "Like, July? As in this month?"

"Yep, isn't it crazy?" His eyes widened with excitement.

"Well, just a bit. It's like two weeks away."

"I know, but I've been planning it in my head and in my bank account for a lot longer. I've been plotting pretty much since I got back from Sri Lanka two years ago."

I leaned my elbows on the table and rested my head on my hands. "Well, I am so chuffed for you. How long are you going for?"

"I'm not sure to be honest. I've bought only a one-way ticket, so I guess I'll see how far my money takes me."

"I'm so jealous. I'll totally miss you!" I reached out and placed a hand on his shoulder. And I really would miss him. We'd been the best of friends since we shared a dorm together at university. I had been unpacking my bags in my room, blubbering away and feeling homesick, despite the fact that I'd only been dropped off by Mum and Dad two hours ago. In walked this tall, slim, tanned, pretty hot-looking guy, smiling at me. I remembered he was wearing a bright yellow T-shirt with a flamingo on the front that diamanté eyes. Pretty hideous, actually. He'd pushed my half-unpacked suitcase onto the floor from the bed, flung himself down, and pulled out a travel size bottle of Absolute vodka from his pocket. He gave me the cheekiest smile, which I eventually came to love. We got pissed that night, giggling and regaling each other with our life stories into the early hours. We'd been firm friends ever since.

He looked at me doe-eyed and dropped his bottom lip. "I'll miss you too, Ell."

"Can you fit me in your suitcase?" I looked up at him pleadingly.

Pete sat up, placed his hands on the table, and broke into a smile. "You know, that's not the worst idea you've ever had. Why don't you come with me?"

I smoothed my long fringe out of my eyes, pushing it over to one side as I smiled. "I was joking!"

"Why not? What have you got to lose?"

I took another sip of wine. "I don't know. But I can't just get up and go with you. I mean, I've no money for starters, which I'd say is a pretty good reason why not."

"Okay, so take the slight issue of no money out of it. Would you come with me then?"

I scrunched up my face and shook my head. "Gosh, Pete, maybe. I don't know. I guess I would think about it."

"You'd think about it? You've just caught your boyfriend at it with some tart from his work, you hate your job, and you've talked so many times about moving back home and out of the city for a change of scenery. So, what's there to think about? What's stopping you?"

I took yet another sip of wine. "I guess you're right. Yeah, it would be amazing if I could come." I pondered. "But none of this solves the money problem!

Pete drummed his fingers on the table, puffing his cheeks out. "There's no way you can get some money together? Could you ask your parents? They've helped you out before, haven't they?"

I shook my head firmly. "I don't know, Pete. I don't know if they'd go for it. It'd be a big ask at such short notice."

"Well, I just think this could be the golden opportunity for you to get out of the life you're stuck in. Leave that God-awful job you hate, travel, meet some new people, and just take a break from the city." Pete picked up his drink, looked up at me from behind the glass, and raised his eyebrows. Soft jazz music played in the background, and the smell of fresh coffee clung to the air. "All I'm saying is, think about it. At least speak to your mum. Tell her this is the trip of a lifetime and it'll be good for you after what's happened."

I nodded, glancing over into a dimly lit corner of the bar where two brown leather Chesterfield couches were tucked cosily away. Whenever Finn and I came here, we usually managed to grab those sofas. They were so comfy and soft, you just sunk right into them. We'd whiled away hours chatting about everything and anything, and now, those couches were occupied by another couple, and those moments we shared would just be fading memories.

"So, you'll at least ask?" Pete said, snapping me out of my thoughts.

I stood up and took a deep breath, feeling light headed as I inched round the table. "I'm sorry, Pete. I need to use the bathroom."

I pushed the bathroom door closed, clicked the lock, and hung my black suede handbag on the coat hook. I turned and stared at my reflection in the mirror. My long hair dangled lifeless around my shoulders, and my fringe kept getting in my eyes. I really needed to get it trimmed soon. My mascara had smudged, and my red lipstick was more "trout pout" than "perfect pout" after I'd reapplied it several times without a mirror and under the influence. Oh, God, I looked a state. *Single, and certainly not hot enough to mingle*, I thought as I blotted my lips with tissue paper and wiped the smudges from around my eyes. Would anyone ever want me again? I leaned closer to the mirror, biting my bottom lip, my eyes welling up. I would be alone for the rest of my life, destined to be a sad, old spinster with twelve cats and three hamsters. I would eventually die, leaving my entire estate—namely my sizeable CD collection including classics from *Boyzone* and *Westlife*—to a cat charity. I sighed and closed my eyes, taking in a deep breath.

Pete was staring down at his phone as I walked over and sat down. "Are you OK? You were a while."

"Yeah, I'm fine. Maybe we should go and get some food soon?"

"Yes, let's do that. But I want you to think about this trip too, okay? I'm not letting you off that easy. You don't have to decide now. Just give it some thought."

I nodded, pulling on my coat. "I will, I promise. Now, Maccy D's?"

It was gone eleven in the evening as I fumbled for my key and unlocked the door, half expecting the usual warm glow of the lamp in the living room and the familiar noise of the TV. Instead, darkness and silence greeted me.

After changing into my pink pyjamas, I climbed into my bed and snuggled down between the cold sheets. I reached for the remote control and switched on the TV. A rerun of *The Royal Family* was playing. The lights of the screen flickered in the dark, sending shadows into the corners of the room. I loved this show and had seen most episodes a million times. As I watched, though, my mind whirled over my conversation with Pete. I knew he was right. I needed something to spur me into change. I needed to find a passion for something again. Maybe asking Mum and Dad wasn't such an awful idea. All they could do was say no, and that would be the end of it. But was I being too hasty? Could I really just get up and go? Finn and I had so much history. We had been living together, sharing money and friends. I couldn't just walk off into the sunset and never come back—could I? It was funny how our relationship had started with a simple hello and was about to end with such a complicated goodbye.

I reached for my phone. The butterflies in my belly starting to flutter about as my fingers danced across the keyboard, texting as quickly as I could. I could feel my breath getting deeper as I hunched over the glow of the screen: "I'm in, Pete. If I can get the money together, I'm in."

And that was it. Message sent.

Chapter 5

As I walked home from work, I dialled my mum's number. I couldn't wait to hear her familiar, comforting voice. After a brief chat—the dogs' latest escapades, my dad refusing to eat his homemade guacamole, her outrage at the postman putting someone else's letters through the door—I decided to seize the moment.

"So, what's going on there anyway?" Mum asked.

I lay the scene. "Well, I haven't heard anything from Finn in a few days, and I'm just feeling a bit fed up really."

I'd called Mum soon after finding Finn's incriminating evidence and, like everyone else, she hadn't been able to believe it. She liked Finn. He and both my parents had always got on well. Finn and my dad loved to watch the football together when we visited home, and there was always plenty of chatter and happy times to be had. But Mum had always had very strong opinions on cheating, and she reminded me of something she'd always said. It was actually pretty much the only piece of advice she'd ever given me when it comes to men: relationships should be given a second chance—except when there's cheating. Never taken anyone back who cheats. This had stuck with me, and I knew I could never take Finn back.

"Oh, love, you're going through a bad time," Mum said. "You come home whenever you need a break from the chaos of it there, okay?"

It felt cool, despite it being July, as I pulled my pink cardigan around me. "Thanks, Mum. And I will. But, actually, I met Pete for a drink last night. You remember him, right?"

"Pete? No, I don't think so. Have I met him before?"

I stopped walking and pressed the button for the crossing as the cars whizzed past me. "Yes, Mum, a couple of times. I guess a while back now. Graduation day at uni? Short, spikey, blonde hair. Tall, very slim. He was wearing that blue shirt with the dancing cactus on it?"

Mum let out a nervous laugh. "Right. Oh yes! How could I forget him?"

"Well, as I say, we went for a drink and got talking about a trip he's going on. And, well, he's invited me."

"Wow! OK, darling. Is he, just a friend or ..."

The crossing started to bleep, and I quickly crossed the road, feeling spots of rain on my forehead. "No, Mum. He's just a friend. He used to have posters of Leonardo DiCaprio plastered all over his dorm at uni. He's certainly *not* into me. Not in that way, anyway."

Mum let out a deep breath. "Right, OK. Carry on then."

"So, the thing is, this trip's in two weeks. Pete's had it planned and booked for months, so I'd just be tagging along last minute. And it's, well, a slightly longer haul then just a sunny holiday to Spain. More ... sort of ... sunny California way."

"Right. OK," Mum repeated slowly.

"I've just been thinking about it, and, well, I think it could be good for me. Take some time out of the city just like you said. Get away from here for a bit. See somewhere new and just relax, you know?"

Mum's voice went quiet as I pushed my phone closer to my ear. "Right, well ..." She paused. "I do think it's a good idea to get out of the city, I mean. So, yes, a holiday sounds fantastic. How long would it be for?"

I had known this question would be coming; I'd been psyching myself up for it all day. Mum hated uncertainty, and so did I, but it was time to take a chance and do something outside the box if anything was ever going to change. The rain started to come down heavily, soaking my hair as I ran over to a shop doorway and tucked myself into it. "Well, this is the thing," I started. "I don't know how long. Pete has a plan, but it's open ended, so he doesn't know when he'll be back. He wants to get as far as his money takes him, and then he'll come home. So, I guess I'd be doing the same." I squeezed my eyes closed as I tentatively spoke those last words.

Silence.

I imagined her face, all scrunched up in horror as she stared down at the floor and considered the chaos of it all. Mum would never get on a plane without knowing exactly where she was staying. She'd need to know every detail of the trip, which wasn't hard since Mum and Dad weren't exactly explorers. They'd been going to the same hotel in Faliraki in Greece for twelve years, Mum declaring the waiters at Faliraki Taverna the friendliest she'd ever known. "And work?" Mum said.

Here we go, I thought as I pulled wet strands of hair out my eyes. "I'm not happy there, Mum. I never have been, you know that. The place makes me miserable. I'd hand my notice in and, when I get back, I'll find something else, something better hopefully."

I could practically hear my mum's eyes roll. "Oh, Ellie! I don't know. I worry about you. I never stop worrying."

"I know, Mum, I know. You say that all the time. But I can't help feeling that this is the right thing to do—just to get away. Then, when I get back, I can start over—new flat, new job, and the problems with Finn behind me." The rain had stopped, and I stepped back out onto the path and continued my fast walk home, staring down at my Converse trainers getting wet in the puddles. Damn it. "It's just ... Mum ... I'd need your help ... with money." I faltered. "I'd pay back every penny when I get home. You know I always do, and this time will be no different. I wouldn't let you down, I promise."

"I know you wouldn't let us down, darling, but I wonder how much you've thought this through. Leaving your job, the flat—it all sounds a little bit impulsive to me. I'll have to speak to your father first, okay?"

The rest of the walk home was a soggy one. The rainwater found its way through my trainers and into my socks, making my toes cold. Mum had asked so many questions, which wasn't surprising, but I didn't have answers to most of them, and as she said goodbye, I had no idea what the decision would be. My fate was in their hands.

I'd been lying in the hot bubble bath for over half an hour; the skin on my fingers had gone wrinkly. Scrolling through my "bath" playlist on Spotify (because everyone has one of them, right?) I hit one of my favourites, Sam Smith's "I'm Not the Only One". I couldn't think of any tune more fitting. How long had Finn been seeing this Louise? Had it been going on for months behind my back? All while we'd been sleeping together in the same bed, sitting at the table eating dinner? One thing was for certain, you don't just get up and go off for a romantic weekend with someone at work if nothing's gone on before. There's always something before. I felt so betrayed. Finn knew I trusted him, and he had abused that. How could I ever trust another man? My phone bleeped. I rubbed my tired eyes and tried to summon the energy to climb out of the soothing water. Then I noticed it was a welcome distraction from my thoughts—a text from Mum. Oh God! I felt nervous butterflies in my stomach. I'd been waiting to hear back from her since yesterday about loaning me some money for the trip. I'd tried to block all thoughts of it out my mind, not wanting to get my hopes up about it. I sat up abruptly, sending a wave of water and bubbles over the back of the bathtub and splashing all over the floor. I pushed the button: "Ellie, I've spoken Dad, and we both agree you should go. We think it will be good for you. Dad has put some money into your account. Let us know if you need anything else. Speak tomorrow. Love you."

I sleeked my wet hair back, my face feeling sweaty in the hot water. I reread the words over and over. I couldn't believe it. This was happening! Oh, my God, this was happening! I was going to California! I felt my breath quicken, and a smile crept across my lips. I sat back, letting the water wash over my shoulders, still staring at Mum's text.

I speed dialled Pete's number. I couldn't get the words out quick enough. "Pete, my parents are going to loan me some money! I'm coming with you!" I started to laugh with excitement and giddiness. I couldn't remember a time I had felt so happy.

Pete began laughing with me down the phone. "Woo hooo! Ellie, this is amazing news. I'm so excited!"

"I know, Pete. I know. I really can't believe this. Do you want to come over tonight? We could book my flight over some Prosecco?"

"Oh, fabulous. And I'd love to, but can we save it for tomorrow? I'm actually out with some work friends. I'll be over at, say, seven?"

"Yes, absolutely! Pete, I need this, I really need this. I feel like it's the beginning of something new for me, you know?"

"Me too, Ell. I have a feeling things are about to get really good. This is the best thing that could have happened to you—a fresh start. We'll have the best time."

I couldn't stop smiling. My heart was still racing. "I'll do some research tonight, have a look at flights and stuff. Okay? This is a new beginning for me, Pete. A road trip to new a new beginning."

I felt exhilarated. I knew it was only a trip, but it signalled, for me, the end of something, the old Ellie—my job, my cheating boyfriend, and London. It would all be behind me, for a while anyway. I'd come back a new woman, ready to take life on again. I was feeling more positive than I had in ages.

"Well, Ellie," I told myself, "there's a whole lot of magic in new beginnings."

Pete had it all planned out, just as I knew he would. I sat watching him intently as he traced his finger down the outline of the West Coast map on my laptop. We'd fly to LA, spend a few days there visiting beaches and all the touristy places, and then we'd pick up a car and hit the road, heading north towards San Francisco, which would be our final destination. I couldn't stop smiling as the butterflies in my stomach fluttered with excitement.

Pete clicked onto Google and typed in "LA hostels". "Obviously we won't be staying anywhere fancy, but I've hit up a few places, got a great little pad for us booked in Beverley Hills. It's really central and looks super cute and cosy. Other places we'll just book on the go." Pete opened a map of West Hollywood on Google and pointed to a street. "See? Pretty central. We'll be able to explore everywhere from there."

I leaned forward, my eyes wide. "Wow! Looks absolutely perfect to me."

Pete nodded. "And we just go as far as we can. Once our money starts to run out, we head home."

I pouted. "But you've been saving for this trip for, like, two years. My money is gonna run out before yours for sure. I'll have to come home alone and end up leaving you behind."

"Well, yeah, that's one option." He pursed his lips.

I drew my eyebrows together. I could tell he was plotting. "And the other?"

"Get a job?"

I screwed my face up in confusion. "What?"

29

"Get a job, Ell. I did it when I travelled around Australia. It was pretty expensive out there, but bar work was easy to come by. I got a cheap place to stay, and after a few of months, I'd saved enough to hit the road again. I made some good friends working there, too. Best thing I did."

I stood up and walked over to the fridge, taking out the chilled Pinot Grigio. "I don't know, Pete. Would it be *that* easy? And what would you do whilst I was working?"

Pete laughed and shook his head. "Typical of you to overthink it, but, yes, I think you could get a little bar work or something else easily enough. And I'd just carry on along Highway One until you were ready to join me. Then I'd come back for you. Maybe I'd even look for work myself. Who knows? I'm just saying, it's something to think about, should the opportunity arise."

I shrugged. "Okay. Well, maybe. I guess that would mean I'd be out there for a lot longer than I thought I'd ever be." I filled my wine glass three quarters full with the crisp cold wine. I had a nervous energy about me tonight, and so far, even a drink hadn't quashed it. I knew I was doing the right thing, but I wasn't used to being impulsive. Any holiday I'd ever been on had been planned meticulously a year or more in advance. Thank God Pete had done all the legwork. But I still felt nervous as I walked back to the couch, slouched back down, and took another sip,

"I guess it does mean that, but what have you got to rush home for? You said yourself, you need to get away. And if you leave your job, which you're gonna do, what's to stop you having a slightly longer holiday?" Pete slouched back next to me, and his mouth curved into a cheeky grin. "And you never know—you might even find love in La La Land." He winked.

I shot him a dirty look. "Love? Absolutely no way! Men are off my radar. Channing Tatum could literally twerk his way down Sunset Boulevard calling my name and I wouldn't look twice." I gave him a hard stare.

Pete gawked at me, shaking his head, mouth open in mock amazement. "You would actually rebuff the advances of Magic Mike? What has Finn done to you?" I rolled my eyes and gave him a poke in his side. He flinched, laughing. "Anyway, you never did say, what does Finn think about this trip of yours?" I gritted my teeth together and sat up straight, turning my attentions back to the laptop. "You haven't told him, have you?" I kept my stare glued to the laptop's screen. Pete gasped. "Are you gonna tell him?"

I shrugged, maintaining eyes forward. "I don't know. I haven't given it much thought. But I guess maybe I will. This week."

Pete nodded. "I think I would, Ellie, even if it's just a two-fingers up to him kind of thing, you know? Show him you aren't rocking in a darkened corner without him and are actually getting on with life and having some fun now he's gone."

"I hadn't thought about it like that, but you're right. I'll tell him. This week, by the weekend."

I leafed through a travel book Pete had brought over, admiring the stunning scenery and picture-perfect beaches. There was a whole chapter for Hollywood—the Walk of Fame, Universal Studios, Sunset Strip, and a tour of all Hollywood's movie stars' homes. I wondered if I'd bump into anyone famous. "Anyway, job or no job, we'll make this the trip to remember!" I beamed.

Pete picked up his glass and held it in the air. "Absolutely! Cheers."

Chapter 6

"The thing is, George, I need this. I really do. And I know it's short notice, but—"

George scoffed and rolled his eyes, throwing himself back on his chair. "Short notice?"

"I know. I'm sorry. I literally only just got the plans for it last night."

George gave me a half smile and took a deep breath, running his hands down is crumpled shirt. "OK, well, I guess I'll consider this your two-week notice."

"I'm really—"

"Don't say you're sorry, Ellie. I understand, okay?"

I nodded in relief.

"Have you told the others?"

"Told the other's what?" I spun around to find Carla stood in the doorway, clutching onto a stack of files and staring at me, her head tilted backwards and her ridiculously perfect eyebrows scrunched together. I could feel a lump in my throat, and my face went hot. I hadn't prepared my leaving speech for her yet.

"Hey, Carla, you okay?" I fidgeted in my chair and looked down at my red shoes. I'd absentmindedly put them on for the ten-minute walk into work this morning, rather than my usual trainers, and now my feet looked pink and felt sore. It was funny. I'd had these shoes for so long, worn them so many times, and yet they still gave me blisters when I walked too far in them.

"Yeah, I'm great, Ell. But what have you—or haven't you—told the others?" Carla tucked one side of her hair behind her ears. I knew she wouldn't let this go. I'd have to just spit it right out.

I gave George a sideways glance. He was shifting awkwardly in his chair and pretending to be engrossed by whatever was on his computer screen; I was in this one alone. "Well," I began, "I've been given an opportunity to go away, on holiday I mean. And, I think with the whole Finn thing right now, it would be good for me to get out of the city and take some time off."

Carla nodded her head as she fiddled with her earing. "Sure, totally! A holiday will do you a world of good." She tilted her head in understanding.

I nervously started twirling the hair in my pony tail around my fingers. "Yeah, I know. But, well, this is a bit more than a holiday. It's more like an extended thing." I studied Carla's expression, but it was unchanged. She stared at me with pursed lips and wide eyes, watching me. "And, well, since I don't have the holidays, my only option is to … well … give notice."

Carla stood up straight, scowling at me. "Leave? As in, *leave* leave?"

I felt tears pool in the corner of my eyes. "Look, I'm only just getting used to the idea, too, but I need a fresh start. You know that, right?"

Working at the bank wasn't my dream job. I'd never set out to be a mortgage account advisor. I had always wanted to be a doctor when I was younger. I'd play dress-up for hours with my pretend stethoscope. Dad used to be my diligent patient; I'd stick plasters all over his hairy legs and arms, and then he'd wince pulling them off. At sixth form college, I'd taken all the sciences. But after the first year, my tutor pulled me in and told me my grades just weren't good enough and, unless I changed my courses, I'd have no hope of getting a place in university, let alone a medical school. And so, I found myself studying the artier subjects—English and media studies. I was surprisingly good at them, and two years later, I got my first-choice spot at uni. My dream of medical school gone though, I'd struggled to really know what to do. Law just sounded interesting at the time. But after final exams, I floundered until I saw the bank's job ad, and a few years later, here I still was. But not for much longer.

Carla's face softened and her lips broke into a pursed smile. "I do know. I do! And I think I'd feel the same if I were you, but it doesn't mean that I'm not gutted you're going." Carla bent down and placed her files on the floor before walking over to me with open arms and hugging me. I hugged her back. We'd been friends from day one, and it was hard to imagine not seeing her every day. Carla pulled away from me, clasping her hands on my shoulders, "So, like, when do you go?"

"In two weeks. The twenty-eighth we fly out."

"Jesus! You don't waste any time, do you?"

I glanced at George, who was raising his eyebrows. "Well, I'm sort of tagging along with a friend who's had it planned for months."

Carla nodded. "That Pete guy?" I nodded back. She squeezed my shoulders and then let go, picking up the abandoned files from the floor and placing them on George's desk. "So, you know, this can only mean one thing, don't you? Emergency planning for your leaving party!" She clapped her hands together in glee. "I'll do some ringing round now, gather the troops, and find a venue."

"I'd just prefer no fuss, if I'm—" But I didn't get a chance to finish.

Carla extended her arm towards me. "Ellie, seriously? When do I ever take any notice of you?"

We laughed. We both knew she was right.

I arrived home to a dark, dreary flat again. It was just after seven, and I had never been further away from that Friday feeling. I felt achy and had a banging headache. I had so much to do now before the trip, but only one thing was plaguing my thoughts tonight—telling Finn. I hadn't heard from him for nearly five days—not a text message, not a phone call, not even an email. I had, admittedly, checked his Facebook page once or twice. OK, maybe like twenty times to see if there were any posts. But nothing. God knows where he'd been spending the nights, and my imagination was running away with me. I hated confrontation. But I knew this had to be done. A little over a week ago I had been living with this man in what I thought was a happy relationship. Now I was scared to speak to him and scared of what he might say. He'd gone from being my best friend to being a stranger in a heartbeat, and I still didn't know how to feel about it.

I walked into the kitchen, switched on the lights, and put on the kettle for a much-needed cup of coffee. While I waited for the boil, I pulled my phone out of my brown leather bag and started to text: "Finn, we need to talk. Can you come over please sometime this weekend? I know it's a

Friday night, but I need to speak with you, so please. Can you come over? Let me know when and I'll make sure I'm in."

After two hours and a million checks of my phone, still there was no reply. *How bloody rude!* I thought, pouring another glass of rosé wine. *I haven't contacted him in days, leaving him to do whatever it is he wants to do, and he can't even be bothered to reply to a message?* Up until now, I'd had nothing to say to him, and every time I thought about him, my stomach turned. I felt sick just thinking about him and her, together, behind my back, and all the lies and the deceit that I had been embroiled in without even knowing. My mind started racing. What was he doing right now? Was he with her? I imagined them together, cocktails in hand, cosying up, gazing into each other's eyes, and discussing how glad they were that their sordid little affair was out in the open. I closed my eyes tight and felt shivers run down my back.

The clink of the key in the lock jolted me upright from the sofa, and my tired, heavy eyes flew open. I sat motionless as heavy shoes clunked along the floorboards. "Ellie?"

Fuck! What was Finn doing here? It was gone midnight, and I was so very ready for bed. I looked down at myself—fluffy fox-print socks and Finn's old faded blue T-shirt. Just wonderful! This was not how I'd envisaged this going. I wanted him to see me looking fabulous and radiant, smouldering in red lipstick and a hint of smoky eye make-up. I wanted him to see what he was missing and that I was managing just fine without him. I wanted to at least be marginally prepared for this. I hadn't seen him in days. Instead, here I was, Friday night, alone, watching reruns of *Sex and the City* in his old T-shirt, crusty dinner stains running down the front, and mascara rings smudged around my tired eyes. I hardly oozed single and fabulous.

Finn staggered into the room, his eyes bloodshot. He was carrying a yellow foam kebab box. I held my hand over my mouth, looking up at him from the sofa in disgust. "Ellie? Hey," he slurred, trying to stand upright.

I put my glass of wine on the coffee table and stood up, looking him over. "Finn, what the hell are you doing here? I'm just about to go to bed. I texted you."

Finn laughed, opening the takeaway box and stuffing a handful of chips covered in tomato ketchup into his mouth. He had been out, smartly dressed in tan-coloured corduroy trousers and a denim shirt, but now he looked dishevelled. His leather belt was half undone, and his skin was pasty. He pulled his black satchel from over his shoulder and tossed it on the sofa, slumping down next to it, making himself right at home. "Yeah, I know. That's why I'm here."

I shot him a dirty look. "Finn, what's going on? Why are you here now?"

Finn finished eating, sat back on the sofa, and clasped his hands behind his head. He looked at me with a confused look on his face. "You texted me, Ellie. Don't you remember? You asked me to come around to talk, so here I am."

I rolled my eyes and turned away from him, walking over to the patio doors and looking out into the brightly lit courtyard below. I looked at Finn's reflection in the window. He sat up, looking at me. "Ellie, I've been thinking about you tonight. Thinking about what we had, and I've missed you. I know I've fucked up big time. I know that, but I figured you might have missed me too, despite everything? That's why you wanted to see me?" As I continued to watch his reflection, he stood up and started to stumble towards me, a smirk on his face. As I turned around, he reached out and took hold of the bottom of my T-shirt, lifting it up, revealing my stomach. With his other hand, he started to stroke my cheek. Then he thrust his waist into mine, grabbing my T-shirt at the sides and pulling me forward.

"Finn!" I pulled away. "What the bloody hell are you doing? Get your hands off me!" Finn's eyes flickered, and he gave a smarmy smile as he reached out to touch my shoulder again. I stepped back, pushing his arms away. "Finn, stop bloody touching me! You thought this was why I asked you here—for some late-night booty call?"

Finn stopped and stepped back, his eyes wide now, his mouth open. "I just, I just—"

"No, Finn! No! This isn't what I wanted. This isn't why I asked you to come here." I felt flustered and hugged myself with my arms.

Finn looked down at his brown leather shoes, scraping them along the floor. "I just thought … you know, for old times. I'm sorry. I mis-read the signs," he muttered as he gave a sort of half shrug.

"What bloody signs? A text message?"

We both stood there in awkward silence. I took a deep breath. I wasn't about to let him get away with it so easily. "For old times' sake? Is that before or after you decided to start shagging your work fuck buddy behind my back?"

Finn kept his eyes on his shoes as he rubbed his neck. "I know Ellie, I'm—"

"Don't say you're sorry again, Finn. Please, just don't." I let out a breath. "I asked you here because I wanted to tell you something. Something important. Well, to me, anyway, it's important."

"What?"

I shook my head. "Will you even remember in the morning if I tell you now?"

He looked up at me and pursed his lips. "Ellie, of course! I've only had a couple." He spread his hands out earnestly.

I rolled my eyes. "Sure you have, but okay. You need to know I'm going away on a trip in two weeks, and I don't know when I'm coming back." There. I'd said it.

Finn looked up at me. I couldn't tell if he understood what I had just said or not. I watched him, waiting for a response. "Where?"

"The States. California."

His eyes narrowed. "Who with?"

"Pete."

Finn nodded and turned, walking over to the sofa. He slumped down onto it and stared down at his shoes, deep in thought. I stood, waiting for him to respond, and finally he broke the quiet. "OK, well I guess I'll move back in here when you leave. And I'll sort things with the flat. Don't worry."

This seemed to be going a little too easily, but perhaps he was happy to be getting rid of me. I nodded, pushing my fringe out of my face. "Okay. Thanks," I managed. I didn't want to talk anymore. I just wanted him to leave. "Finn, it's late. I'm tired. Can we talk another time? We can sort everything else through email."

After another awkward, strained silence, Finn picked up his takeaway box and man-bag and walked towards the door. He stopped in the doorway and looked at me. "I'm sorry for coming here like this tonight. After what I've done ..." He stopped and shook his head. "Ellie, I did love you. I really did. And I never set out to hurt you. I hope one day you'll forgive me."

I didn't say anything, and neither did he. We just stood there in awkward silence until he broke the quiet and looked straight at me. "I know I can't take back what I did, but I just want you to know, I'm glad you've found some happiness in it all and you're just getting on with life."

I looked up at him and rolled my eyes. I could feel myself getting angry. "How very noble of you. Thanks for all your support." I spat my words out in clipped tones.

Finn's eyes widened. He'd known me long enough to hear the sarcasm in his voice. "Well, I'm gonna go. Email me any other details, okay?"

I didn't say anything as he pulled his black satchel around his shoulders and hooked his long hair behind his ears. I could feel his gaze on me, but I kept my eyes on the floor, arms firmly crossed. I just wanted him to leave. How dare he come here, let himself in like that, and then completely patronize me? I felt so angry, my face was hot. He was glad I was getting on with my life? Glad I'd found some happiness? What the hell did he think I was going to do? Of course, life goes on! Shit happens, and people move on. And that's exactly what I was going to do.

His footsteps clinked along the wooden floorboards, through the hallway to the front door. The catch clanked as he opened it to let himself out. But then a loud thump made me jump. I ran to the doorway to find Finn, face down, legs apart, arms outstretched, and his black satchel wrapped around his neck. Several ketchup-covered chips were strewn across the floor in front of him. And, next to his feet, was one of my red high heels. I gasped and put my hand to my mouth, part in shock and part to stop him from seeing a smile creep over my lips as he squirmed and shuffled to sit up.

"Damn shoes, Ellie! Fucking hell!" he yelled as he stood up and headed for the door. "Why do you always have to leave them lying around in the hall like that?"

I said nothing in reply. I just slowly bent down, picked up my red shoe by the heel, walked back inside, and closed the door behind me.

The next few days were a blur of packing, lots of goodbyes, and of course a fabulous leaving party thrown by Carla at the last minute. Despite my best efforts for it not to, the night had run well into the wee small hours, involved lots of vodka and dancing. It ended with the mandatory chicken kebab on the way home.

Then, it had just crept up on me, and in a complete whirlwind I found myself, skinny mochaccino in hand, at Starbucks in Gatwick Airport. "I still can't quite believe I'm here with you. It's crazy!" I hissed.

Pete took a sip of his steaming hot latte. "Tell me about it!" His eyes danced with joy. "I never thought this moment would come. I've been planning it for months, but I'm so glad you're here with me, Ellie. We're gonna have so much fun."

I smiled and nodded, taking another sip of my coffee. I looked out the terminal window and watched a plane effortlessly glide from the runway into the sky. I wondered where it was heading and how the hell such a colossal thing could making flying look so effortless.

Pete took hold of my hand and smiled. "This trip won't let you down, Ellie. I have a funny feeling you're in for the time of your life. Who knows? You might not want to ever come back!"

My eyes narrowed. "Oh, God, you and your funny feelings." We both laughed as I took hold of both his hands and looked straight at him. His eyes were glistening. "Pete, this time, I really hope your funny feeling is right."

Chapter 7

My reflection stared back at me though the opulent window of Chanel, and I could hardly believe I was here, standing on Rodeo Drive. I looked through the glass at the chic, stylishly dressed mannequins, adorned in sparkly handbags and lush cashmere jumpers. Then I looked down at my own faded blue skinny jeans, black peplum T-shirt, and my red high heels. There was no way I was going into that shop! Besides, I was hardly in the market for a pair of £1,700 purple crocodile-skin loafers anyway. I was definitely more a "Primarni" than Armani kind of girl.

I couldn't help but smile to myself as I imagined walking into the boutique. I wondered what the shop assistants would think of me. I felt a serious affinity with Julie Roberts in *Pretty Woman*, but I never dreamed of getting the makeover or the gorgeous rich guy at the end. I wondered, as I moved along the tree-lined road in the warm morning sunshine, when I would meet somebody new, or if I even wanted too after Finn.

"So, excited about tonight much?" Pete beamed at me, abruptly interrupting my procrastination. I could feel the excitement pulsing through every word he spoke. He was loving being here, and so was I. From the moment the plane had touched down three days ago, I'd felt it. The heat had hit us as soon as we stepped from the plane, the sunshine roasting our skin. Pete had that weathered, olive complexion. He could rub oil all over himself and never burn; he'd just emerge a shade darker each day. I, on the other hand, had lathered myself in factor-fifty and still managed to burn my neck and arms, my pale complexion never thanking me for the sun's rays. My freckles had started to come out all over my face as they always seemed to do in the sunshine. I used to hate them as a teenager, always trying to find the thickest foundation and concealer to cover them up. Now, though, as I neared thirty, I felt they added a hint of youth and drew the eye away from the fine lines starting to form around my eyes.

And the best bit was that I was a million miles away from home. London, even after only three days, was a hazy memory, consigned to my "I'll get back to you" box. I was on holiday and, apart from checking in on Mum and Dad while I was away, I refused to let my life back home creep into my thoughts. This was my time to get my head straight and get some perspective so I could return home refreshed and ready to face normal life again.

"Absolutely! I can't wait. Gonna have my heels on, drink some wine, dance all night long. Pretty standard stuff." I mocked shaking my hips and holding and imaginary glass of wine. We both laughed.

Pete put his arm round my shoulder. "So, I spoke to a few guys back at the hostel this morning, and Carl, the guy who works on the bar, mentioned a fabulous club not too far from us. Fancy it?"

I grinned cheekily at him and raised my eyebrows. "Oh, Carl has suggested a fabulous club, has he? And will Carl be coming along with us by any chance?" I peered at him through my wide-open eyes with feigned innocence.

"Maybe." Pete smiled back and poked me in the side playfully. I guessed that was all I was getting from him for now. "Fancy a pre-evening cocktail somewhere before we head back?" he asked.

I grimaced, looking down at my shoes. "Sure, but my feet are really aching in these now. I could do with getting them off." I winced slightly.

"I have no idea why you insisted on wearing those to come down here. I knew you'd start moaning." Pete rolled his eyes accusingly.

I playfully pushed him, knocking him off balance. "Hey, I'm not moaning, and I told you, this is Rodeo Drive! I had to inject a bit of glamour, right? I couldn't rock up in my Converse, could I?"

"Well, you could, theoretically," he mused.

"Pete," I countered, "let's just find us some cocktails."

Getting back to my room, I fell onto the bed. My feet ached, and I was looking forward to a long soak in the bath before hitting the town later. I pulled my heels off and looked down at my sweaty, red, blistered feet. How could a pair of shoes I'd had for years and worn to work like a million times, still tear my feet to shreds? I lay looking up at the white-painted ceiling and stretched my arms out, closing my eyes and allowing my mind to wander back to the day just gone. There I stood, staring at my reflection in the Chanel window on Rodeo Drive, and I'd smiled to myself. I was actually here. Dreams did come true.

Two hours later, Pete and I found ourselves in the quirky, tropical-style beer garden of our hostel. The small, but perfectly formed, circular space was very cosy, the walls covered with bamboo screens. Palm trees were scattered about the grounds in mosaic-covered terracotta pots, and there was a little waterfall in one corner of the garden. Wooden benches with colourful cushions were spotted about, and beach loungers were clustered together. Fairy lights hung from a wooden veranda, and candles were burning on the tables. A small bar was tucked over to one side of the garden. A tall, blonde, good-looking guy with tattoos down one arm—though I wasn't sure of what, as they all seemed to merge into one—stood wiping some glasses with a cloth. He looked up, smiled, and motioned us over. I gave Pete a cheeky grin and nudged his arm. "I'm gonna play a wild card here. That's Carl, right?"

Pete looked down at me, smiled, and gave me a discreet shove back. "It is. He's gorgeous, right?"

"Oh, absolutely!" I concurred.

Pete did his usual confident strut in Carl's direction, hands in his navy chino pockets, his navy-and-pink floral shirt and bright yellow tie ensuring no one would miss him. I often wished I could take just a smidgen of his confidence for myself. That would do. "Hey, how are you?" Pete smiled.

Carl gave a huge, toothy smile back. "I'm great, Pete. How was your day?"

"Amazing. Thanks for the tips. We had a wander down Rodeo Drive and the farmer's market. Such an great atmosphere down there!" Pete turned to me. "This is Ellie, by the way, my partner in crime."

I reached out and took his hand.

"Nice to meet you. You look fabulous, by the way," he generously offered in a long, slow American accent.

I felt my cheeks go red as I blushed. I'd never taken compliments well and preferred not to get them, from strangers anyway. They always made me feel a little awkward and self-conscious. "Um, thanks," I said, smiling and looking down at my black strappy sandals. "Will you be coming along with us later to the club?"

Carl's eyes lit up. "Sure! I have a few friends heading down that way tonight, so I'll head over when I get finished here."

"Great," I replied with genuine enthusiasm.

"So, what can I get you guys? Mojitos?"

Pete beamed. "Oh, Carl, you know me too well already."

"Take a seat. I'll bring them over," he offered kindly, throwing a tea towel over his shoulder and grabbing some cocktail glasses. He looked as if he meant business.

Taking the weight off my still-aching feet, I sat down on a cushioned metal chair under the fairy-lit veranda. "Well," I said, "you seem perky tonight, and might I say, particularly cheesy."

Pete smirked. "What?"

"You know what." I rolled my eyes and began to mimic my friend, "Oh, Carl, you know me too well," I teased, and we both laughed.

"Well, you know, I'm having a great time. I'm absolutely loving it."

"And from what I see, it's not just the place you're loving." I threw him a cheeky wink.

"Well, you know what? He's hot and, even better, I think I stand a chance there."

Pete gave me a nudge, and we both giggled again as Carl came over and placed our cocktails on the table before rushing off back to the bar to wait on a group of four girls who had suddenly appeared there. "Anyway, aren't you having the best time too?" he checked.

I took another sip of my mojito. "Aww, Pete, I am! I just love it here. It's got such a great vibe. The beaches, the villages … it's amazing."

I looked down into my glass, running my finger along its rim causing speckles of sugar to fall onto the table. "I guess I'm just a little worried about the whole money thing, you know? I'm having such a fab time. I'd love to stay as long as I can, but the dream is going to come to an end soon—much sooner than I'd like."

Pete placed his elbows on the table, leaning his chin on his hand. "Look, I'm not gonna let you starve, OK? I've got your back for a while, and if you're loving it as much as you say, maybe give some more thought to the job thing we talked about." Pete motioned over to the bar. "Carl there, he's from Florida. He came out here last summer. Been here ever since. The hostel gave him a room here for really cheap, and he works the whole summer. Loves it. You should think about it too, Ellie."

"Oh, really got to know Carl there, have we?" I teased again.

We both laughed and took another sip of our drinks. "Seriously Ellie, just give it some thought."

"I will, Pete, I will. I can't imagine going back home right now, what is there for me?"

Pete nodded. "My point exactly."

I stirred my mojito with its black straw and nodded in agreement. It seemed like a crazy thing to be thinking about, staying out here and working. But was it really? Maybe I needed to start thinking outside the box, take some chances. I had been sensible all my life, never taking too many risks. And look where it had got me. No job. No money. Nowhere to live. A cheating boyfriend.

"Come on, drink up. Let's get another round in." Pete grinned. "A certain amount of lubrication is needed for this evening's activities."

I glanced over at Carl. "Erm, what kind of lubrication are we talking about here?"

We both laughed, and Pete winked. "Just drink up."

We'd been in Avalon about two hours when Pete went missing. He'd told me he was just nipping to the bathroom, but nearly forty-five minutes later, he was nowhere to be seen. I'd texted him, but nothing. Oh, God, what if something had happened to him? What if he'd been attacked in the bathroom? He could be lying in a cubicle bleeding to death and I wouldn't know. I sighed and shut my eyes. *Calm down, Ellie. You always thing the worse. I'm sure he's fine. He probably just got held up cueing at the bar or something.* I willed myself to believe it. I opened my eyes and looked down at my black strappy sandals. The damn things had been pinching at my heels all evening, and I couldn't wait to tear them off. I smoothed my fringe away from my eyes and picked up my bag, but before I could stand up from our table, I heard Pete's familiar voice shout over at me. Thank God! I put my hand to my chest and scowled at him. "Where the bloody hell have you been?"

"Ellie, I'm sorry. I got caught up with Carl. You OK?"

"Well, yeah, apart from being left to sit here on my own twiddling my thumbs." I sulked.

"I know, I know, I'm sorry. But look, Carl has a friend I want him to introduce you too. Come on."

Frowning I picked up my bag and inched my way out of the booth, through a crowd of people, following Pete to another table on the other side of the dark club. Different coloured lights flashed from every direction, and the music was so loud, a mixture of house and dance. It had been a long time since I'd been to a "proper" club back home, preferring to relax in bars with a nice glass of wine and good conversation. I could hardly hear myself think in this place. I suppose you could officially call me old.

Two guys, Carl from the hostel and another guy I'd never seen before with short dark spikey hair, black rimmed glasses, and a thick beard, were chatting animatedly as we walked over. *Not bad*, I thought as I smiled awkwardly. Was Pete trying to set me up here? I certainly wasn't up for it, and he well knew it.

Pete beamed as Carl looked up as us and smiled back. "Hey, guys!" Carl said, managing to absolutely nail a pink fluorescent vest top and pink-rimmed glasses. His muscular arms were framed perfectly by the sleeveless top. And that tattoo! I'd never seen anything like it. His arm was covered right up to his shoulder.

Pete took centre stage and did the introductions "Guys, this is Ellie. And Ellie, you know Carl, and this is his friend Aaron."

Aaron smiled warmly and extended his hand. "Nice to meet you, Ellie. Pete's been telling me a bit about you."

I shot Pete a dirty look. "Oh, has he now?"

"So, Ellie, Aaron is a good friend of Carl's, and turns out he's a recruitment consultant here in Hollywood," Pete said. "I figured, after our conversations about working over here, he could give you some advice, point you in the right direction, you know?" Pete was smirking at me, looking too pleased with himself.

I looked from Aaron to Pete, not sure what to say.

"And I told him a little bit about you. How brilliant you are, of course. How you're looking for a new challenge." Pete winked at me and then kept the momentum going. "Aaron, why don't you sit next to Ellie so you guys can have a chat. I'll go and get us some more drinks. Gin?" Pete widened his eyes and me and started doing a shuffling motion with his hands as Arron scooched over in his seat, making space for me. Awkwardly, I sat down and watched Pete trundle off through the crowd of people in the direction of the bar.

"Aaron, I'm sorry, Pete can be a little overbearing at times. Once he gets an idea in his head, that's it. I'm sure the last thing you want to be discussing on your weekend off is work."

"I don't mind, Ellie. I'm happy to chat, but sure, weekends are for having some fun, right? So, how's about you give me your email, and Monday I'll send you a couple of things that may just interest you. How does that sound?"

I frowned. "Interest me?"

"Yeah, we have a few job vacancies at the moment—some pretty good opportunities, actually, have just come in. I'll send you a few things I think may be of interest to you. You can just send over your CV if you want to apply."

"Wow, that simple eh? Thanks! I'll certainly have a look."

Aaron handed me his iPhone, and I typed in my email address. "Thanks again," I repeated earnestly.

"No problem. You could be just what we're looking for to fill a role for one of our VIPs actually. He's British, and I believe he's looking for a Brit to fill the roll, so that could be perfect for you."

"VIP? What kind of role?"

Aaron smiled. "Monday."

Chapter 8

A professional, extremely organized, efficient, and enormously flexible individual is required. This individual must take work very seriously, be discreet and unobtrusive in all matters and be able to manage multiple projects at one time. The job is 24/7. A confidentiality disclosure agreement must be signed before employment begins.

"OK," Pete said flatly as we sat on my bed staring down at the small, brightly-lit screen of my iPhone, reading through the email Aaron had sent me as promised this afternoon. I had been surprised to hear back from him at all, but I couldn't deny I was intrigued.

"Do you see me as a personal assistant? Really? I mean, I struggle to organize myself! And, anyway, we don't even know who I'd be working for. Why are they being so hush hush about it? If I'm applying for this, I'd like to know who I'm working for." Pete shrugged, and I continued my protests. "And you know, this seems a hell of a lot more intense and permanent than bar work. I don't know if I want to get into something so deep. It's like a proper job." I scowled.

"Ellie, the way I see it, this if perfect for you if you can get it."

I screwed my face up. "How do you work that one out?"

Pete threw himself back on the bed, placing his hands behind his head. "I mean, sure, it's more intense than you wanted, and serving pizza and chips all day would *definitely* be easier. But look at the pay check!" Pete sat bolt upright, causing me to flinch. He grabbed my phone and scrolled down to the pay and benefits section of the email. "Starting salary: $70,000. Own car. Spacious living quarters. And look at this, 'The applicant must be able to travel internationally and be flexible for working on location. All travel expenses covered by employer.'"

I watched Pete's eyes light up. I grabbed my phone back from him and looked down at the email. I smiled and jabbed him playfully in the side with my hand. He winced. "Maybe you should apply," I told him. "You're more excited than I am!"

Composing himself, Pete retorted, "Ellie, darling, I don't have the employment credentials. Let's face it, I've gone from bar to restaurant to bar again back home. And I don't think my references would be the best, you know? Let me remind you of my brief stint at The Grills on the West End. That bitch Wendy hated me. Remember when she came over to me, three days into the job, and told me she didn't think I had it in me to serve steaks and that my customer service was abysmal? She said I looked angry at every customer just because I stood with my arms crossed while waiting to take their order. Absolute whore she was." Pete clenched his teeth together and then his voice softened. "But, for you, this is just too amazing to miss out on." I rolled my eyes as Pete threw himself back on the bed, placing his hands on his stomach. The room, despite the air conditioning was stifling. Sweat dripped down my nose. "Who cares if you mess whomever this person is around?" he said. "Apply! If you get it—and it's a big if—do it for a few weeks, a couple of months, get some cash together, and off we go again. You'd never make that kind of money in some crappy restaurant. You'll have no living expenses with this, and it'll be a hell of a lot more interesting than serving up burgers in a pinny."

We both laughed. I raised my eyebrows. "Erm, excuse me, but what's wrong with a pinny?" Pete tutted. Joking aside, I could see that what Pete was saying made total sense, but I just wasn't sure if it was worth the hassle. Then again, I'd have to get the job first. Maybe I'd just apply and go from there. Chances are, I'd never hear back anyway.

"Have you seen much of Carl since Friday night?" I said.

Pete shook his head, and a smile started to cross his face. "No, it's his weekend off, though I did see him in my dreams last night."

"Oh, shut it." I laughed. There was silence for a few minutes, both of us in deep thought, and then, decision made, I threw myself down next to Pete on the bed. "OK. I'll go for it. Why not? What's the worst that can happen?"

Pete's eyes sparkled with excitement, "Do it, ASAP, like today. Okay?"

I bit my lip, feeling butterflies in my stomach and then took a deep breath. "It does sound pretty amazing, doesn't it?" I said.

Pete turned his head to look at me and smiled. "I'd say it does."

The LA sunshine warmed my pale skin as Pete and I strolled along Laguna Beach. For a sunny morning it was pretty quiet. As I looked out to sea, I saw a thick mist dancing on the surface of the water towards the horizon. I wondered if maybe a storm was on its way in and the locals had decided to stay home. I looked down at my bare feet, damp sand tickling in between my toes. Leaning down, I picked up a greying broken shell, dusted it off, and held it up towards the sunlight. It was pretty, and when I looked at it closely, tilting it one way and then another, spots of pearlescent pinks and yellows appeared in swirls of colour on its rough surface. It was funny how something that was damaged could offer such beauty. *A memento from here*, I thought as I placed it in the pocket of my shorts.

It was Wednesday, two days after posting my CV, and I hadn't heard anything back from Aaron. Pete and I had decided to head over to Orange County and do some exploring. It was so pretty down there, and it reminded me of some of the coastal villages I'd visited in Spain. The side roads were all lined with terracotta-coloured houses and shops. Lush palm trees lined the pathways, and the waves made a continuous drumming sound as they hit the shore.

Pete and I slowly wandered along the shoreline. "I could get used to being down here," I said. "It's truly stunning, isn't it?"

Pete kept his gaze out to the ocean, his straw trilby shading his eyes. He looked dapper today—blue denim shorts; a black, loose-fitting shirt; and flip flops. He'd already caught the sun, and his golden tan glistened under the sun's rays. "Sure is." He sighed contentedly.

We sat down on the warm sand, facing out to sea, the sunshine licking our faces. Pete pulled out a bottle of water from his satchel and gulped some down, offering it to me. I took hold of the bottle and sipped it. It was so cold the condensation on the outside of the bottle wet my hands as I sipped it. Water had never tasted more delicious.

"So, I spoke with the hostel this morning," Pete told me. "We're paid up until tomorrow night. After that, if we want to stay in LA, we'll have to look for somewhere else, which is a shame as it's so nice, hey?"

I screwed up my face. "Wow! Yeah, that is a shame. What do you think we should do then?"

"Well, we've been here well over a week now, and I feel like we've pretty much seen everything on the list. We could move on up the coast? I could pick the rental car up tomorrow morning, and we could head up north to Santa Barbara? I've shortlisted a few places to stay on Trip Advisor, so it's just a case of ringing around and getting booked into somewhere for a few days. How does that sound?"

"I think that sounds amazing, Pete. I agree, it's probably the right time to move on." I watched the waves as they clashed against the worn rocks.

"And the job?" he asked. "It would be an amazing opportunity."

"It would have been, you're right, but I'm not holding my breath for it. I reckon I'd have heard something by now. Plus, I can't hang around here waiting forever, can I?"

Pete nodded, taking his trilby off and running his hand though his spikey blonde hair. "Sure. I mean, I guess we aren't going too far north yet, so it wouldn't be hard to get back if you needed to."

"Well, it's an option if it ever gets to that, but honestly, money is okay so far, you know? I'm budgeting. I don't want to spend this trip worrying about some job I was never going to get anyway. I'm just gonna continue exploring, have the best time, and if I have to, then there'll be other jobs and other things I can do. Worst case scenario, I get another few weeks out here, then I pack up and get my sun-tanned butt home." We both laughed.

"Them butt cheeks haven't seen the light of day," he said. "What are you talking about, girl?"

"Plenty of time, Pete, plenty of time. Did you not see my thong bikini in the suitcase?" We both laughed again, and Pete pushed me onto my elbows. I lay in the sand for a few moments, eyes closed, listening to the drumming of the waves. It was so relaxing, I could have stayed there all day. "Think you'll stay in touch with Carl?"

"Doubt it. I added him on Facebook, so I guess in that way we'll stay in touch. But, different lives, you know?"

"Well, yeah. I suppose you're in two different worlds. He's a Hollywood boy, and you're ... well ... not." I scrunched up my face. "Long-distance relationships are tricky."

Pete closed his eyes and positioned his face directly below the sun, leaning his arms behind him for balance. "Yep, it'd be doomed before anything even began."

Chapter 9

The ocean was mesmerizing as the sun's rays danced on the surface of the water, creating diamonds of light that flickered between the waves. As the car sped along, I looked out to the ocean, the view framed in palm trees. I took a deep breath and shut my eyes. Santa Barbara had been about an hour and half's drive from LA, and it felt like a different world. It was a beautiful place, and a feeling of freedom and energy overwhelmed me. I could feel my heart beating faster as I longed to arrive at our destination and start exploring. The clicking of the car indicators broke my thoughts as Pete suddenly pulled over to a lay-by. The car chugged abruptly to a stop, forcing us both forward, tightening the seatbelt across my chest. Pete gave me a coy sideways glance. "I'm still getting used to this right-hand driving, okay?"

I rolled my eyes and giggled. He continued excitedly, pointing to the top of the road ahead. "Anyway, I think we're pretty much here, according to the satnav, anyway."

I brushed my hair out of my face as Pete pointed to a large white-painted building. Lush palm trees and pretty pink-and-yellow-flowered shrubs framed the Spanish-style house perfectly. "That's where we're staying? Wow! It looks amazing. Well done you!" I smiled and gave Pete's shoulder a squeeze.

"Yep, come on. Let's get there and investigate."

As we drove up the thin winding road towards the building, those butterflies of excitement caught me again. This place seemed quiet and tranquil, and I was looking forward to spending some time by the sea, taking in the breathtaking views after the hustle and bustle of city life in LA. Pete slowed down as we neared the house. A small black-and-white sign at the front of the house said Drew Residence.

He squinted his eyes as he looked up at the pretty cottage. "Yep, this is it."

Peeling my sunglasses off, I looked up. "It looks quite continental, doesn't it?"

"I know what you mean, but let's not get too excited till we get inside. It wasn't expensive, but I did get a cancellation, so you never know. We could have dropped on here."

I put my glasses back on and leaned back in the car seat. "You know, I'm sure we passed a Hilton Hotel half an hour or so ago. We can backtrack if we have to."

Pete gave me a scowling look, and we both laughed. We didn't care where we stayed really. Who would when you had the beauty of Santa Barbara on our doorstep?

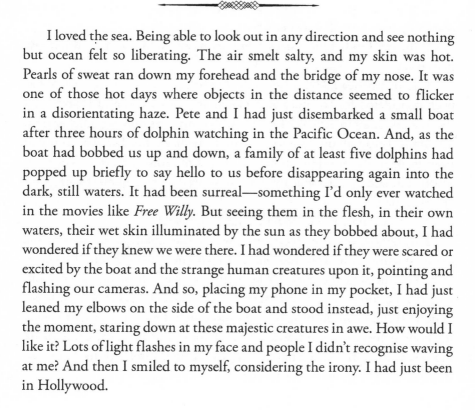

I loved the sea. Being able to look out in any direction and see nothing but ocean felt so liberating. The air smelt salty, and my skin was hot. Pearls of sweat ran down my forehead and the bridge of my nose. It was one of those hot days where objects in the distance seemed to flicker in a disorientating haze. Pete and I had just disembarked a small boat after three hours of dolphin watching in the Pacific Ocean. And, as the boat had bobbed us up and down, a family of at least five dolphins had popped up briefly to say hello to us before disappearing again into the dark, still waters. It had been surreal—something I'd only ever watched in the movies like *Free Willy*. But seeing them in the flesh, in their own waters, their wet skin illuminated by the sun as they bobbed about, I had wondered if they knew we were there. I had wondered if they were scared or excited by the boat and the strange human creatures upon it, pointing and flashing our cameras. And so, placing my phone in my pocket, I had just leaned my elbows on the side of the boat and stood instead, just enjoying the moment, staring down at these majestic creatures in awe. How would I like it? Lots of light flashes in my face and people I didn't recognise waving at me? And then I smiled to myself, considering the irony. I had just been in Hollywood.

It was still early as we lay on the beach. Pete sat down and fell backwards into the sand placing his straw trilby over his face to shade it from the sun's piercing rays. Even he had caught a little sun. The end of his nose was bright red after our hike yesterday up to Knapp's Castle. It hadn't been a long walk, but the views at the top of the hill and the scenic ruins were stunning though we'd forgotten our sun cream and were paying for. I sat down next to Pete and pulled a bottle of water out of my bag. "It's been a fabulous two days. I really feel like I've been on holiday with the beach and the sunburn."

Pete didn't look up. "My nose is a state. I look like bloody Rudolph!"

We both laughed as I lay down next to him, taking my iPhone out of my pink rucksack. I scrolled through. There was a text from Mum asking how I was doing, and a ton of emails, all sales stuff as usual. As I scrolled further, however, there it was ... "Pete! Fuck, Pete! It's an email from Aaron." I nudged him in the arm and he sat bolt upright, his trilby falling onto his knees.

"Go on!" he said excitedly.

"I've got an interview! Jesus." I read and reread Aaron's short paragraph, searching for more of an explanation, something else.

"Oh, my God, Ellie, that's fabulous news. Will you go? What else does it say?"

I shook my head. "Not a great deal to be honest. Just that my CV has been considered for the post of personal assistant to A, and I have been shortlisted for an interview." I kept reading, my eyes moving quicker than my brain. I read aloud, "Interviews are to be held this Tuesday. You will need to be at Beverly Hills hotel at 10.45 a.m. Your interview will be at 11.00. The successful applicant will know on the day and meet with A for an assessment."

Pete's eyes narrowed. "What? Okay, who is A?"

I shrugged, my eyes piercing down at the small phone screen, the words starting to morph into one as I read and reread them. "I have no idea. I'm guessing the client? The VIP? They're still being cagey about who this person is. Why?" Pete stared at me in silence as I shook my head. "I don't think I can do this, Pete. It's too much. I'm just starting to enjoy my holiday here. I want to watch more dolphins, lie here, get a tan, drink mojitos at that little shack bar around the corner. I don't think I'm up to this, you know? It just seems too much."

I'd been waiting for this email for days, checking and rechecking my inbox, hoping I'd hear something, and now here it was, and I didn't know what to do. Aaron had told me there'd be interviews, but I had honestly never thought I'd get through the paper sieve. I had no idea of what to expect. Who would be interviewing me? What should I wear? What would they ask me? Nothing. And it was Sunday. The interview was Tuesday morning. I would have to get back to LA today to prepare, find somewhere to stay. Oh, God.

"Okay, Ellie, I can see from your face you're going into meltdown here. Don't panic. We can sort this."

I shook my head, put my phone down, and fell back into the sand. "I don't know, Pete. I think it's all too much."

"Oh, come on, Ellie, do this." Pete lay next to me and put his hand on my arm, squeezing it. His voice went soft and quiet. "I saw you in London. That night we went for drinks just after you'd broken up with Finn, you were a mess. And now you have this amazing opportunity. No one likes interviews. No one wants to do these things. But what the hell have you got to lose?" I kept my eyes shut. "If you don't get the job, that's okay. We'll move on to our next adventure. You'll stay a few more weeks, and then you'll have to head home, penniless and jobless. But you go, you get it? Take it. There's nothing for you back home—no job, no boyfriend, no flat."

I rolled my eyes. "Jesus, Pete, tell it like it is, why don't you? Hand me a bloody razor blade."

We both laughed as Pete continued his pep talk. "If you don't go, you'll never know. We can carry on for, what? Four weeks tops? And then you said yourself you'll have to go home. To what? But take the interview, and if you get the job, do it for a few months, earn a shed load of money, get your bills paid, a house to stay in, a car, the works, and then ... well off we go again."

I looked at Pete. He stared back, and I knew he was right. This job offered something new along with more money than I had ever earned before and a free place to stay in an amazing city. In my time off, I could explore, make friends, and as Pete said, after a little while, move on. Why was I being so cautious?

"I just think, go, do the interview, see how you get on, and go from there. Make the decision when you need to."

I nodded. It was time for change. Maybe I wouldn't get it anyway. But as he said, what did I have to lose? "Okay, I'll do it. I'll go back to LA tonight or tomorrow, and I'll go and see what happens."

A smile formed over Pete's lips as he leaned over and hugged me. "Fabulous, and *so* the right decision. I just have the best feeling. I'll drive you back today, and we can get a room booked in LA for you on the way. That won't be a problem."

I looked down again into my phone, the sunlight making it hard to see the screen. I was covered in sand and felt weary after the boat trip's early start. I picked up my blue flip-flops and stood up, brushing down my green T-shirt and blue denim shorts. "Time for lunch and a mojito before we hit the road?"

Pete winked. "Most certainly."

"What's your favourite movie character?" Pete paused and looked at me. "That was a question?"

"Yep, first one. It kind of caught me off guard. I was expecting the usual 'Tell us a little about yourself' or 'Where do you see yourself in five years?' But no, movie characters."

The interview had lasted half an hour, and the majority of it was a blur. Walking through the Beverley Hills Hotel entrance with its black-and-white-striped ceiling and red carpet, I felt like a fraud. I couldn't believe I was doing this, but at the same time, I felt surprisingly calm. I looked down at my red high heels, which blended with the carpet, as I made my way up the steps and through the glass doors. I hadn't been waiting long before a young, twenty-something brunette girl with a huge, cosmetically enhanced trout pout came over to me and asked me to follow her. I duly had, awkwardly pulling the waist on my black pencil skirt round to where it should be and smoothing over the front of my new cream shirt with the palm of my hand as I walked behind her. I'd felt OK up to that point, but then the sweat appeared on my nose, and suddenly I felt very self-aware and so out of my depth. The girl certainly wasn't fond of small talk as she silently motioned me over to a small sofa covered in grey fabric. I sat there, sweating and alone, for only a few minutes before two guys walked in, both also in their twenties and dapper looking. One was working an amazingly well-groomed beard and thick, black rimmed glasses. The other was clean shaven with short, spikey hair. He was wearing a short-sleeved denim shirt and black skinny jeans. They were polite and they smiled, and then they hit me with it.

Pete looked at me in bemusement, a smile creeping onto his lips. "And what did you reply?"

"Well, Pete, you know my favourite movie of all time." This wasn't a question. He knew of course.

"Oh no, *Labyrinth*." Pete put his hand to his mouth, covering a smile. "You didn't say Hoggle did you? Please tell me you didn't!"

I pulled a face at him. "Behave. No, I didn't. Sarah of course. I said, 'Like Sarah, I'm resourceful and take on creepy muppets all the time in real life.' I was actually pretty impressed with my quick thinking." Pete didn't say anything. He just nodded and gritted his teeth together. I stared, wide eyed at him. "What? Oh no! Was it rubbish?" Pete started laughing. My eyes began to water, and I grabbed a tissue to blot them dry. I didn't know whether to join in his laughing or cry.

"Oh, Ellie, only you. I can't believe you said that. What did they say?"

"Not much. Just an 'okay', and I think one of them sort of smiled, but then they both just closed the books they'd been writing in, stood up, shook my hand, and left." I shrugged. "Then trout-mouth girl came back and escorted me out." We laughed until my belly started to ache.

"Jesus! Well, it's done. Guess it's just a waiting game now."

"Well, not long. They said the successful applicant would be told on the day, so anytime now."

"So, I guess we better go and have some drinks to calm our nerves, hey? And since we find ourselves back here in LA for the night, cocktails down on Sunset Strip?"

"Oh, God, yes! Let's do it." I beamed. I wasn't going to let the interview get me down. What was done was done. I couldn't change anything.

I walked into the bathroom and looked in the mirror. I was still dressed in the black skirt and cream blouse I'd worn to the Beverly Hills Hotel earlier. My hair was still in a tight chignon bun high on my head, and most of my make-up was still in place despite the heat, which usually melted it off my face. A quick change, and I'd do. After a few mojitos, the interview would be a distant memory.

———————◆◇◆◇◆———————

Ellie,

Congratulations. I have the pleasure of writing to let you know you are the successful applicant for the position of personal assistant to A, pending any issues arising from the assessment. A is very much looking forward to meeting you tomorrow at Café Latte in Beverly at 2.15 p.m. prompt. Just be yourself, and if you have any questions, call me.

P.S. Sorry I didn't get back to you yesterday as promised. We have been so busy here this week. Say hi to Pete for me.

Regards, Aaron

I stood in my hotel room, towel wrapped round me, water dripping from my hair onto the tiled floor.

I read the words over and over again, expecting some subliminal message to appear telling me that, actually, this was all a dream, and everything was in my imagination. I perched myself on the edge of the bed, turned my phone screen off, and looked in the full-length mirror. I twisted my long strands of hair around my fingers and drained the now-cold water onto my towel. I felt a shiver despite the warmth of the room.

Was this the start of a new chapter? Could I really make it out here, even if it was just for a little while? I felt bubbles of excitement mixed with nervousness swirl around in my tummy. I stared down at the blue bobbled rug and combed my fingers through my thick, wet hair. Who was A? It had all been so secretive. A wealthy businessman? A lawyer? A popstar? And what if he or she didn't like me? Was the whole point of the "assessment" a chance to just suss me out? I wasn't going to even try and begin guessing. Tomorrow was only a few hours away, and I needed to make some preparations. What was I going to wear? Should I get a manicure? All perfectly acceptable ponderings.

After the interview yesterday, Pete and I had ended up having a pretty heavy session down on Sunset Strip. It's safe to say that both of us were pretty drunk by the time we arrived back at the hostel later that night. For a time, I'd forgotten all about the interview, but every so often I'd checked my emails until eventually, at eight o'clock, I gave up any hope of hearing anything. I just assumed that was it, and I'd knocked back a few more gins and elderflower tonics to drown my sorrows. Since the interview, I'd thought about the job interview a lot, and I was glad in the end to have gone. I'd warmed to the idea of the job more and more, and whilst I never thought I'd get it, there had been a very slight glimmer of hope, and I'd held it tight. But as I clambered into bed last night, the room spinning as I closed my eyes, I'd felt that the hope had gone.

This morning, I was so hungover, my head hurt between my eyes and I felt sick to the stomach. Pete had woken in a slightly better state and had decided to head back to Santa Barbara, since we were still paying for the hotel there until next week. There was a Spanish Festival going on in the town, and the streets promised to be bustling with music, dancing, and local food stalls—pretty much everything Pete loved. I'd decided to hang around for just a couple more nights, and had made my decision that, if I hadn't heard anything from Aaron by Thursday morning, I'd link back up with Pete, and we'd continue are journey. But now, much to my complete shock, I guessed my travel plans were postponed. I had a coffee date.

Chapter 10

It was 2.17 p.m., and here I was in a side booth of the small, quirky café A had chosen for our meeting. Aaron had sent me a text when I was on my way there, asking me not to sit in a window seat, and instead to pick a side booth out the way of any passers-by. *What a weird request,* I thought. Was A some sort of recluse? A total nut job? I had to hand it to A, though, crazy or no crazy, this place was pretty cool. A tiled floor of black-and-white squares, sage green walls, and red bauble lights hanging from the ceiling made the atmosphere eccentric, yet strangely relaxing. The colourful, mismatched chairs and cushions, retro café signs, and old vinyl records spread across the walls furthered the eclectic feel, and Bob Marley's "One Love" was playing in the background. I could quite easily sit here all day, inhaling the comforting aroma of freshly brewed coffee and reading a good book.

Twenty minutes later, and still no sign of A. I wondered if I should ring Aaron and get him to chase up whoever this person was, but I didn't want to come across as pushy. How long should I be expected to wait? My second latte was gone, and I was caught up on current affairs thanks to having read some local newspapers. I was the only one in the café now. I was standing up to go to the bathroom when, out the corner of my eye, I saw a black Mercedes with tinted windows pulled up outside. Damn it, I couldn't see who was driving. Was this A? Trying not to look too eager, I sat back down and held my phone in front of me, pretending to read from it. With a sneaky sideways glance, I saw the driver's door open and a young guy get out. Okay, maybe not.

I realized I was holding my breath only as I let out a disappointed sigh. This guy was way too young and scruffy looking to be A. He slammed the car door shut and started to walk towards the café, placing his keys into the back pocket of his jeans before stuffing his hands in his front pockets. He was tall and athletic looking with longish blonde hair tucked behind his ears and partially covered in a grey beanie hat. He walked with a real swagger as he sheepishly looked from left to right as he walked through the door. I felt my face go warm as he walked in, the café door making a loud ding noise. *He may not be A, but he's almost certainly a hottie,* I thought to myself as I stood back up, placing my phone in my bag and slowly edging my way out of the booth. I would give A ten more minutes, and then, that was it, I was going. What a total waste of time this had all been.

As I walked past the café counter, I glanced over at two waitresses giggling between themselves. One whispered to the other, and I guessed "hot guy" was causing a bit of a stir. I smiled to myself and headed for the bathroom.

"Ellie?" A man's deep, husky, British accented voice behind me stopped me in my tracks. I turned around and black Mercedes guy stood in the middle of the room looking at me. He slowly took his beanie off and allowed his hair to fall from behind his ears. "You're Ellie Gibson, right?"

Oh, my God! Charlie Robinson! I stood staring at him, my mouth drying up. Charlie Robinson, super-hot, super-famous actor person was looking at me and had just said *my* name.

"You are Ellie, right? Sorry I'm late. I got tied up with something."

I couldn't speak, and my heart started to beat out of my chest. Could you actually see someone's heart beating fast? Okay, now was the time to say something—anything—but I couldn't remember any words. *Act natural, just do something, pick something up, smile, do anything you would normally do.* Nothing. I just stood there, staring at his lips, his eyes, his hair, his lips. Oh, God.

He took his hands out his pockets and walked towards me. "Ellie, are you okay?" His thick, perfectly groomed eyebrows drew together, his eyes on me. A bead of sweat trickled down the bridge of my nose, and I took a huge gulp. A clatter of cutlery from behind the café counter startled me back to the room. We both looked over at the two girls, who were clambering around to pick things up from the floor. I watched them, licking my lips and trying to regain some composure. He turned back to me, and I finally spoke. "Err, sorry. Yes, I'm Ellie."

He started laughing, combing his huge hands through his golden locks. "Great, and I'm sorry about that whole A thing. It just prevents people who have other intentions from applying for the job, you know? I'm Charlie. Great to meet you. Shall we sit?" He smiled again, flashing his flawless Hollywood teeth as he motioned over to the seat. We sat down opposite each other. "I have to know the right person is applying for this job for the right reasons."

"Of course. Completely understand. No problem," I said awkwardly. I could feel my cheeks burning, and my hands felt clammy as I rubbed them together under the table.

"Were you going somewhere?" Charlie asked casually.

"Yes. Sure. I'll just ... I'll be back in two seconds, okay?" I quickly stood up and inched my way out of the booth. Charlie picked up the drinks menu. He shook his head. "I pick this menu up every time, even though I always order the same thing." He smiled, rolling his eyes and placed the menu back down on the table. "I'm having an espresso. What can I get you?"

Trying to seem breezy I turned around and smiled. "Oh, anything. A black coffee's fine. Thanks." I could feel his eyes on me as I hot-stepped my way through the bathroom door, closing it behind me. I leaned my back against it and shut my eyes. Oh, God, I hoped I hadn't made a total idiot of myself. Had I been rude? Should I have shaken his hand? I felt flustered. *Damn it! Pull yourself together, Ellie.*

I knew I should have made more of an effort with the make-up and got my hair blow-dried. Damn, I looked a right bloody mess. My nails at least, thank goodness, had been treated to a last-minute French manicure yesterday, and I'd pick up a new lippy from Sephora, but I still felt somewhat inadequate now against his absolute fitness. After a few deep breaths, I opened my eyes. *OK, here it is. Charlie Robinson is sitting out there, drop-dead gorgeous, but he is now my boss. He's not just super-hot though. So far, he actually seems pretty normal, even making a joke of himself, and I'm going to be living in his house, doing chores for him, hearing his telephone calls, speaking to his family members and friends. No one will believe me. This is too insane.* I shut my eyes again and shook my head. My mind was whirling.

I thought back to my flight into LA. *Celebrity* magazine was running an article on Charlie about his new film. He was in London at the premier, suited and booted with some gorgeous blonde girl in tow. I hadn't thought a great deal about it at the time. I'd only looked at the bloody pictures. I rolled my eyes and could feel my neck getting hotter as I got more flustered. I needed to pull it together. Now!

I walked over to the oval mirror above an old-fashioned white sink and looked at myself. *Calm down, Ellie. If you mess this up, it's over. Be normal. Take a breath. He's just a human being, like you. Remember what they say—when you get nervous in front of people, picture them naked. Right, like imaging this guy stark naked is going to help this situation.* I rolled my eyes, pulling my new Charlotte Tilbury lipstick out my bag—Red Carpet Red. *Well this was certainly fitting,* I thought as I dotted a small about onto each lip and smudged it across. Didn't want it to be too "out there" of course. Nice and subtle, just a hint. I smoothed my long fringe to one side and traced my fingers under my eyes, wiping away any trace of caked foundation and mascara. Right, I'd have to do.

Charlie was at the counter when I slid back into the booth. The two waitresses were beaming up at him as he handed them a piece of paper and a pen. He was tall—definitely over six feet—and his body looked so toned and muscular. My eyes wandered down to his bottom. Oh my, it fitted quite nicely in his jeans. He turned, and I flushed, instantly throwing my eyes back up to his, hoping he hadn't caught me admiring his backside. He smiled and walked over to me, placing his espresso and my black coffee on the table. As he intertwining his fingers, a thick, silver, bohemian-style ring on his thumb reflected the light. "So, I'm sorry," he said. "I don't have too long this afternoon. I have a production meeting for a new project at four o'clock. I just wanted us to meet, and I guess get a little better acquainted before you start."

I smiled, taking a sip of coffee. Charlie seemed so natural and at ease with himself, oozing a confidence that I could only ever dream of having. When I first met someone, I always felt somewhat awkward, conscious of what the other person thought about me. I worried about not saying enough and coming across as shy or saying too much and being seen as over-bearing. I worried about what people thought of my hair, of my shoes, and if they noticed that one eyebrow was ever so slightly thicker than the other. I tried to push these thoughts out of my mind and tried to remind myself of something Mum once said to me: "People are too busy worrying about themselves to be worrying about you." Which, I guess, since I was worrying about myself all the time, was probably true. Sometimes remembering this helped, and sometimes it didn't. And I could pretty much say that, right now, those words of advice were not easing the awkwardness I felt.

"Sure," I replied, trying to sound normal but cringing inside, my eyes wandering down to his plump and kissable lips as he sipped his drink. I wondered if this could be some kind of out-of-body experience. Maybe I'd drunk too much coffee this morning and was having a caffeine-induced hallucination. Anything was more possible than Charlie Robinson sitting before me, sipping his espresso.

Placing his cup on the table, he folded his arms and sat back against the booth. "So, I already know quite a bit about you. Is there anything you want to ask me?" His eyes were burning into mine as my face went hotter. I shifted in my chair and took another sip of coffee (possibly not the best idea since the hallucination theory was still in the air). I looked down at the table. To look at him was too difficult. He was way too beautiful for me to be talking to. I cleared my throat. "Oh yes. Lots of things, I guess. Um, just not too sure where to begin."

He smiled and looked down at the table, his long blonde hair falling over his face. He quickly swept it back behind his ears. "How do you like LA?" he asked.

I forced my eyes up to his, but couldn't hold his gaze. I looked back down at my mug "Oh, I just love it. My friend and I spent over a week here exploring. It's got a wonderful feel."

Charlie nodded and smiled back, taking another sip of coffee before placing it down and tracing the edge of the cup with his finger. "Yeah, I love it here. It's home now, you know?"

I smiled and started to fiddle with my silver drop earring. *Come on, Ellie*, I scolded myself. All I had to do here was act normal, ask some questions, and not get all geeky. I could do this. I'd been in enough social situations to hold a conversation, just not one that had involved an international movie star, but I was mature enough, and this job depended on me not acting like a complete moron right now. I took a deep breath. "Where in the UK are you from? Your accent doesn't give much away."

Charlie gave a little laugh to himself and twisted his thumb ring. "Manchester originally, though I moved down to London when I was twelve with my parents for their work. Get home as much as I can, and I miss some of my home comforts, but you know, work's busy. Your application said you're from London too. Whereabouts?"

I nodded, pushing my fringe away from my eyes. "Yeah, Fulham."

Charlie's eyes widened, and he gave a huge grin. "No way, I grew up in Battersea. We were so close—that's crazy!"

I couldn't help but smile back, a tiny bit of my unease starting to lift, my shoulders relaxing ever so slightly. He seemed genuinely excited that we had grown up so close, which was, in all fairness, pretty remarkable. It made him, for that moment, much less of a movie star and more of just a normal, albeit amazingly handsome, guy.

Charlie took another sip of his coffee, keeping his huge grin, and I couldn't help but stare at his perfectly white, straight teeth. I wondered if they were real, or like a lot of things in this town, paid for. Either way, he had the most beautiful smile.

"Imagine if our paths have crossed before," he said. "I used to go to that little cinema, the independent one down Berry Street." He looked up past me towards the ceiling. "Did you ever go there? Damn it, what was it called?"

I nodded and smiled, feeling all a flutter inside. "The Arthouse." I used to go there all the time as a teenager. It was the place to be seen when you were fifteen and looking to get off with the fit guy from physics. I'd shared a kiss of two with Daniel (the fit boy from physics) in the alleyway next to the cinema. I'd be dolled up to the nines with hoop earrings and the latest Top Shop dress I'd saved up three months' pocket money for. Life was so much simpler back then.

"Yes!" Charlie almost jumped out his chair. "That was it. God, I used to love that place. Those green velvet chairs and the pink-and-white-striped boxes they served popcorn in." I giggled as he spoke. I loved that place. So many happy memories. "And remember Bob?" Charlie beamed.

I did a little jump up in my chair, the excitement of our unexpected shared past momentarily consuming me. "The cinema usher? Of course. He was so lovely."

Charlie placed his elbows on the table, leaning closer to me. "I used to spend hours chatting to him. I'd sit on that little step outside while he brushed up, and I'd make him tea while he cashed the tills. We'd chat for hours about movies." Charlie looked down at his hands, fiddling with his thumb ring. "I wonder where he is now."

"It's still open, you know. Maybe he still works there?" I said.

"Doubtful. He must have been in his fifties back then, and we're about fifteen years on." I nodded. I couldn't believe that we'd hung out in the same spot and never bumped into each other. I would almost certainly have remembered him. I looked up from my drink, his eyes on me. "It's a small world, hey?" he said. "How did we not cross paths? I'm pretty sure I would have remembered you."

What did he just say? Complete brain freeze took over me. He would have remembered me? In what way? I wanted to ask, but the words wouldn't leave my mouth. Charlie Robinson thinks he would have remembered *me*? I tried to bring my attention back to what my face was doing, since clearly my mouth had stopped cooperating. Carla always told me my face said everything—that if I was pissed off or embarrassed, I didn't need to speak—and I feared this was one of those moments. I tried to smile.

Charlie shifted in his chair. "My dad still lives in Battersea actually. He has an apartment there. My mum ... she died, a few years back now." He looked down and picked up a spoon that was lying on the table, twirling it in between his fingers.

I threw my hand up to my mouth. "Oh, I'm so sorry."

Charlie didn't look up from his cup as he continued to twist the spoon in his hands. "It's okay. It was a good few years ago now. I just wish Mum could have been here to see what I've achieved, since it's down to her—her encouragement—that I'm here at all."

I nodded, taking another sip of coffee, my eyes leaving his. A silence fell over us, and a pang of self-awareness hit me again like a brick. Shifting in my chair and clearing my throat, I searched my brain for something else to say, but after the excitement of our shared teenage past, my mind had gone blank. I forced my eyes up again to see him staring at me. I could feel the back of my neck getting hot and my mouth drying up. What was he thinking? My tummy started doing summersaults as I looked back down.

Eventually, his eyes still all over me, he said, "What brings you to LA?"

"Gosh … erm, I needed a holiday. My friend, Pete, was coming here, had the whole trip planned, and I just jumped on board last minute." I shrugged.

He sat back, slouching in his seat, relaxing into the red leather cushions. "How come so last minute?"

"Well, some personal issues at home prompted a bit of a change in direction." How much should I tell him? My mind was racing, as I didn't want to lie, but I hardly wanted to start divulging my relationship woes to him. I'd keep it brief, to the point. I took another sip of coffee.

Charlie's eyes narrowed, and he sat back up, listening intently. "Personal issues?"

"Just guy problems. All sorted now." I shook my head to show it wasn't a concern.

He smiled and took his black leather wallet from his back jeans pocket. He took out some dollar bills and placed them on the table. "Ah, OK I won't pry into that anymore."

"No, it's fine. He's long gone. I'm just glad the whole thing had a silver lining, bringing me here."

Charlie smiled. "Positive thinking—I like that."

We both picked up our cups and sipped our coffee in silence. I hoped I hadn't got into personal stuff too soon, but he had asked, and I wanted to be honest. I was surprised at how normal he seemed because, of course, I'd never met a big Hollywood movie star before. I once bumped into the guy who plays Ian Beale on *Eastenders* on the Northern Line between Chalk Farm and Camden Town, and another time I chased after David Beckham's car when he was leaving a book signing in the West End, but all I can hope is that, during that incident, Becks didn't actually see me. This was different. Sitting here chatting with Charlie was just surreal. He looked down at his silver Tag Heuer watch. "Ellie, I'm going to have to get moving. I'm sorry we couldn't have more time here. We haven't even touched the surface, but I'm glad we did this."

I smiled politely, hoping this wasn't just his quick escape. "Sure, great to meet you."

Charlie pulled out his mobile phone from his jeans pocket and looked down at the screen. "So, I'm guessing you're okay to start tomorrow? Here's the housekeeper's mobile number. Her name's Jessica. Give her a call. She'll give you all the info you need, okay?"

"Tomorrow? Wow, yes, fine, absolutely."

He looked up from his phone and beamed at me, his perfectly white teeth sparkling. His beautiful blue eyes glistened as he looked at me. He started to stand up, inching his way out of the booth. Sam Smith's "You Know I'm Not the Only One" started to play in the background. "I love this song. One of my favourites," he said.

"Really? One of mine too, actually."

Charlie ran his fingers through his hair again, sweeping it behind his ears and placing on his grey beanie. "OK, well, see you tomorrow, Ellie. Make yourself at home. I'm likely to be in meetings and rehearsals all day, but I'll be about at some point. And don't worry, Jessica is great. She'll show you the ropes. I won't go hard on you, it being your first week and all." He looked at me without smiling, and I felt my cheeks flush crimson. Charlie pulled his sunglasses over his eyes, pushed the café door open and sauntered out, jumping into his car and driving off.

I sat there in a daze. Had that just happened? Or was I about to wake up in my hotel room, this morning not even started yet? I looked over at the counter. The two giggling waitresses were sending daggers my way as I smiled politely and picked up my bag from the table.

I felt as if I was walking on a cloud as I headed out into the warm LA sunshine. He wasn't what I'd expected at all. He seemed normal, kind, thoughtful, not to mention drop-dead bloody gorgeous. Had I already mentioned that? I was really going to have to watch myself here. I couldn't go getting a crush on my boss, though it was going to require some serious willpower. I had to remind myself he was a Hollywood movie star with pretty much the entire earth's population of women to pick from, if he hadn't already. We hadn't even got close to talking about his relationship status. But, the point here was that he wouldn't look twice at a plain Jayne like me anyway, so no point crushing on someone so wildly out of my league. I would be the consummate professional, working hard and getting the job done. But, who knew, Charlie Robinson and I could become friends, and that was exciting enough.

Of course, I went straight back to my hotel room and spent the remainder of the afternoon stalking Charlie on the internet. I googled, read his latest news feeds, browsed several thousand photographs and videos. I read his Wikipedia page, his Facebook fan page, and his twitter posts. I felt that I knew this guy better than he knew himself by the time I was finished. Most of his pap pictures saw him glaring at the camera, shooting the photographers dirty looks as they invaded his privacy. I wondered how he felt about that. I looked at photos of him eating, walking a dog, chatting with friends. But, despite that, he had a definite sparkle about him, and he oozed charisma. He exuded confidence in the way he walked and looked into the camera. In his interviews, his sultry deep London accent gave me goosebumps all over. Occasionally I'd here a slight American twang, but I guessed, living here, that was only normal. He was funny, charming, intelligent, creative, and artistic, and as I flicked through the images, I wondered if he even knew some of these photos existed at all. Did he even know they'd been taken? It must be an odd life to have strangers taking pictures of you getting on with living your daily life, and you don't even know it.

My eyes felt tired and sore as I rubbed them and sat up, leaning back on my arms. I picked my phone up off the bed, and it felt warm to touch. Maybe I'd spent a little too long in stalker mode doing "research", but one more hit before I was done. Clicking on Google I searched "Charlie Robinson girlfriend". Lots of images of Charlie at red-carpet events with the same tall, slim, and very attractive brunette girl. The internet, which of course is always right, said he was dating make-up artist to the stars, Mia Luce, and had been for several months. It was also speculating that the pair had recently got engaged. *Well*, I thought, as I threw myself back on the bed and rubbed my temples, *I guess I would find out pretty soon if Mia Luce was still on the scene, or anyone else for that matter.*

I looked again. More pictures of Charlie with various gorgeous blondes and celebrity types. Charlie with Emma Stone; Charlie with Reese Witherspoon. I put my hand to my mouth and shut my eyes. I had to stop looking now. This wasn't good for me. There was research and then there was this crazy bunny-boiler shit. Time to turn off. I had to get to know him for him, not for what TMZ.com told me about him. This was all way too surreal. Time to check in with Pete. He'd calm me down and put things into perspective.

"*Fuuucccckkkk! No! No!* I don't believe you. Who is it, really?"

"Pete, honestly, I'm not joking. It's him."

I thought Pete was going to explode with excitement as his high-pitched, raucous voice pierced my ear, forcing me to hold my phone at arm's length. I could still hear him quite well. "But, he's, like, a full-on celebrity person! Like, movie star celebrity person!" Pete couldn't even get his words out in an orderly sentence, they just spewed out of his mouth as quickly as his mind raced. The excitement was ridiculous, but I felt it too.

I sat smiling, hitting the speakerphone button and placing my phone on the bed. "I know, Pete, I know. I'm as stunned as you. Imagine my face when he walked in. Can you even imagine?"

"So, let me get this absolutely one hundred per cent straight here."

Oh, here we go, I thought, *another summing up from Pete.*

"You, Ellie Gibson, land in LA for a holiday and apply for a PA job for which you have no experience, which just turns out to be the PA for international Hollywood hottie Charlie Robinson. You now get to go live in his house, you get to drive his cars, and he gives you a shed load of money to do this. Man, am I sorry I didn't go for that job now."

We both laughed. "I know, Pete. I'm, like, pinching myself right now. I mean, can I believe any of this? I'm still expecting to wake up any minute now. Stuff like this doesn't happen to people like me."

"Well, what was he like? What did he say?"

"It was weird. He walked in, called my name and, well, a lot of it feels like a blur, but he was sort of normal and not what I'd have expected at all. He was chatty, friendly, and of course super sexy. I wanted to poke him just to make sure he was real, but I didn't want to seem like a complete weirdo, so obviously I didn't touch him at all, or poke him, but then he just said, 'See you tomorrow,' and he left."

"I bet you wish he wanted to poke you though, huh?" We both let out a fit of giggles. I threw myself back on the bed, holding my stomach as a stitch crept in.

"Well, fuck me. I can't believe it," Pete said, after regaining his composure.

"I know, Pete. I know."

I took a deep breath and sat up on the bed, looking over at myself in the long mirror hanging on the back of the door. "So, I'm starting tomorrow. I've literally got tonight to get my head around it, pack up, calm the fuck down, and get myself out of this crazy fan mode. It's exactly what he doesn't want, hence all the secrecy. I get it now."

Pete was quiet on the other end for a moment, contemplating his next question. "Was he as hot as he is in his movies?"

"Hotter, Pete. So much hotter." We laughed again.

I could hear the smile in Pete's voice. "You crushing?"

"Erm, of course. Who wouldn't be? But he's my boss now, and the whole A thing was to stop any crazies from applying for the job, so I have to stay professional. It's why he hired me. And, anyway, I'm just another employee to him. He has the pick of Hollywood's most beautiful women. I hardly think he'd look twice at me."

Pete tutted loudly. "You do yourself an injustice, Ellie. It's time to get some confidence. You are drop-dead bloody gorgeous, and he'd be lucky to have you."

I scoffed. "OK, Pete, whatever. Please don't say stuff like that."

Pete went quiet. I knew he hated me being down on myself, but I wasn't under any illusions. Charlie wouldn't look twice at me. I didn't completely hate the way I looked. I'd just come to realize, as I'd got a little bit older and a little bit wiser, that I was simply average. I was average looking, with an average job, an average ex relationship, and just an all-round average life. I didn't expect anything special, wasn't particularly good at anything, and had never been called beautiful—well apart from Mum and Dad, of course, but they didn't count. People always said I looked nice when I made an effort to dress up. I liked to shop, throw on some new make-up, and try different hair colours from time to time. But I was just average. And someone like Charlie would quite simply never be interested in me. I was fine with that. I would admire him from afar, and that was enough. But I hated those comments from Pete. Sometimes he was so flippant, and he knew compliments made me feel uncomfortable. Changing the subject, I said, "Anyway, where are you now? Still in Santa Barbara?"

"Yep, but I think I'll spread my wings and head up to Monterey and Carmel tomorrow. I'll miss you, though. Kinda wish I still had my travel buddy."

"Pete, I will so miss you too, but I'll be back with you as soon as I have enough to pay for us both to stay in a swanky five-star beach-front hotel, okay?"

We laughed, but I really meant it.

"Can I have dinner thrown in? Maybe even a glass of wine? Because, when you think about it, you'll realize that it's me who pretty much got you this job after all. You know, the support, the encouragement …"

"Pete, forget the wine. Once I'm back on the road, lets order a bottle of champagne! Make it two. We'll be back doing our Thelma-and-Louise thing in no time. Just give me a month or so to make some cash, and then I'll be done, and we'll be hitting it large."

We laughed again. "I'll hold you to that. Now go and get ready. Big day for you tomorrow."

Chapter 11

"Hi! I'm Ellie," I said into the speaker. "Charlie Robinson's expecting me."
I was doing my best to sound confident, while inside, as the huge, black
wrought iron gates, towered over me, my stomach was turning. A deep
buzz started up, and the gates slowly opened. The woman on the other
end of the intercom said nothing as the crackling on the speaker stopped.
Hesitantly, I walked up the steep, winding drive heaving my black suitcase
behind me. As the majestic white-walled villa came into view, I stood
staring at it, admiring its floor-to-ceiling windows and lush, beautifully
preened gardens.

I was struck by how much of a Spanish feel the property had—quite
traditional and very cosy. Not what I had expected from Charlie. But then,
I had no idea what to expect from him, full stop. I didn't know him. Not
yet. The driveway was huge, with four sporty-looking, gleaming motors
parked up. I took a deep breath, stepped up to the door, and rang the bell.
I could feel my heart pounding as I stood, and I quickly ran my fingers
through my fringe, pushing it to one side. A minute or so later, the door
swung open and a small, blonde-haired, pretty woman opened the door.
"Hi, come in. You must be Ellie." She didn't smile as I walked through the
door and into a colossal hallway. I looked up at the most amazing staircase
that seemed to go up for miles. Three huge pieces of modern abstract art
hung side by side on the dark-blue walls. The place was huge, with doors
heading off in every direction.

"I'm Jessica, Charlie's housekeeper. Nice to meet you." She smiled,
the corners of her eyes scrunching up as she did so. Was that a fake smile?

73

"Wow, thanks. What a great house. It's stunning!"

"Yeah, it's amazing, eh? Charlie really loves it here. He's really into his art, as I'm sure you can tell, and has quite contemporary tastes. He's been here a couple of years now and has really made the place his own."

I nodded. "It's certainly magnificent."

Jessica started walking into the kitchen, and I followed. The room was massive, one of the biggest kitchens I'd ever seen. Light grey cabinets, wooden worktops, a huge island, and a kitchen table big enough for ten people framed by bi-folding doors that let out to, of course, the most magnificent infinity pool overlooking the Hollywood Hills. I stood in awe, realizing that I'd been holding my breath. What a stunning place. And this was going to be my home for the next few weeks.

"So, I will show you to your room," Jessica said. "You can drop your bags there, and then I'll give you the tour of the rest of the house and your office. That sound OK?" Jessica started to move before I even had time to answer, so I followed. As we walked out of the kitchen and back into the hallway up the sweeping staircase, I briefly looked at colourful paintings as well photographs of Charlie with friends and family members looking happy. I continued to follow Jessica up a second staircase and onto another landing. This place was a Tardis. I'd need my satnav to get around it. At the end of the landing was a white door, which Jessica opened. As I followed her into the room, my suitcase dragging behind me, the scent of lavender hit me instantly.

"OK, so this is your bedroom and that's your bathroom. There's a bath, though I'm not sure how much chance you'll have to use it," she said, pointing to another door at the end of the large bedroom. All white walls, white bedsheets—pretty much everything white. She pouted, "If you want to put photographs up, pictures, whatever, you can do."

"It's amazing. Thank you."

She nodded, glaring at me a moment and then turned her gaze to the small window above the bed, which was decorated with white wooden shutters. "And just outside you get a good view of the pool."

I walked over to the window and peered out. There was the most wonderful-looking, crystal-clear infinity pool. It seemed to just hang over the Hollywood Hills. The water sparkled as it lightly rippled about. Cream-cushioned sun loungers lined the side of the pool, and a small terrace in the corner housed a dining table and huge wood burner. "I'm guessing he has some crazy pool parties down there?"

Jessica raised her eyebrows. "Actually, not so much. Charlie has a pretty small circle. He's private, you know? His friends come over for a beer and video games. And, sure, he has the odd evening out there, but to be honest, the pool doesn't get used that much. You're welcome to use it if you get any down time—and Charlie is out, of course—but you probably won't get much of a chance. You'll be pretty busy." I nodded, continuing to stare out into the hills. Jessica certainly enjoyed reminding me how busy I'd be here. Starting to make her way out of the bedroom, she stood in the doorway. "And if you want to follow me, I'll show you your office."

I walked into the small room next to my bedroom. Jessica folded her arms. "Everything you'll need for your crazy days, including laptop and phones. And if there's anything else you need, just pick it up yourself and bill his accounts." I looked around. The office was small but perfect—plain white walls like the bedroom, a dark wood desk, black leather swivel chair, and a little succulent plant positioned perfectly next to the laptop computer, which was switched on and ready to go. "Your username and passwords are written down on that little stickie note."

"That's great, Jessica. Thank you. You're super organized."

She pursed her lips together, and her expression hardened. "Well, honey, you have to be. Now, obviously you can use the main kitchen, but if Charlie is having guests, he'll probably want you to keep a low profile, get some takeout, or whatever. Generally you'll know well in advance." I watched her mouth as she spoke. Her lips were so plump and pouty, she must have had fillers in them. Jessica's eyes widened. "And you know that this is a probation period, right? Your first month here is just a trial to see if you fit in. Charlie has to like you. You'll be working closely with him."

I nodded, forcing a smile. Why did this conversation feel so awkward? "Of course."

"We've had few crazies apply for jobs recently. A cleaner we employed not long ago left a pair of pink thongs on his pillow—used, would you believe? And we think she stole some underpants of his too. Had to let her go."

I gasped. "Wow! That's awful."

"So, anyway, have a look around, get acquainted with the place, and I'll meet you in my office. It's at the other end of this landing. When you're ready—in, like, ten minutes or so, okay?"

Before I could say anything, she'd turned and walked out. I made my way back to my bedroom and shut the door, throwing myself onto the queen-sized bed, legs and arms stretched out as I stared at the plain white oval-shaped lampshade above me. I felt the sheets between my fingers. They felt soft—luxurious even–and had that freshly washed lavender smell. Nothing felt better than fresh sheets. I closed my eyes and stretched out further. My mind wandered to thoughts of Charlie and the amazing life he had here in LA. He was so lucky to have made it to where he had, but then he was also super talented. The hotel I'd been staying in had Netflix, and I'd managed to get some reruns of an American TV series he was in called *All About Us* before he made it big in LA. It was a sit-com that followed the ups and downs of three young married couples. It was funny, and he was terrific in it. I could see why Hollywood had snapped him up. I replayed our coffee shop meeting again in my head, remembering his beautiful smile and the way he had looked at me. I could feel my breath quickening as I remembered him leaving the coffee shop, the waitresses staring over at him. He had been talking to *me*. I closed my eyes, but before my thoughts could wander to anything more inappropriate, my phone dinged. My eyes shot open and I sat up and grabbed it from my bag. It was Mum: "Darling, update soon. I miss you. Let me know everything's okay. Mum X"

Making a mental note to reply later, I looked over at my suitcase but decided it could wait. After fixing my messy bun into a slightly less-messy bun, tucking a few loose strands into the bobble, and applying a fresh layer of nude lipstick to my dry, cracked lips, I stepped out of my room and made my way down to Jessica's office. As I got closer to the slightly ajar door, I heard Jessica's hushed voice, which sounded slightly strained. Was she on the phone, or was someone else in there with her? I edged slightly closer forward but couldn't hear anybody else's voice. Not wanting to interrupt what seemed like a tense conversation, I turned and started to head back to my room, but then I heard my name. What? I shouldn't be ear-wigging, but she had clearly just said my name in a conversation that sounded pretty tense. Naturally, I edged myself forward a little more towards the door, held my breath, and listened. "Yes, I know. Well, let's see, shall we? Let her bed in, and I'm sure the cracks will start to show. How she got this job I'll never know. I'm completely baffled. But, Charlie said give her a chance, so that's what I have to do—or at least have to *look* like I'm doing. Give me time, okay?" Silence. I held my breath in hard, unable to believe what I was hearing. Her heavy America accent was grating on me as she hissed her words down the phone. "I know, I know. Look, give me time. My hunch is he'll be advertising for another PA again very soon, and next time, I'll make sure you're in the running. Okay? You know it would be great to work with you. Friends back together again. We'd have such a laugh. Okay, I gotta go. I'll call you later."

The conversation ended, and I stood there, staring at her office door. I wanted to barge in there and confront her, let her know exactly what I thought of her and whatever little scheme she was planning against me. But I couldn't do it. My legs wouldn't move me forward. I felt upset, confused, and furious all at the same time. But I had to play this cool. Whoever it was she was talking to, and whatever it was she was trying to do, I was now aware of a plot against me, and that gave me the advantage. I had the upper hand and was one step ahead. As my dad always told me, "better the devil you know". I'd say nothing to Jessica, but the knowledge protected me from being too open with her. I'd could watch my step and play all the right cards.

I took a few deep, calming breaths, fixed my fringe out of my eyes—it really needed trimming—and strode into the room with a smile. Jessica's eye's widened, and her voice was high pitched. "Ellie, that was quick!" I said nothing. "Okay, so I'm leaving shortly. I'll show you around the rest of the place real quick, and then I have to go. Let's head outside."

I continued to smile through gritted teeth and followed her down the long corridor and the two flights of stairs we had come up earlier. The stairway smelled of warm vanilla as we quickly descended onto the ground floor. I looked around again, still unable to believe the grandness of the place. A chandelier made of intertwined stag's antlers hung above me, each point holding a miniature cream lampshade. It was certainly an interesting piece of art, and I wondered if they were real stag's antlers or purely decorative as I followed Jessica out the front entrance of the house and onto the driveway. The LA sunshine made me squint.

"OK, so here is the front door key," Jessica said, holding it out for me. All the other keys for windows, the cellar, and the cars are in a cupboard in the kitchen. You'll find them, don't worry. Charlie can always show you later."

I looked at each car in turn—a silver Aston Martin, a red Maserati, a very expensive-looking black 4 x 4, and a black Mercedes with completely blacked-out windows. Wow, would I be driving these? I honestly didn't think I had the nerve too. I hated to reverse at the best of times. All of my accidents had happened when I was reversing. I lacked complete spatial awareness when going backwards, so in one of these … well. Never mind that I'd be driving on the "wrong" side of the road! Perhaps I'd better let Charlie know before he handed me the keys.

Jessica continued. "Each one has its own keyring with a description of what that key opens, so you'll have no problems with it. Mostly, car wise, you'll use the black Mercedes. You can use it for whatever. There are no restrictions really. It's all insured for you, so all you have to do is drive it." Jessica looked at me, waiting for a reaction. I didn't give one, keeping my gaze on the cars. "Just figure out Charlie's schedule for the day—where he needs to be taken—and in between, you might get some time for yourself. But it really is twenty-four seven."

I nodded. Without giving me any time to respond, Jessica motioned me back through the front door and into the house. She pointed to her left. "The living room is through there. The kitchen you've seen already. Oh, the coffee machine makes an amazing brew, and you'll need plenty of it, that's for sure." Jessica faked a smile again and rolled her eyes. I was starting to get onto her game. She was trying to scare me and unsettle me into thinking that things were going to be chaotic and I'd be unable to cope. She was trying to zap me of my confidence to do the job before I'd even started. *I know what you're doing*, I thought, and I simply smiled back.

I continued to follow her out of the kitchen and down another long hallway, this one with dark wood flooring and cream walls. "There's a bathroom through there, and at the end of this corridor is Charlie's leisure room. He has his music stuff in here, his gym equipment, and some film stuff. He likes to keep this room as private as he can from the staff. It's his little man cave." Jessica pushed open the door, and I peeped inside the room. On one side was a gym area with all kinds of scary looking weights and machines. On the other side, four guitars hung on the wall. A set of huge speakers, a keyboard, and a set of drums took up the rest of the space. Wow, was there no end to Charlie's talents?

Jessica closed the door quietly and turned around, giving me a side glance as she quickly scurried back down the corridor and down the hallway. "There's usually always a member of staff around if you need anything. We have two cleaners, a cook, a gardener, and a driver, but the driver works only part time, mainly when Charlie has big red-carpet events and stuff like that. Charlie's generally pretty laid back about who drives him to places. As long as he gets there he doesn't mind."

I nodded, following Jessica back into the kitchen. She picked up her black leather rucksack from where it lay on the countertop. "OK, look, I'm sorry it's been a quick tour. I'd hoped to stay longer, but I need to get to an appointment this afternoon, so I'll leave you to explore on your own. I've left my cell number on your desk. Text or call me if you have anything urgent, and I'll be back tomorrow morning at six."

I folded my arms. "Great. Thanks."

Before I could say anything else, Jessica was making a beeline for the front door. As soon as she slammed it behind her, the house was suddenly very quiet. I looked up at my reflection staring back at me from a wood-framed mirror mounted on the wall. I recognized my face, but I felt that, behind the exterior, everything had changed. I could never have predicted six months ago that I'd be standing here in the kitchen of one of the biggest stars on the planet. It was beyond dreamlike, totally surreal, and I hadn't processed it all yet. I needed time to sit down with a brew and think. But there had been no time for that. Since the interview, everything had happened to quickly. And if Jessica's warnings were anything to go by, I'd have even less time now. Still I found myself expecting to wake up in my London flat, Finn fast asleep beside me, the last weeks all having been the worst nightmare. Or was it the best dream? I wasn't sure, but with every moment that went by, I had to keep hoping that it wouldn't end.

Chapter 12

As I climbed the vast spiral staircase, I examined the framed black-and-white photographs lining the walls. There were photos of Charlie with groups of guys; Charlie with two young girls who couldn't have been older than twelve or thirteen; and then one of a much younger Charlie, his hair short and spikey with an older lady, her hand resting casually over his shoulders as she stood above him. They were both smiling, and I wondered if she was Charlie's mother. I suddenly felt a twinge of guilt for looking at these intimate, beautiful photos. I turned away, quickly climbing the rest of the stairs to the first floor. Turning left, I started to walk through the landing into a corridor. I could see two doors, and one of them was open. Well, Jessica had said get acquainted with the place, so I guessed I should have a little nosey round. I pushed the door further open and walked into a huge bedroom. A king-size bed dominated the centre of the room, and a gigantic flat-screen TV was mounted on the wall opposite it. Dark grey walls, crisp white sheets, and shelves full of trinkets, trophies, and more photographs. I realized almost instantly this must be Charlie's bedroom, and I knew I shouldn't have come in here.

"Hey!"

I felt the hairs on the back of my neck prickle up and I spun round. "Charlie!" He stood there, looking at me, his beautiful, soft lips curving into a smile. My mouth felt dry and I felt my face go crimson. "Charlie, I'm so sorry. I didn't realize this was your bedroom. Jessica told me to just come up and have a look round, so I ... well, the door was open and I just ..." I took a deep breath. "I'm sorry. I've literally been in here thirty seconds, and I was about to leave."

Charlie gave a dismissive wave of the hand. "It's fine. Don't worry. You settled in?"

I couldn't take my eyes off his face, but I was conscious that I had to try to. It was rude to just stare, but I couldn't help it. He was even more handsome than I'd remembered from the café and from the zillion photographs and videos I'd viewed online. In person, he was just divine. His face had more stubble than it had had yesterday, and his hair was smoothed back off his face, tucked behind his ears. His baggy jeans and plain white T-shirt made him look effortlessly cool and a little bit rugged. Not what I'd expected from a movie star at all. I could feel my cheeks burning, and the more I thought about them burning, the worse it got. I could only hope he hadn't noticed. "Yes, thank you. Your house is stunning." I smiled what I hoped was a warm and genuine smile and not a I'm-totally-checking-you-out kind of smile.

Charlie rubbed his beard, looking at me. "Thanks. I tried to make it as homely as possible, a sanctuary surrounded by madness, you know?"

I nodded, pointing to a floating shelf on the wall that held three colour photographs in black frames. "I love your photos. The people look so happy on them."

Charlie looked over and smiled, "Yeah, that's my mum there, and my niece and nephew, who came to visit not so long ago. I took them on a tour of the beaches. They had a blast." I nodded, watching his gaze fall over each photo in turn, his eyes glistening, his Adam's apple protruding in his throat. "I miss them all so much. I even find myself missing the little things from home—cheese on toast, cottage pie, Cadbury Freddos, Quavers."

I pulled my face, and Charlie smiled. "Wow, you have such distinguished taste!" I couldn't help but laugh. Here I was, standing in Charlie Robinson's bedroom, and he was telling me he missed Quavers.

"The little things, you know? I just miss them sometimes."

"I know. I'm only teasing."

We both laughed, and he turned his gaze away from the photographs, back to me. "So, I guess we'd better sit down and have a chat about stuff."

"Yeah, that'd be great."

He looked at me, smiled, and I felt my heart melt. My forehead and the bridge of my nose started sweating again. It was so hot in the house. My lips had gone so dry. I needed water desperately. I looked away from him, pretending to observe his photographs, hoping he wouldn't notice the mini breakdown I was having. I ran my tongue along my bottom lip to moisten it, and I pushed some stray strands of hair out of my face. I wished Charlie would turn away. I could feel my heart pounding. How was he doing this to me? "OK, well, I'll go and put on some coffee," he said. "I'll see you downstairs in five?"

"Yes, perfect. See you shortly."

I side-glanced him as he walked out the room—through *his* bedroom door—leaving me standing there. I exhaled, relieved that he was gone. *Damn it! Why did he have find me here?* I'd been there for all of two seconds, and then he'd walked in! Typical. I licked my bottom lip again, took a deep breath, and headed downstairs. If this was going to work at all, I had to get past the "hot boss" thing and get on with it. I had to just forget that he was a movie star, treat him like a normal guy, and remember he had simply employed me to do a job, just as George had done back home at the bank. I smiled to myself, remembering home and the office I'd left behind. It was never really so bad.

I walked back to my bedroom and sat on the edge of the bed. I closed my eyes and took some deep breaths, still flustered that Charlie had caught me snooping. I opened my eyes, glancing down at my suitcase on the floor, clothes spewing out over the sides. My mum had packed me a "travel survival" bag, which I'd tucked in the mesh insert of the suitcase and then forgotten. But now I remembered. Jumping off the bed I grabbed the small bag and opened it to find a Cadbury's Freddo tucked in between a packet of hankies and a box of plasters. God knows what Mum thought I'd get up too in between London and LA. I tucked the candy in my back jeans pocket and headed downstairs. The coffee machine was bubbling away on the countertop, and Charlie was leaning into the open fridge. "I have Pinot Grigio if you'd prefer something a little stronger?"

I smiled, looking at the clock on the wall. "It's only four o'clock! Besides, don't think I should be drinking on the job, do you?" I raised my eyebrows at him.

"Oh, OK. Very professional. I like it. It was a test, really, you know—a probation test, and you passed!" He smiled, and I smiled back. I *thought* he was joking. At least I hoped he was. "A little later then," he said. "Please help yourself to it—to anything in here. Just make yourself at home." I walked over to the breakfast bar and watched him pour milk into two mugs. "Coffee then?"

"That would be perfect. Thank you. You want some help?" I walked to the coffee machine and stood next to him, taking hold of one of the cups. This was the closest we'd been, and he seemed taller now as I looked up at him. I could feel the heat of his body, and he smelled woody, earthy—like sandalwood. He stopped what he was doing and stared down at the cups. After a silent moment, he turned to me and smiled. "No, it's fine. Go and relax. I do know how to make a coffee, you know."

He took the cup out of my hand, and my skin brushed his. I felt the hairs on my arms prickle as goosebumps popped up. I was smiling, and I had no idea why. I needed him to stop doing this to me. I walked over to the breakfast bar, my knees feeling weak, and sat down on a wooden stool as I watched him place the coffee mugs under the machine, which gurgled some more as it filled them. Charlie turned and looked at me, his hair falling from behind his ears over his face. I felt a sudden flush and looked away, hoping he hadn't noticed. Was this going to happen every time he looked at me? I was going to have to start reminding myself, every minute of the day I was with him, to recite my new mantra: "Remember: too hot for you. Forget international movie star!"

"So, your bedroom okay?" His voice snapped me out of my thoughts.

"What? My bedroom? For the coffee? I erm …"

Charlie beamed as he walked over to me and placed a cup in front of me. "No, I mean, is your bedroom okay for you? Not shall we go up there now." He raised his eyebrows.

Oh. My. God. Floor, swallow me now! "Oh, of course, sorry. I was joking." Bright red. Bright, bright red. "Sure, my bedroom's perfect. Everything is great."

"And the office? Jessica has filled you in on everything, right?"

I smiled, picking up my mug and taking a sip. "Oh yeah, she has, and I'm ready to get going."

"Good. She's great, is Jess. You'll get to know her well. Hopefully you guys will become good friends."

I nodded graciously, knowing full well that we would never be friends. Not after I'd heard her plotting against me on the phone. I wondered again whom she'd been talking too. One thing was for certain—whoever it was, she was very familiar with her, or him. I couldn't tell from the conversation if the person was male or female, but from the sound of it, they had worked together before. I couldn't understand it. If the person she was in cahoots with wanted this job so much, why hadn't he or she just applied for it like everyone else had done? It didn't make any sense. It was on the tip of my tongue to tell Charlie, but no, I would hold my cards tightly to my chest—for now.

"Most Tuesday afternoons, I go to DeLatte and meet with my friend Jo. It would be great if tomorrow you could drive me there. About midday. Then I've a couple of meetings across town at about three o'clock."

"Yeah, no problem," I said.

"Tomorrow evening, for dinner, I need you to pick up some ingredients." Charlie handed me a cookbook. A yellow stickie note marked a page and contained a list of ingredients that were not already in the pantry.

I opened it up to a recipe for Thai red duck with rice. "Wow, sounds delicious. You like to cook?"

"Absolutely." He beamed at me. "My mum loved cooking and was always trying something new. I used to stand on a kitchen chair when I was little next to her while she was busy at the cooker making dinner. I'd watch her stir things, sieve things, and she'd let me help." I could hear his voice breaking ever so slightly as he spoke. He took another sip of coffee as he looked out to the garden through the huge, open bi-folding doors. A slight breeze trailed through, very welcome on my clammy skin. "Since our conversation in the café yesterday," he continued. "I've thought about home a lot. I'm sure the Arthouse Cinema was even somewhere in my dreams last night, though I've forgotten now." He ran his hand through his hair, taking in a deep breath and letting it out slowly. "Don't get me wrong, I love LA. But I guess it would be nice to try and get home a little more often. Maybe even rent a place in London for a while."

I nodded. And there was me a few weeks ago, desperate to get away from the place. Charlie sipped his coffee, looking down at the worktop. I decided to seize my moment. "So, I was just going through my suitcase, and my mum … she did this little … well, anyway … and I remembered she gave me this!" I pulled out the Freddo and handed it to him. "I'm guessing they don't sell these in LA?" Charlie laughed, shaking his head. I smiled, pushing it further in his direction, "It's yours, to ease your current homesickness."

We looked at each other, and he took it from me, tracing it with his fingers. "Ellie, that's so nice of you. Thank you."

"It's nothing. You can enjoy it with your brew."

He nodded, looking straight into my eyes, but I couldn't hold his stare. And so, once again, I looked down at my mug. After a few silent moments, Charlie jumped up and cleared his throat, combing his hair back behind his ears. He seemed suddenly jittery, and I felt an instant panic. What if he thought the Freddo was too much? That I was getting too friendly or personal? Had I overstepped the mark and judged the whole thing wrong? I watched him walk over to the sink and place the cup on the drainer. He dried his hands and then turned his stare back to me. "Anyway, I have a couple of friends coming over tomorrow night, so I thought it would be nice to make something rather than order takeout."

I nodded, feeling awkward about the subject change as his mobile started to beep. He looked down at the screen before turning it off, bringing his attention back to me. "So, I know you don't have any PA experience, but that's OK. It can be a learn-on-the job thing. But, really, I just need you to do for me whatever I need you to do." He paused and looked at me. "Within reason, of course." I felt a flush creep all over my face, and my neck was hot. I avoided his eyes as I took another sip of coffee and looked over to the garden. Maybe I'd imagined his mood change a few moments ago. "Does that sound okay? Don't worry though, I'll go easy at first."

Almost spitting out my coffee, I gulped it down and placed my cup on the countertop, bringing my eyes back to him. I jumped off the chair. I'd spent way too long with Pete and his dirty mind. "Yes, fine. Whatever you need. I'm gonna use the bathroom. Sorry, I'll be right back!"

Charlie stood up, watching me. "It's OK, Ellie. I'm going to hit the gym now anyway, and then I'm heading out to some friends for a jamming session, so I'll catch you later. Get acquainted with the place and make yourself at home."

I took a deep breath, feeling relieved to get some space between us. "OK, sounds good. Have a good night. You know where I am if you need anything."

"I sure do. Thanks, Ellie."

I didn't look up at him as I walked out and headed back up the stairs to my room. I shut the door behind me, turned around, and leaned against it, closing my eyes, my forehead pressed against the cool painted wood. That was intense. I had to assume that, if this was going to work, I'd just get used to being around him. It was just a crush I was experiencing, and after a few days I'd be over it and I'd be able to get on with doing my job without turning into a tomato and a blithering wreck every time he spoke to me. I stared down at my suitcase. Tomorrow I would swing into action as official PA to Charlie Robinson, on duty and ready to go. I was going to be good at this. I wanted to be. Organized and super-efficient, that was me. And how hard was it going to be? As Charlie had said, I just had to do whatever he wanted, within reason. I could do that. And I didn't want to give Jessica any excuses to get her claws into me. I knew she wanted me gone, and I wasn't about to help her with that.

Chapter 13

The hazy morning sun streamed through the white shutters of my bedroom window as I peeled my eyes open. What time was it? I'd set my alarm for 6.30, but it hadn't gone off yet, or at least I hadn't heard it. Panicking, I snatched my phone off the bedside table—6.15. I could hear male voices chattering outside. One was most definitely Charlie's distinct, soft, and husky British voice. The other guy spoke in a low, Southern American accent. *They're sure up and about early*, I thought as I kneeled up on the bed and peeked out of the window through a gap in the shutters. Yep, there he was—semi-naked Charlie in the swimming pool, leaning against the side, water glistening off his bronzed back, his shoulders broad and his wet hair sleeked back from his face. Was that a tattoo on his arm? What was that? I squinted, but I still couldn't make it out. I looked away, feeling like a compete perv. Why was I starting to go red? He wasn't even in the room! I guessed it was going to be another of those days.

I rubbed my eyes and observed myself in the full-length mirror opposite the bed. The remnants of yesterday's mascara were smudged under both eyes. I was in desperate need of a refreshing shower and a strong cup of coffee. *Well, here goes. My first day.* I jumped out of bed. Twenty minutes later, I was ready to take on whatever Charlie's day had in store for me. I looked at myself in the steamed-up bathroom mirror—blue faded jeans, pink T-shirt, blue Converse trainers, and my hair fixed in its usual messy bun. No one had said anything about a dress code, so I'd opted for comfy and practical as I took a deep breath and started to make my way downstairs, the smell of coffee welcoming me as I entered the kitchen.

Jessica was sitting at the breakfast bar as I walked in. She looked me up and down without smiling. I forced a smile. "Morning, Jessica. How are you today?"

She didn't look at me. "Great. Everything is running smoothly. How was your first night? Sleep well?"

I nodded. "I slept fine, thank you. Is Charlie still in the pool?" I looked out towards the opened bi-folding doors.

"No, he left about ten minutes ago. Didn't say where he was going, but he spoke to you about his coffee this afternoon with Jo, right? So, I'm assuming he'll be back for that later." Jessica didn't take her eyes off the newspaper as she spoke, her long, blonde, perfectly straightened hair flowing down her shoulders, black rimmed glasses perching on her nose. I was glad I'd decided to dress casually. Jessica had done the same, in black jeans with a hole in one knee, a plain black T-shirt, and Nike trainers. She was ridiculously slim, and her jeans hugged her pert bottom perfectly. I wondered how old she was. Twenty-seven or twenty-eight maybe? I always looked at people's hands when trying to guess their age. It was a bit of an obsession of mine. Fine lines and wrinkles on the face along with dark circles and ages spots could be covered by good make-up. And of course, in LA, you could never be sure how much Botox and fillers people had injected into their foreheads. But the hands always gave the game away. I discreetly glanced at Jessica's hand. Not a wrinkle. She was definitely still in her twenties.

I walked over to the fridge and took out some milk. As I started to make my coffee, I could feel Jessica's stare on me. I didn't look up at her. "He's easing you in, you know," she said. "It won't be at a snail's pace for long. So enjoy the next couple of days while you can."

I folded my arms and kept my eyes on the coffee machine. I had imagined she'd be the last person to offer advice, considering she was trying to oust me. I couldn't trust a word she said. "Thanks. I'll do that," was all I could muster. I could hear Jessica sip her coffee and take another bite of her toast as I filled my cup and walked over to the glass doors leading out to the pool. "Who is the guy in green overalls?" I asked.

Jessica started leafing through a newspaper as she spoke without looking up. Her nails were perfectly manicured with a nude-coloured varnish that looked great against her golden tan. I couldn't imagine ever being so well groomed, but I did know I would never be so rude. "Oh, that's Noah. He's the caretaker, handyman, and gardener here. Worked for the previous owners before Charlie bought this place, and he just ended up staying on. He's part of the furniture and pretty much knows everything about the place, so if I'm not here, Noah's your man." Before I could reply, she stood up, folded her paper in half, and picked up her mug and plate. "Anyway, busy day ahead. I'm interviewing for a new cleaner, so I won't be around. If you need me, just call. Catch you later."

I didn't say anything as I watched her quickly move out of sight. I was glad she was out the way. I felt self-conscious around her, as if she was watching my every move, waiting to strike. I looked around. Charlie's style was pretty informal and natural. I liked it. Picking up my coffee, I walked into a huge, bright room just off the kitchen. Two rust-orange sofas sat on the dark-coloured wooden floor, and several paintings on canvas adorned the cream-coloured walls. The natural earthy tones made the room cosy and inviting. I could just imagine lighting the candles and snuggling on the sofa with a glass of wine and a good film.

I perched myself on the edge of one of the sofas and finished my coffee. I felt as if I should be doing something, but it was only 8.30 in the morning. I picked myself up and walked through to the garden. Noah was sweeping the poolside and didn't seem to notice me as I got closer. "Hi, Noah. Nice to meet you," I said, approaching him. "I'm Ellie, Charlie's new PA." I extended my hand and Noah shook it, smiling. He had a nice, friendly face and was maybe in his late forties. Lots of wrinkles on the hands, and his face was very weathered. His skin was golden brown, and he didn't strike me as the kind of guy who applied factor-fifty sun cream. "I'm told you've worked here a while?" I offered.

"Yep, seventeen years I've been caretaker here. Charlie moved in about three years ago, and he's been incredibly good to me, keeping me on, you know?"

I smiled. "Sure, that's nice. I guess I'm just finding my feet right now, first day and all."

Noah nodded, placing the broom against a stone wall. "Of course. It's been a pretty quiet couple of weeks for Charlie because he's taken some time off," Noah said. "But things can get pretty hectic round here."

"Hectic? In what way?"

Noah folded his arms and raised his eyebrows. "Well, Charlie can be pretty demanding at times. But can't they all?"

"Demanding?"

"Well, you know. You'll find out for yourself soon enough. But, these people—they're not like you and me. They live in another world—a world that revolves around them." Noah picked up the broom and started sweeping again, brushing leaves away from the poolside. "Keep things professional. He's a great guy, but he isn't our friend. He's our boss. I think sometimes, when we work so closely with him, that gets forgotten, you know? Just my advice to you. That's all." Noah kept his eyes on the ground as he continued to sweep. I wrapped my arms tightly around my body, feeling awkward and not sure how to respond to this. "You'll get used to things," Noah continued.

I raised my eyebrows. What did Noah mean when he'd said 'sometimes, when we work so closely with him, that gets forgotten'? What was he implying? Had Charlie been involved romantically with other staff members? This surprised me, since Charlie had taken such care to make sure no closet fans had gone for this job. He had, no doubt, been looking for a professional, genuine person. Getting involved with staff just didn't seem like something he would do, but then, how well did I actually know him? I wanted to press Noah further, but as kept his eyes down to the ground and was busying himself, I got the feeling he didn't want to be questioned. "Sure! Well, thanks."

Noah nodded again, maintaining his focus on the ground. "Well, if you need anything, Ellie, I'm here all week. Weekends off." He looked up at me and forced a smile. "I'd better get on. I have a to-do list as long as my arm today. I'll see you later." Noah turned and walked towards the large square wooden outhouse at the bottom of the long, luscious green garden.

As I walked back into the house, replaying the conversation with Noah in my head, another thing he'd said— 'They're not like you and me'— bothered me. What did he mean? Charlie had seemed pretty damn normal to me, but again, I had a lot to learn about him. I pushed my fringe out my eyes and pulled my brown tortoise-rimmed sunglasses from my head and over my eyes, turning around from the kitchen to stare out over the hills, down to the hazy city below. Did he mean Charlie was a little crazy? A bit of a man-diva? I could cope with that if it meant I got to stand here with the California sunshine beaming down on me. I could pretty much cope with most things if it meant I was here.

The front door opened, and Charlie strolled into the kitchen, one hand in his pocket. He looked so relaxed—light blue jeans, Vans trainers, and a plain black T-shirt. His hair was tied in a small bobble. Black sunglasses shaded his eyes, and he flashed me a wide smile. "Hey, Ellie, how are you? All set to go?"

His smile had the ability to make me flush in an instant, and I had resigned myself to embracing it, blaming it on the hot weather, should anyone notice and enquire as to why I suddenly looked the shade of a beetroot. I closed my laptop and stood up from the kitchen chair. "Yeah, I'm just—" I didn't trail off, I got interrupted!

"Great, I'm just gonna freshen up. I'll be down in five."

I nodded and watched him saunter out the kitchen and hurriedly make his way upstairs. A few moments later, I was out on the driveway, climbing into the driver's side of the black Mercedes. Thank goodness I'd had some driving practice over here with Pete. This whole other-side-of-the-road thing was pretty confusing. Pulling my black shades on, I watched the front door, waiting for Charlie to appear. He'd said he'd be down in five minutes. Twenty minutes later, there was still no sign of him. I rolled my eyes and took a deep breath, switching the engine off and climbing back out. Before I could reach the door, it swung open and Charlie came bounding out. "Sorry. Took a call. Let's go."

I forced a smile and climbed back into the driver's seat. Charlie pulled his shades off and clinched back his hair, placing the glasses on his head as he sat down next to me. I looked down at the air conditioning controls. It was on full blast, so why did it feel so hot in here? I felt a bead of sweat trickle down my nose, and my palms felt damp on the leather steering wheel. The more I thought about how hot and sweaty I was, the worse it was getting. I could smell his vanilla aftershave as I started to pull off the driveway. I felt anxious and self-conscious and could feel him watching my every move. "OK, let's go. I'll try not to kill us both. I'm not used to this side of driving yet," I mumbled.

Charlie gritted his teeth. "Jesus, not filling me with massive amounts of confidence here." He tugged at his fastened seatbelt dramatically and smiled. "Just checking."

We both laughed, and I felt strangely at ease being with him. It was funny—he had the ability to make me weak at the knees and flustered by simply looking at me, and yet sitting there I felt at ease, joking with him and laughing. My mind wandered as we sat in comfortable silence, Charlie texting on his phone. I glanced down at his fingers tapping away on the screen. They moved quickly, and I wondered how they would feel dancing all over me. There he was, pushing me up against the wall with his waist, holding my hands about my head and kissing me hard, fast, like I'd never been kissed before. "You okay, Ellie? You missed the turning." I snapped out of my daydreaming, face crimson. *Shit!* "Oh, God. Sorry. I was in another world there," I said coyly.

"You know where we're going, right?"

I nodded, keeping my eyes on the road. "Yep, just got a bit confused." I looked down at the satnav. It had reworked the route. "We can get off at the next junction, and it's only added a few minutes. Sorry about that." I didn't look at him. I couldn't.

"You were smiling, when you missed the junction. I was watching you, wondering if you were gonna pull off. What were you thinking about?" he pressed.

I was hardly going to tell him. I laughed nervously and feigned complete innocence, scrunching my face up and wafting my hand dismissively in the air. "Oh, nothing! Just the sunshine, you know, makes me feel happy." *Busted!* I thought, as I turned my face on an angle in the hope he wouldn't see the lie in my eyes. I had to change the subject. "Anyway, you meet your friend every week here?"

He nodded and rested his head back on the seat. "Yeah, it's the only time we get to catch up."

"Have you known him long?"

"A few years. We worked together on a movie. He was in production. Great guy, and so down to earth, which is pretty hard to find in this town."

The satnav on the car interrupted our conversation. Charlie pointed out the window. "Park out front. The owners don't mind me going there."

I nodded and pulled over. Charlie pulled his sunglasses off his head and over his eyes.

"Do you want me to come in with you, or shall I wait here?" I asked.

He looked at me and pulled his face. "Come in, of course. You can't sit out here. Get a coffee." Charlie opened the car door before I had a chance to reply and bounded straight through the entrance. I grabbed my laptop bag and purse and awkwardly followed behind. He was already walking towards a corner booth away from the window when I walked in. I could hear him greeting a dark-haired guy who sat opposite him. Guessing it was Jo, I walked over and smiled. Charlie looked up at me and smiled warmly back. "Jo, this is Ellie."

I extended my hand, "Nice to meet you."

Jo gave me a warm smile, looking at Charlie as he did so. He had lots of tattoos, all in black, no colour, going right up to his neck and all pretty much blending into one. I could just about make out some skulls, a few snacks, and a rose without staring too much.

"Ellie," Charlie said, "can you grab us two cappuccinos please, extra hot. And get yourself one."

"Oh, sure, OK. I'll be right back." I left them chatting and walked over to the small counter.

"Two cappuccinos?" A tall, skinny, and handsome guy smiled at me from behind the counter. He had the most strikingly warm hazel-coloured eyes and luscious, long, thick eyelashes. Why was it some boys were blessed with the most amazing lashes and we girls have to fake up to achieve that? *Boys are very undeserving of those*, I thought as I smiled back, unable to tear my eyes from his. His hair was long, straight, and held back in a pony tail. And he had the smoothest, slowest, most sultry American accent I'd ever heard. I could definitely listen to it some more. I blushed. "Yes, please."

"Sure. And for you?"

"Oh, err, a skinny latte please."

He smiled. "On the house for you, ma'am. I'm Ross Wadey, by the way. Nice to meet you. I'm guessing you're Mr. Robinson's new PA?"

I scrunched up my face, confused. "Who?"

Ross wafted his tea towel in the air towards Charlie's table. "Mr. Robinson?"

I smiled and shook my head, feeling slightly embarrassed at the confusion. "Oh, right. Sorry. You mean Charlie. Yes, I am."

"He lets you call him Charlie?"

"Erm, yes, why?"

Ross pulled his eyebrows up, his eyes wide in disbelief. "Oh, his last PA told us to refer to him only as Mr. Robinson, and we weren't to speak to him or look at him unless he approached us first."

"What? That doesn't sound like him."

"Well, he's been coming in here for over two years now, most Tuesdays, to meet that guy. Never spoke to him, and he never leaves a tip."

"What? I can't believe that."

I looked round at Charlie and Jo. They were chatting and laughing. That didn't sound like Charlie at all. Perhaps Ross was confusing him with someone else.

"I'm guessing you're new?" Ross asked. "Like, in the last twenty-four hours new?"

"Well, yes, I am."

"I guess you'll soon get to know him then. His last PA said he was a bit of a nightmare to work for, but then, aren't they all?" Ross laughed and turned to the coffee machine, springing into action. Watching baristas make coffee had always mesmerized me. Back home, on lazy Sunday mornings, I used to love sitting in my local Starbucks, people watching or reading a good book. I'd often find myself observing the coffee-making process, enjoying the way the baristas glided along the machine, flipping handles, and pressing all kinds of buttons. It was remarkable, but it looked way too confusing for me. I was happy just to drink the result. I glanced over at Charlie again. He was still smiling and talking animatedly to Jo. What Ross had just said about them all being the same—hard work—was the exact same thing Noah had said that very morning in the garden. Maybe they were right, and Charlie was just easing me in before hitting me with his diva ways.

"Maybe he's mellowed a bit. You never know," Ross offered, frothing the milk up and pouring it into the waiting cup. "There you go," he said, handing me my latte. "I'll take the cappuccinos over to Mr. Robinson's table."

Ross placed the two cups on a tray. I took a sip and watched him confidently stride over to Charlie's table. I hugged the cup in my hands.

This was a welcome caffeine hit. After this pit stop, I had been directed to drop Charlie off at his studio in West Hollywood. Then I had to tackle the shopping and task list for Charlie's dinner party tonight. The list was as long as my arm. I turned back round. Ross was heading back over in my direction, staring down at the floor, and Charlie was staring straight at me. He wasn't talking or smiling. He was just glaring at me, looking a little pissed off, his lips pursed together, the skin in between his eyes all crinkly. Oh, God, what had I done?

I turned away as Ross came over and stood behind me, softly placing his hand on my shoulder. "Come through to the back. We have a staff room. You can chill in there until they finish up, if you want."

Grateful for the relief from Charlie's eyes, I picked up my bags, and Ross grabbed my cup as I followed him past the counter and into a small side room, which was brightly lit. There was a small TV in the corner, a kettle, and a fridge. I huge staff shift rota hung from the wall. I sat down. "Thanks, Ross. I appreciate this. Can you give me a heads up when they look like they're ready to leave?"

Ross smiled, wiping his hands on a tea towel. "Will do, Ellie. I'd better get back out there. I've got some customers."

Ross disappeared, and I checked my phone. A text message from Pete: "Hey. Need an update. Monterey is beyond stunning. I sent you an email. Reply."

Within minutes, Ross was back in the doorway. "Ellie, it looks like they're winding up."

"Wow, that was quick. OK. Thanks, Ross."

He folded his arms across his chest, "So, I guess I'll be seeing you next week?"

"Sure. Unless his plans change."

Ross's eyes lit up, and he smiled. Did everyone in this town have the most perfect teeth? "OK, Ellie. See you then."

I smiled back and walked into the front of the café. Charlie was standing next to his booth. He motioned me over. "Ellie." I walked over, luging my laptop bag over my shoulder. "Jo has last-minute RSVP'd for tonight. He's coming along too for the meal, so I'm gonna need two more seats, one for him and one for his girlfriend. That makes eight. Okay?"

I looked at Jo and nodded. "Sure."

"And I don't have time to cook tonight now either. I have a few things I need to do this afternoon, so I need you to ring Rose. Tell her she'll need to work tonight. From say five until late."

"Rose? I haven't met her yet, I—"

"My chef. Did Jessica not mention her and give you her number?"

"No, I don't think so, but I haven't had chance to—"

"Okay. Well, get her number from Jessica and call her up. I'd do it sooner rather than later. You don't want to piss her off by giving her too short a notice."

I looked down at my watch. It was one o'clock. He wanted Rose at the house by five, and he didn't want *me* leaving it short notice? He had to be joking. I looked for signs—hoped for signs—of humour. Nothing.

"Okay, we're done here. Let's go." Charlie nudged his way out of the booth and walked past me, placing his shades over his eyes before he got to the door. I looked down at the tip tray on the table. A twenty-dollar bill. He had left a tip.

Chapter 14

We drove in awkward silence up through the winding curves of Mulholland Drive, the afternoon sun beaming down on us. I was a little confused, struggling to read Charlie. He had acted pretty diva-like in the café, requesting me to ring his chef Rose, whom I'd never met, and ask her to drop everything and just head into work within the next few hours. He showed no regard for what she might be doing, and even worse, expected me to do his dirty work for him. *Maybe this is what everyone has been warning me about.* And this was only the beginning. Ross had warned me, but he'd also said Charlie never left a tip, and yet he'd left a handsome twenty-dollar tip, and he'd only had a couple of coffees. I guessed it was only day one, and I had plenty of time to suss Charlie Robinson out. For now, he'd requested I drop him at a friend's house and leave him there whilst I got on with my errands in preparation for his dinner party tonight.

Charlie pointed out the window. "It's just on the right, up there." I slowly pulled up the secluded, narrow side road to a large black double gate. Beyond was only a long sweeping driveway surrounded by lush green shrubs and trees. I looked at him, but his sunglasses firmly masked his face. He didn't look up as he jumped out of the car. "Keep your phone close. I'll call if I need anything."

Before I could reply, he'd slammed the door and headed towards the intercom. I waited as he spoke and watched as the gates slowly opened, letting him through. He didn't look back as he paced down the driveway and out of sight. *I'm sure you will let me know*, I thought as I started up the engine and pulled off into the road.

I spent most of the afternoon taking three shirts and a tuxedo to the dry cleaners, trawling toy shops for a wooden train set to be sent urgently to London—a birthday gift for his seven-year-old nephew, Lucas. I took several phone calls; one from his manager who was desperate to get hold of him but couldn't, and two from Noah, querying outside seating arrangements for the evening's dinner party. And, of course, I called Rose. To my surprise she'd been OK about it, as if she was expecting it. And she not only agreed to work the shift, but offered to pick up the groceries she'd need for the meal on her way in. I wondered how much Charlie was paying her. It must be a considerable amount for her to be so accommodating.

But, as I spent my whole afternoon scurrying around after Charlie, it struck me as odd that I was almost living this person's life for him—buying birthday presents for his relatives, speaking to friends and colleagues on his behalf, checking his emails, and organizing his parties. It seemed that all Charlie did was show up, enjoy the ride, and take the credit for other people's hard work. It really was the oddest life, and I was still getting my head around it all.

It was just after five o'clock as I started to head back to the house, all jobs ticked off the list. I was feeling pretty good as the warm LA sunshine flooded the car. The Bluetooth in the car started ringing, interrupting the radio. I looked at the screen: Charlie. I was surprised to only now be hearing from him. He'd been off the radar all day, and I wondered if the house I'd dropped him at this morning was the home of his love interest. He'd never mentioned his friend's name. I'd realized by now that that part of his life was super private. No one had mentioned it or even hinted anything about it. "Hey, Charlie, I'm just heading—"

Charlie cut me off. "Ellie, I need a shirt. A floral shirt. Where are you?"

"Sorry, what?"

Charlie's voice was high pitched, almost frantic. "A floral shirt! Can you pick one up?"

I pushed the indicator on the car and hastily pulled over to the side of the road. "Pick up a shirt for you?"

"Yes, I need one for tonight," he said matter-of-factly.

I scrunched up my face, completely confused. "Erm, OK. But aren't you staying in tonight?"

"Ellie, can you get me a floral shirt? Blue maybe. I need it to go with dark-blue jeans, okay?"

"Charlie, I—"

"My friends will be round at seven thirty. Send me some pictures of shirt options. I'd like to look them before you buy one."

"Charlie, I literally—" And the call disconnected. What the hell was that? Did that conversation just happen or had I dreamed it? It was gone five o'clock. I was pretty much back at the house, away from town, with two and a half hours until his friends arrived, and he wanted me to go out and just magic up a blue floral shirt? Was he out of his mind? Where would I even find one at such short notice? This had to be a test. He was testing me, that was it. He had to be. Who else would do this? I sat, staring at the road, shaking my head. After a few moments in recovery, I pushed the indicator back up, took a deep breath, and did a U-turn in the road. If this was going to be his game, I had to step up to it. I hit the Bluetooth button on the steering wheel. I didn't want to make this call, but I had to. I gulped hard, waiting for her to answer,

"Ellie?"

"Jessica! Hi, I need your help."

I could literally hear the smile in her voice. "Ellie, you OK? You sound a little panicky."

"Charlie just called. He wants a floral shirt—in two and a half hours from now. Help me!"

"Oh!" the smugness was sickening.

I shrugged my shoulders, forgetting she couldn't see me. "Where can I go? What shops does he like?"

"Okay. West Hollywood, The Grove. Loads of shops there and not too far from the house."

I leant over and tapped the address into the satnav. Thirteen minutes from me. Great! "Okay! Thanks, Jessica. I owe you."

"For this dinner party tonight, I presume?"

Glancing down at the directions on the screen, I continued following the busy road ahead. "Yes, for tonight."

"Well, I can't promise you'll find anything there, but that's your best bet."

I let out a long sigh. "Okay, and thanks again."

The call went dead on her side as I pulled off the freeway, following signs for The Grove. The air con was blasting my face, but I still felt hot, and I could feel my heart pumping in my chest. I needed to get in here and get out fast. The pressure was on.

Just over an hour later, I was back at the house, blue floral shirt in hand. God knows how I'd pulled this one off, but I'd remembered visiting the same mall with Pete during one of our sightseeing tours, so it was a little familiar at least, full of designer stores. And it seemed, as luck would have it, that floral prints, even for men, were very much in vogue this season. Finding something hadn't been too difficult, especially with no budget to worry about. In my flurry of panic, I'd forgotten to text him a picture of it. I just hoped he liked it.

As I walked into the hallway, the most delicious, fragrant, spicy smell hit me. A dark-haired lady in her mid-fifties perhaps (her hands were quite wrinkly) was busily working away in the kitchen over the Aga stove. The windows were steamed up, and used spoons and forks were strewn all over the counter tops. A pink floral apron clung to her heavy-set frame, and her hair was clipped up in a tousled bun. She was stirring something in a huge copper pan with a wooden spoon.

I smiled as I walked over to the breakfast bar and placed a blue paper bag on the worktop. Inside was the floral shirt, folded and wrapped in white tissue paper. "Hey! I'm guessing you're Rose? Lovely to finally meet you. I'm Ellie." Rose looked up and gave me a warm smile as I extended my hand. "And I'm sorry about the last-minute phone call. I—"

She let the spoon drop into whatever it was she was stirring and wiped her hands on her pink apron before shaking mine. "Ellie, so lovely to finally meet you, and don't worry about it. I've been working here for three years now since Charlie moved here. I know he can be a little spontaneous at times. You'll get used to it." She looked at me, her eyebrows drawing together "You look flushed. I'm guessing Mr. Robinson has kept you busy today?" She smiled and picked up the spoon again, stirring the contents of the pan briskly.

I laughed awkwardly, pointing to the shirt on the counter. "Yeah, you could say that. Last-minute shirt purchase from the mall. I just hope he likes it. It feels odd buying clothes for someone else." Rose smiled again, though she didn't look up as she continued to stir whatever was in the pot. "How are you getting on with dinner?" I asked.

"Great. Looks and tastes delicious, if I do say so myself. Hopefully Mr. Robinson will enjoy it."

I shook my head. "I'm sorry again that you had to come in at such short notice."

Rose's eyes glinted as she pulled her stare up from the pot of sauce and looked at me. "Don't worry, Ellie, really. I had no plans, and anyway, Mr. Robinson is a kind and genuine man. I'm happy to come over. But, like all of them, what he wants, he wants, and he pretty much always gets. You have to be ready for his call. It's a twenty-four seven job."

Before I could say anything else, my phone beeped. Pulling it from my jeans pocket, I saw a text from Charlie: ""Ellie, don't worry about tonight now. I'm having dinner out. Let Rose know she can go home." I stared down at the words, reading them over and over, my mouth going dry and my heart beating hard. The colour drained from my face as I kept my glare on the screen.

Rose stopped stirring and looked at me, motionless. "Everything okay, Ellie?"

I couldn't respond. I could feel the anger brewing up. Was this guy actually for real? He had called Rose in to work at the last minute without any regard for what she might be doing on her day off. He'd asked her to cook a three-course meal for him and his friends, and he'd sent me off on a wild goose chase for a bloody, ditsy floral-print shirt that he now had no intention of wearing. The pair of us, not to mention Noah and Jessica, had wasted all bloody afternoon busting our arses for this guy, who then sends this? With no explanation whatsoever. Oh, he has decided to eat out now. Decided to eat out. Just like that.

Rose walked over to me and started to untie her apron. "He's cancelled, hasn't he?" She shook her head and walked over to the sink, washing her hands and staring out of the window as she spoke. "Don't be too ruffled by it, Ellie. He does it all the time. Their lives—the way they live—it's so different from the way you and I live. Charlie can be very chaotic. His plans change in an instant. They don't think about all the running around people do for them, or the efforts we go to. They pay us well, and it's our job. The trick is not to take it personally." Rose turned around.

After drying her hands on a tea towel, she walked over to me and put a hand on my tense shoulder. "The good news is, we have this delicious Thai red duck curry here and an amazing vanilla cheesecake—calorie free of course—that I believe is now all ours, as it won't keep." She winked at me. I looked up at her, and my mouth curved into a smile. Rose smiled back and walked over to a cupboard. Taking out two dinner plates, she motioned over to the pots that were steaming away on the Aga. "Can I interest you?"

I nodded. "Absolutely!"

I lay on my bed, staring at the ceiling. It was gone ten in the evening, and I hadn't heard anything else from Charlie. Rose had gone home. The huge house was empty, and I was still reeling. I just didn't understand how Charlie could behave like that—to be so rude and take such liberties. I got the feeling, though, that Charlie didn't think he was being rude. The people around him, like Rose, just seemed to accept his behaviour as an occupational hazard, and they just got over it. I thought back again to my conversations with Noah, Jessica, and Ross. Maybe they had genuinely been trying to warn me about this, and I'd just been too naïve to believe them. I peeled myself off the bed and stood up, undressing before climbing into the shower and letting the warm water wash away my frustrations. As I shut my eyes and put my head under the water, my phone bleeped from the bedroom, the sound breaking into my weary thoughts. It was late. This couldn't be Charlie now, could it? I turned the water off, grabbed a towel, and walked over to the bed, water dripping all over the beige carpet. His text read: "Ellie, I need the bulb to my bedside lamp changed this evening before I'm home. Thanks. C"

"Thanks C?" This guy was incredible. As if I needed a reminder of who was texting me, asking to change a bloody lightbulb at this time of night. Was the day ever going to end? Did he not think I might actually be in bed right now, shaking off the pointless day? I shook my head, resigning myself to the fact that I was going to have to sort this, and there was no point standing around moaning about it. I threw my phone onto the bed, grabbed my bathrobe and slippers, and wrapped a towel around my dripping wet hair. I headed out onto the landing. Right, bulbs. Where the hell would I find them? Making my way downstairs and into the kitchen, I squinted as I switched on the overhead spotlights. Okay, store cupboard. Jessica had mentioned that a box of household items was kept in there. After a quick search, as luck would have it, I found a huge box of bulbs—all different watts, shapes, and sizes. I carried it upstairs. Charlie's bedroom door was open partway, and I used the box to push my way in. I switched on the ceiling light and threw the box onto the bed. I found the black spotlight on his bedside table and took the old bulb out. I squinted my eyes to read the wattage. *Right, I'm winning here*, I thought to myself as I rummaged through the box looking for a matching replacement. The towel fell off my head onto the bed, leaving my hair to fall down over my shoulders and over my face, still wet. I swept it behind my ears and continued searching. *Ugh, come on bulb! Please let me find the right one. There's like a thousand in here, and I just want to get this done and get to bed.*

"Hey!"

My heart jumped into my throat as I spun round. "Charlie!"

He stood in the doorway, his arm up against the frame, smiling. "Sorry. Did I startle you?"

I grabbed the straying towel that had fallen from my head and pulled it up against my chest. "Yes. I didn't know you'd be back so soon." I smoothed my hand over my face, remembering I had zero make-up on, three spots on my chin, and I could feel my cheeks burning as his eyes focused on me. I couldn't believe he was seeing me like this.

He smiled, leaning his arm against the door frame. "I didn't expect to be back so soon, but I got tired and a little bored, so ..."

I didn't say anything as I turned back to the bulb box, trying to act un-flummoxed by his presence. This was difficult, though, as he looked so good—black skinny jeans and a khaki-coloured T-shirt that fit tightly around the arms, showing off his toned biceps. His hair was tucked behind his ears, his face looked stubble free, his skin ridiculously flawless. He sauntered over, stood beside me, and took the old bulb out my hand. He looked at it closely before placing it on the bed. "Here, I'll find it," he whispered. His mouth was so close to me I could feel his warm breath on my neck. I didn't look up at him. I couldn't. I allowed my hair to fall over my cheeks, shading my damp crimson skin. I watched him as his unusually big hands started to sort through the box, my eyes gliding down his body, past his shirt to his black jeans and then to his crotch. Not many people in my life had taken my breath away. In fact, I don't think anyone had up to that point. Charlie didn't even need to try. He just needed to look at me, speak to me, and I felt breathless.

"You OK, Ellie?"

I looked up, startled and embarrassed. I threaded my hand nervously through my hair. "Yes, fine."

He nodded and smiled and then turned back to the box. Finally, he held up a bulb and walked over to the offending spotlight. "Well, I think this is the one." He pushed the bulb in and clicked the switch. The light illuminated his beautiful face. "Ahh, there we go. All sorted. Thanks for helping, Ellie."

I pushed my hair behind my ear and forced a smile as I turned away and walked towards the door. I could feel his eyes on me and hoped he wasn't pissed off that I hadn't sorted the light sooner. I turned around and looked straight at him. "Do you want anything else before I head to bed?"

I guessed I should at least ask, out of politeness, but I hoped he would say no. Instead, he said nothing and just looked at me, his eyes narrowing, then he smiled. "I don't think so, Ellie, unless there's anything you need from me before bed?"

Sure, thanks Charlie. Since you ask, I'd like you to pull off my dressing gown, push me against the wall, spread my legs, and fuck me until I'm a sticky hot mess. How's that? Of course, this wasn't my reply. Instead, I said, "No, no. That's fine. Have a good night, Charlie. I'll see you in the morning."

Flustered, I turned to leave. As I started to close the door behind me, he said, "Ellie?" I stopped, my heart skipping a beat, and peered back into the room. "Goodnight." He smiled.

I hurriedly closed Charlie's bedroom door and walked up the stairs to my room. I couldn't believe he had walked in on me when I looked the way I did. I lay on my bed and let my hair fall on my shoulders. I found myself staring at the white ceiling lampshade again, but as I did so, something didn't sit right. Charlie had texted me ten minutes before he found me in his bedroom while I was rummaging through his spare bulb box. If he had been on his way home and minutes away, why not change the bulb himself? Or at least tell me he was on his way home, allowing me to at least get dressed. And why have me faffing around when he had no problem changing the bulb himself? I closed my eyes, taking a restorative breath. I was too tired to think about anything anymore. Sleep was calling me.

Chapter 15

My phone bleeped from my bedside table, startling me out of sleep. It was 5.45 in the morning, and Charlie had just sent me four text messages, one after the other. The first: "Ellie, I'm at the studio this morning. Can you meet me there by 8 a.m.? I've left a list of things I need picking up on your desk." This had quickly been followed by a second message: "Sorry, Ellie, that shirt—not so keen. Return it." And the third: "Oh, and my publicist, Damian, has been trying to reach me. Can you call him, see what he wants? Let me know." And the final message: "Forgot to put a Starbucks coffee on the list of things I need. Black, no sugar."

I lay there, propped up on my elbows, eyes half open, staring at the messages, rereading them. Charlie was unbelievable. Couldn't he do anything for himself? He was a grown man for God's sake. My head was spinning, and I started to feel as if I'd done a day's work before I'd even dragged myself out of bed and jumped into the shower. I guessed I'd better make it a quick one. Whilst I let the hot water wash over my tired eyes, I tried to remind myself of how lucky I was to be here. I mean, was running to the store and picking up a Starbucks in the warm LA sunshine really that bad? I had to show resilience. I wasn't going to cave in despite the craziness of Charlie's life and his constant demands. I hadn't known what to expect going into this job, but I was heading along a very steep learning curve. I told myself it was only for a short time. I'd get some spending money together, and then I'd be back on the open road with Pete. I was sure Charlie wouldn't have a problem finding someone to take over from me. It seemed that Jessica already had someone lined up anyway. Reaching for the towel, I climbed out the shower cubicle and stared at myself in the mirror, smoothing the lines around my eyes with my fingertips. *Better get your face on, Ellie. Another busy day.*

The morning went by smoothly, partly because I'd previously memorized the route to the supermarket and the local Starbucks. I'd ticked off pretty much everything on the to-do stickie note Charlie had thoughtfully left for me stuck to my laptop screen, and I'd made several of his calls. I was winning, and I smiled to myself as I pulled up at Charlie's studio. This wasn't so hard. At the reception desk, a pretty, blonde-haired girl smiled at me.

"Hi. I'm here to see Charlie Robinson," I told her.

"And you are?"

"Ellie."

"Okay. Just take a seat over there, Ellie. I'll call through to him now." I walked over to a cosy, black leather chair and sat down, shifting in the seat and playing with my earing as the girl picked up her phone and dialled. "Ellie for Charlie," she said into the receiver. The girl nodded, looked up at me, and pressed a buzzer, which opened a side door. "You can go through. Up the stairs, turn right. Charlie's in room ten."

I smiled and headed up the stairs, Starbucks in hand. When I walked into the room, Charlie and another man were sitting at a desk looking into a computer screen. Charlie had the same grey beanie hat on he'd worn on our first meeting, and a blue, short-sleeved denim shirt that showed off his muscular arms and golden tan. *He is so hot*, I thought, as I walked in and smiled, trying not to blush and succeeding. Maybe I was getting used to his presence now, and he was no longer sending me into a blithering, melting hot mess just by looking at me. The other guy was much older, well into his fifties I reasoned. It was in the hands again. His hair was greying and unkempt, but he had the most well-groomed beard I'd ever seen. "Hi," I said cheerily.

Both men looked up at me, but neither smiled back. Charlie stood up and walked over to me. "Hey, thanks, Ellie. This is Brian." I looked over at Brian and smiled, giving a little wave, but he didn't look over, continuing instead to stare at the screen. Why were people so rude in this town? Charlie reached out and took the Starbucks cup from my hands. "I'm guessing that's mine?"

I smiled and handed it to him. "Oh, yes. Sorry."

Charlie took a sip and then looked at me, screwing up his face. "Ugh! I'm sorry, Ellie, but it's a little cold. I can't stand cold coffee."

My face flushed, and I side-glanced Brian, who now decided to stare over at me. "Oh, I'm sorry. I got here as fast as I could. The traffic was—"

Charlie handed the cup back to me and walked back over to his desk before sitting down. "Don't worry. It's fine." He picked up the phone next to the computer. "Sarah, can you bring me a black coffee, please. Great. No sugar. Thanks. You're a star." Charlie was silent as he placed the phone receiver down and looked up at the computer screen.

I just stood there and started to fiddle with my earing, feeling awkward as hell. I inched forward towards him. "Was there anything else you needed?"

Charlie kept his eyes on the screen. "No, that's fine, Ellie. I'll see you later."

I looked down with repulsion at the Starbucks cup in my hand. I could feel my face and neck burning hot, but this time, from anger. I'd run around like a crazy person all morning, doing everything that he'd asked of me, and then I'd walked in here to be treated with such contempt. Why would he treat me like this? I looked up at him, but he wasn't even looking at me. It was as if I'd simply vanished into thin air, both of them now engrossed again in self-congratulating conversation about how awesome a job they'd done. I had no idea what they were talking about, and I wasn't interested. I envisaged myself walking over to the desk and pouring the damn cold coffee all over the computer keyboard whilst shouting "Get your own next time!" before casually walking out. But, of course, I didn't. I pulled my car keys out of my jeans pocket and silently left the room without saying a word.

I made a slow drive back to the house, feeling irritated. Charlie was such a difficult person to work out. During our first meeting, he'd been so pleasant. But the more I was getting to know him, the more I was starting to dislike him. Sure, he was still ridiculously hot, but I wasn't flushing and getting so worked up every time our paths met. Maybe he was becoming a little less attractive to me the more I got to know him. The person I'd thought I knew now seemed completely arrogant, rude, and egotistical. I didn't mind his requests, the to-do lists, and all the running around. It *was* my job. But his diva ways were already wearing thin, and I was only a week into the job. I wondered how much longer I could last. I hated to admit defeat, but did I need this? Was Charlie acting the way all celebrities acted? Maybe I just needed to give it more time, get used to him, and get to know him better. I felt certain there must be another, gentler, kinder side to him. Surely, I could stick it out for another month or two before the road called me back. After all, no one had said anything terrible about him. I knew he had to be a good person deep down, and I'd seen flashes of that already. Maybe I just needed a little break after a pretty steep learning curve. *I'll speak to Charlie later*, I thought. *I'll ask about some personal time*. I knew that would do me good. I could just head down to the beach, laze for a couple of hours, read a book, catch up with my own emails, and ring Mum.

By the time I arrived back at the house, I'd talked myself into feeling better and decided to cheer myself up with a shopping trip. I did have a blue floral shirt to take back after all.

I'd expected Charlie back at some point that afternoon, but he never showed. At 10.30 p.m., after I'd heard nothing, and after I'd got caught up on all his emails and phone calls, I clicked my laptop shut and headed upstairs for a nice long, warm soak in the bath. I climbed into the tub, letting the bubbles envelope me. After smearing on a strawberry-enriched facemask and pinning my damp hair on top of my head, I shut my eyes. This was nice and just what I needed. Spotify played out on my phone. Camila Cabello's "Bad Things" came on as I sunk further into the warm water, letting it massage my tense shoulders. My mind wandered to Charlie. I didn't want it to, but I found myself envisaging him—his beautiful face and his big hands as he searched through the light bulb box last night. I thought about the way he'd looked at me, or at least the way I imagined he was looking at me. I pictured him standing in front of me, looking the way he did with those entrancing blue eyes. He was smiling at me, and I was blushing. He walked over, his body touching mine, his breath brushing my cheeks. I could feel his chest moving quickly as his eyes bore down on me. His blonde hair fell over his face as he took hold of the back of my head and pulled my face towards his. He pulled my body closer to his, and I could feel him protruding against me. He ran one hand down my neck, then my back and ran his other fingers through my wet hair. Then he moved his lips down to my neck, onto my stomach, kissing and stroking me as he moved further down, making my whole body tingle with pleasure. He kept looking up at me, but I pushed his head down further with my hands as he ran his fingers down my thighs, and then up to my knickers, making me shiver in anticipation for what was next.

Beep!

My eyes flew open. Damn! Another text message, and of course it was from Charlie. Who else at this time? But this was no longer surprising. I was getting used to messages at all hours. "Out in the club tonight. Will be home in the morning, C."

I read and re-read the message. He certainly wasn't one for going into detail. I pulled myself up out of the soothing water and wrapped a towel around my body, feeling guilty and little bit angry at myself for my dirty thoughts. He'd treated me like crap today, and here I was fantasising about him in my free time. I should be thinking about someone else—Channing Tatum or Zac Efron. Just anyone else, not Charlie. But he'd crept into my mind as much as I tried to keep him out, and it was beyond annoying. For a fleeting moment I felt a twinge of jealously. What was he doing tonight? Who was he with? These moments, though, really were fleeting, as I reminded myself that it made no difference to me where he was or who he was with. *Time for bed, Ellie. Time for bed.*

The buzzing woke me. It was dark, and the blue light from my flashing phone illuminated the ceiling. What time was it? I reached over to my bedside table and grabbed it. Charlie? What the hell? "Hello?" That was all I could muster in a croaky voice as I attempted to sit up but instead slumped down against the wooden head board.

"Ellie, sorry to wake you. Can you come pick me up?" Charlie slurred his words. He sounded drunk.

I squinted in the darkness. "What? What time is it?"

"About three in the morning. I'm not sure. Lost track of time. I'm in Santa Monica at the Ocean View Hotel. See you in thirty." The phone went dead.

I lay back down on the bed in silence, the light on my phone switching itself off, plunging me into complete darkness. Three seventeen in the morning? Was this guy on another planet? My eyelids felt heavy as I leaned over and switched on the bedside spotlight. Could he not have just called a taxi? It's not like he was stuck for cash. Switching my bedside lamp on, I pulled myself up out of bed, walked wearily into the bathroom, and switched on the light, squinting as my eyes adjusted to the brightness. My reflection greeted me with a caustic look as I rinsed my face, put my glasses on, and brushed my teeth. After throwing on my jeans and a grey cardigan, I grabbed my car keys and headed out into the balmy night. I was glad of the darkness shadowing my heavy eyes, make-up free pale complexion, and unbrushed hair.

I jumped into the driver's seat and pulled out onto the road, the satnav guiding me in the background. When I flicked on the radio, Drake's "Hotline Bling" was playing. I giggled to myself. A more fitting tune could not have been on. I drove down the empty highway, street lamps overhead illuminating my way. Fifteen minutes into my journey, the Bluetooth sounded, breaking the music. Charlie. I rolled my eyes. "Hey."

"Hey, how far away are you?"

I looked at the satnav. "I'll be with you in ten minutes or so."

"OK. Great." The line went dead again. Unbelievable.

Twenty minutes later, I pulled into the swish-looking hotel courtyard. Bentleys, Porsches, and other expensive-looking sports cars were parked up like glistening trophies. I stopped outside the entrance, and a smart-looking guy wearing a black suit and tie came over to me. I wound my window down and gave a half smile. I really wasn't in the mood for this.

"Hi, welcome to Ocean View. You want me to take your car?" He beamed. You wouldn't have thought it was the middle of the night.

I looked towards the reception entrance, expecting Charlie to come bounding out, but I didn't see him. Where the hell was he? "No. It's fine thanks. I'm just here to pick someone up."

"OK. No problem. You can stay here for ten minutes for a pickup, but after that you'll need to move."

"It's OK," I promised. "I won't be long." I smiled and wound my window back up, pulling over into one of the parking bays. I dialled Charlie's mobile number, but it just rang out. Damn it. I hadn't thought I would be getting out the car. I looked a complete mess. He knew I'd been minutes away. Why wasn't he answering his bloody phone and looking out for me? Rolling my eyes and letting out a sigh, I pulled down the rear-view mirror. *Great! Just great,* I thought as I observed the bags under my eyes and pimple on my chin. *Just fabulous. I'm about to walk into one of the poshest looking hotels I've ever seen in my life looking like I've been pulled through a hedge backwards.* I pushed my lips together to prevent a scream surfacing and heaved open the car door. I jumped out and headed towards the conveniently bright reception area.

The place was contemporary and luxurious with duck egg–blue, retro-style lounge chairs and wooden tables, colourful modern art sprawled along the walls, and huge floor-to-ceiling windows. I could only dream of staying in a place like this. Keeping my head down, I made a beeline for the reception desk and, of course, as luck would have it, a beautiful blonde woman, about six feet tall, super slim, and wearing an elegant, slinky red dress that glided along her curves stood beaming at me with her perfect pearly whites. "Hi. Welcome to Ocean View. Are you picking up?"

I pursed my lips together. "Hi. Yes, I am."

The girl looked down at the computer and was poised to start typing. "What's the company name?"

I shook my head. "Company name … erm, what?"

The girl's eyes narrowed, the top and bottom of her long, and obviously fake eyelashes, almost touching. "Yes—your cab company name?"

"Sorry, cab company? What?"

She just looked at me, her flawless, dewy skin mocking my huge red pimple. "You're a cab driver, right?"

I shook my head again and put my fingers to my temples. "No, sorry. I'm here for Charlie Robinson. Do you know where he is? I've tried reaching him on his mobile, but he isn't picking up."

"Oh, right. Hang on." This girl vanished into a side room and, after a few minutes, emerged, wearing one of those forced wry smiles. "Charles won't be too much longer. If you take a seat over there." She pointed with her French manicured finger to a seating area by the door.

Charles? Since when was his name Charles? I smiled to myself and walked over to a blue three-seater couch. I hugged my cardigan for comfort, feeling so out of place and self-conscious. I felt eyes on me, though I suspected that, in reality, nobody was taking much notice at all. I wished Charlie would just hurry up since he'd dragged me all the way out here at this hideous hour. He'd pestered me on the drive up here, and now here I was sitting waiting for him. Typical. I pulled my phone out my jeans pocket. Nothing.

"Hey!" Charlie stood in front of me. His hair was sleeked back from his face, he looked sweaty, and his eyes were bloodshot and glazed over.

I smiled and stood up, "Hey. Good night, Charles?"

He smiled back, getting the joke. "It was OK, you know." He looked me up and down and raised an eyebrow. "Let's go," he said, pulling my arm as we started to walk towards the door. I glanced over at the blonde women at reception. She was staring over at us. I smiled at her, and she looked away.

After I climbed back into the car I reset the satnav. Charlie rested his head on the seat and shut his eyes. I side glanced him. *Sure—must be hectic, all this socializing,* I thought as I drove in silence. The sun was just starting to peep up through the buildings as we headed back onto the freeway. After a few minutes, Charlie lifted his head and looked at me. I didn't look at him; I kept my eyes firmly glued to the road. "How was your night, Ellie? Thanks for picking me up, if I didn't already say."

I nodded and smiled. "Sure, that's OK. Erm, yeah, it was fine. I went through some of your correspondence, watched a film, and went to bed. So not as exciting as your night."

"I think a movie and bed sounds great. These parties, they get pretty tiresome. You feel like you have to go because you want to support a friend, or you have to go because it's promoting your work and it's in your contract, but they become tedious."

I scrunched up my face. Who was he kidding? "Yeah, I can see how attending party after party every weekend can become tiring," I rolled my eyes.

"Geez, you climbed out the wrong side of the bed." He smiled and poked my side.

I flinched away and waved my hand towards his, forcing him to stop. "Well, I wouldn't be *out* of bed right now if it wasn't for your late-night taxi call, right side or wrong side."

He looked and me and started laughing, and I had to laugh back. I could give as good as I got. After a few moments, Charlie rested his head on the seat. "I'm serious, though. This lifestyle from the outside seems pretty great, but sometimes it's nice to just chill out at home. Be alone, be yourself, you know?"

I nodded. I did actually get that. "You friend wasn't there tonight? Just work people?"

"The word *friend*, especially in this town, us very loosely defined. There were a couple of people I would call friends there and then just some acquaintances, you know? There are very few people I trust or people I'd call friends here."

"Why'd you stay here if that's how you feel?"

"Well, I came here—a good few years ago now—as a nobody. I worked hard, made a couple of friends—people like Jo who weren't interested in fame or fortune—and eventually I got my break. Very few people were interested in me until then, and all of a sudden, I've got people cueing up to take me out for drinks, and invites flooding in for parties." He turned his head to look out the window and combed his hair back off his face. "Fame brings quite a few unpleasant people your way. You're caught in this world where there are plenty of people around you, but somehow you feel alone. It's hard to know where to turn and who to trust, especially when you've been burnt a few times. I just like to keep things simple, keep my circle small." He took a deep breath, and then turned his gaze back to me. "But I guess I stay here because my work is here, and I have a life here now. But it has its downfalls. I like to keep things as real as I can in the mist of it all."

I nodded, keeping my eyes on the road. He took a deep breath and shifted in his seat, resting on his side to face me. "You look deep in thought," he said.

I looked at him again and smiled. "Yeah, just, you know, thinking about what you just said, about feeling alone. I've been there."

Charlie raised his brows. "How so?"

"Ahh, you know—dead-end job, dead-beat cheating boyfriend, moving back home with my parents at twenty-nine, and feeling just a tad out of my depths in trying to pull myself back up." I could feel my eyes welling up, and I turned my face away from him. I didn't want him to see my tears. Why was I revealing this? I shouldn't have said anything, but I felt a sudden comfort with him. He'd opened up to me, and I wanted to give him something in return. "I guess I felt like there was nothing left for

113

me in London, and whilst my family and friends have been great, like you said, there are people around you, but you still feel alone sometimes and you know that no matter how many people have your back, you're the only person who can pull you out of whatever rut you're stuck in."

The satnav interrupted us, directing me off the freeway at the next exit. I pushed the fringe from my eyes and took a deep breath. I hoped I hadn't shared too much. "I'm sorry. I shouldn't be ..."

"Sorry for what?" He scrunched up his face.

"I don't know I just ..."

"You're real, Ellie. I felt that as soon as we met." I turned to look at him, and his eyes narrowed on me. I felt myself getting nervous again as I fumbled through my brain, thinking how to respond. "I hope I can trust you," he said. "We spend so much time together, and you know so much about me already—personal things. I've built a wall around myself since I've been out here. Not to stop people getting in, more to protect what's already inside me." He shifted in his seat and ran his hand through his hair again. "I don't want Hollywood to change me. I have seen what it can do to some people. I've lost a few friends to its curses—drugs, egos, mental breakdowns. I let few people in, Ellie, but when I do, they're usually locked in for good. And I want you in. I know you won't let me down." He looked down at his hands, twisting his silver thumb ring.

I felt my heart beating and I gulped hard. "I won't Charlie. I promise you." I glanced over at him again, his head now resting on the seat, his eyes closed. I wondered if he would remember this conversation in the morning. We'd not known each other long—little over a week—but during that time, I'd seen so many different sides to him—movie star Charlie, at-home Charlie, confident Charlie, and now vulnerable Charlie. It was exhausting trying to get to know him. I imagined it was even more exhausting to be him.

As I pulled up to the house just after five o'clock, Charlie had been lightly snoring for the last ten minutes of the journey. After I gave him a firm nudge in his side, we made our way into the kitchen. I walked over to the cupboard, grabbed a glass, and filled it with ice-cold water from the fridge dispenser. Charlie sat at the breakfast bar, head in his hands.

"I'm going to get back into bed, Charlie. Unless there's anything you need me to do before I go." He looked up at me, his hair falling onto his face. I shrugged my shoulders and raised my eyebrows, prompting as he sat in silence.

He stood up and slowly walked round to me. I could smell alcohol on his breath. "No, Ellie. It's fine. Unless there's anything you want from me before you go?"

I looked down at my glass and took a sip of water. My mouth was dry, and my face was suddenly on fire. "No," I managed. "That's fine. See you later." And off I went back to bed.

Chapter 16

"Two cappuccinos?" Ross gave me a half-hearted smile as I walked over to the counter. The familiar and comforting bubbling and hissing of the coffee machine instantly relaxed, me and after running around on errands with Charlie all morning, I needed a Zen moment. I nodded. "Yes. Thank you, Ross. How are you?"

Ross grabbed two cappuccino cups from the top of the machine and placed them underneath the spout. "Okay, you know?" I nodded. I didn't know him well enough to enquire further, but he didn't seem as chipper as he had last week.

"How's living in Charlie's world working out for you?" He raised an eyebrow. There was something about the way he asked, a hint of sarcasm in his voice. Charlie did come here every week, but Ross didn't know him, did he? Not well enough to have a real dislike for him or know so much about him. Maybe Ross was just having a bad day.

"Well, it can get pretty … how shall I say it? Eventful, you know? But I think it's going OK, so far."

Ross nodded, placing two steaming cups of coffee on a tray. "Want to come through for a coffee? I'm due my lunch break now anyway, so I'll see you in there shortly. I'll just take these over to Charlie's table." Before I could reply, Ross was over at Charlie's booth, which was tucked away in the corner of course, and a few moments later, Ross and I were sitting side by side in the small, brightly lit, extremely stuffy staff room. "You working this weekend?" Ross asked

"I work every weekend, but no firm plans yet, if that's what you mean."

Ross shifted in his chair and removed the red-and-white-striped tea towel from the apron around his waist. He twisted it around in his hands, seeming on edge, nervous. "Sure. Well, if you get some free time, do you fancy doing something?"

I looked up from my coffee cup to see Ross blushing. Was he asking me out on a date? It had been a long time since a guy had asked me out, or even flirted with me. I was not one of those girls who got admired often. Occasionally, when drunk, I'd bemoan, usually to Carla, that I must be the ugliest girl in the world as no man ever flirted with me, and I certainly never got asked out on dates. Carla always promptly assured me that I wasn't, in fact, the ugliest person she'd even seen, and suggested I go for body dysmorphia counselling. She always suggested it was my quiet attitude that kept people away. She used to say to me that men didn't know how to take me, that I didn't give much away. She was probably right. I wasn't much of a flirt myself. And, of course, being with Finn for all those years, it had never bothered me. Carla used to say I gave off an air of being "taken." And I used to reply that, if that was the case, why did she always get eyed up on our Friday evening post work drinks? We'd had this conversation drunkenly several times without ever really having reached a conclusion.

I was out the game now, thrown back on the shelf, and the idea of dating again petrified me. But it was harmless fun, nothing serious, and it would be nice to get to know Ross, even if we just became friends. It would be nice to have someone to hang out with when I had time off, if that ever happened. "Erm, sure. How's Friday at seven?" I smiled.

"Great. Will your boss be okay with that?"

"I am allowed personal time, you know? He doesn't have me permanently chained to him or anything."

We both laughed, and he blushed some more. He pushed his thick, black-rimmed glasses closer to his eyes as they had started to slide down his nose. "Of course. I'll look forward to it then."

We smiled at each other and finished our coffees. A date! What was I going to wear?

We were driving down the busy highway on our way to a red-carpet press event for Charlie's new movie, but he seemed anxious, fiddling with his thumb ring, biting his lip. He'd been quiet for the last twenty minutes, slumped in his car seat. Maybe it was the whole thing about press and cameras at these things—too many flashing lights and journalists intruding on his privacy. But he knew the script, and he had told me it was all part of his job. He'd certainly dressed for the occasion—smart navy-blue chinos, a loose white shirt that set off his caramel tan, and brown suede brogues. His hair was sleeked back off his face, and he looked achingly handsome. I was hoping to skip the cameras, Jessica having informed me this morning that I could drop Charlie at the front with all the fanfare, and then nip round to the back entrance, sneaking in, away from all the craziness. *Should be easy enough*, I thought.

I'd been meaning for a few days to ask about taking some personal time, and no better time than when I was driving, since I didn't have to give him eye contact. I could just pin my gaze to the road as I spoke. "So, any plans for this weekend? There's nothing in the diary."

Charlie also kept his eyes ahead on the road. "I'm not sure yet. One of the guys has asked me to head over to his cabin in Big Sur for the weekend, but I dunno. I've some scripts to read over, and I just feel like taking it easy, ordering pizza, watching some movies." I nodded. This was sounding good. No major plans then. I could surely skip out on Friday night with Ross. Charlie shifted in his seat and pushed both sides of his hair behind his ears. "Perhaps you could join me?"

Shit. I took a breath in, thinking how to word this best. "Yeah, I mean, that would be nice, on Saturday night maybe? But I was actually going to see if I could take some personal time on Friday evening, if you didn't need me for anything."

Charlie turned his head towards me. I could feel his eyes burning into me. As I had planned, I kept my eyes glued to the road. "Okay. What are your plans?"

"Well, you know that guy from DeLatte? Ross? He has offered to take me sightseeing, show me a few of his local haunts, you know?"

Charlie didn't respond. He turned his head away from me, instead looking out of his passenger window. Okay, so why did I all of a sudden feel like I could cut the atmosphere with a knife? This was awkward. What was he thinking? After a minute or two, his voice toneless, he sliced that silence with that knife. "OK. No problem."

I didn't say anything. Charlie, instead, filled the silence with a phone call to his publicist.

We pulled up outside the front entrance of a huge, white, nondescript building in downtown LA. A red carpet was laid out from the road to the doorway, and photographers and journalists lined one side of it, two and three deep. On the other side, fans stood—mostly young girls holding banners and pens and books—looking out for their idol. Burly-looking men wearing black suits, white shirts, black ties, and ear pieces lined the carpet, holding everyone back. This was the first time I'd taken Charlie to anything official like this, and I hadn't been sure what to expect. My heart was in my mouth as I pulled up to the front entrance. One of the security men walked over to the passenger door and flung it open. Lights flashed from every direction, and people from both sides of the carpet started screaming Charlie's name. He jumped out without saying anything, waving at the crowds, his lips working a huge Hollywood smile. The security man slammed the car door shut. I re-adjusted my eyes to the daylight after being blinded by the flashing bulbs, and I pulled off, looking for a side road to turn into so I could access the back of the building. None. This place had a back entrance, right?

Jessica had specifically said this morning this place had one. Don't get dressed up, she'd said. You'll be behind the scenes all day. No one will be looking at you, so keep it low key. And I'd done just that. Charlie hadn't mentioned my casual outfit, but then he'd seem so absorbed in his own stuff, I doubt he would have noticed whether I'd rocked up wearing Louboutins or loafers. I turned the car around and drove past the building's front again to the other side. Nothing. What the hell? I pulled the car over and watched as a navy-blue Aston Martin pulled up at the red carpet. Charlie had disappeared inside, and now two guys jumped out, and another tall, thin, smartly dressed guy with a bald head and glasses handed one of them a ticket and immediately jumped into their car, driving it away. Valet parking. They must have assumed when they saw me dressed in jeans and a black T-shirt with 'Bonjour' written on the front that I was just Charlie's ride and let me drive off. I rested my head on the steering wheel, letting out a quiet grunt. *For fuck's sake.* I was going to have to pull out front alone and get out of the car dressed like this, and conspicuously walk down that red carpet. Alone. And in Converse. This was certainly not how I imagined my first red-carpet moment would play out, not that I'd ever really imagined one at all. *Fuck.* I grabbed my bag and pulled out a small, pink-encased compact mirror. Opening it, I grimaced. I wiped under my eyes, bit my teeth together to check I had nothing stuck in them, and smoothed my lips together. I closed my eyes tight. Why was this happening to me? I ran my fingers through my fringe, combing it to one side. Finally, I clicked the mirror closed. Maybe I could ring Charlie and tell him there'd been an emergency at the house and I'd had to leave. But that would be lying, and I really didn't want to go down that road. I looked over at the chaos again. The photographers were having a quiet moment. No one was about. Perhaps I could seize my chance? Sneak in. They'd hardly notice.

The Bluetooth started ringing. Charlie. He was whispering "Where are you?"

"I, erm …"

"I need you to get up here."

I put my head in my hands. "Charlie, I'm … lost."

"You're what? Where are you?"

"I'm just … erm … in the car, sitting outside. I thought I would park up round the back and come in the building that way, you know, avoid the cameras, but … well, there is no back." Charlie went silent. I closed my eyes and rested my head against the steering wheel. He's going to sack me. That's it now.

"So, you're out front, and you don't want to come through the photographers?"

"Sorry! I'm not, um … I'm not used to this, and I'm dressed …"

"It doesn't matter what you're wearing. Just, pull up close and wait for me. I'll come out and get you."

"What? Can you—"

"I'll be there in five, okay? Just pull up out front, and I'll come to the car. Look like your handing me something—anything—and then jump out, okay? Then walk up with me." I opened my eyes and exhaled, not realizing I'd been holding my breath. Tears pooled in the corners of my eyes as fear and a little relief engulfed me. "Okay, I'll be there in—"

The line went dead. Did he sound pissed off with me? I couldn't tell. He'd just made his big Hollywood entrance and was having to come out to get me in front of the world's paps again, something he hated doing. All the cameras would be on him. No one would even notice little me in the background.

A few moments later, lightbulbs started flashing. And there he was, slowly walking down the carpet towards the road, waving and smiling at both sides of the crowd as he went. He was a natural, so calm and in control, oozing charm and charisma as he strolled along effortlessly. He stopped to shake someone's hand and looked over to me. I pulled up, and he opened the passenger door.

He smiled. "Hey, you OK?" I nodded, my mouth dry, my heart beating fast. "Come on. Follow me." I jumped out, and lightbulbs continue to flash. Charlie leaned over to me, and I felt his breath on me as he whispered, "Give me the car keys. I'll sort it. Head in. I'm right behind you."

My whole body went goosebumpy, and for a split second I felt light headed. Beads of sweat started dripping down my nose, and my legs felt weak as the lightbulbs kept flashing. All the while, people were screaming Charlie's name. A girl no older than thirteen was crying and looked as if she was about to have a heart attack, throwing her arms towards him as one of the security guys held her back. I put my head down and made a swift beeline for the entrance.

The coolness of the building hit me as I stood watching Charlie in awe as he swooned his way down the carpet once more, smiling and shaking hands with adoring fans as he went. He stopped at the entrance facing the crowd, gave one final wave, and turned to head inside. He looked at me and smiled, his face sweaty. He let out a sigh and put one hand on my shoulder. My whole body trembled. I thought I'd got over Charlie and his ability to turn me into a wreck. Obviously not. "You okay?"

"Yeah. Charlie, I'm sorry,"

He shook his head, his eyes burning into mine. "Don't be. You didn't know. I should have told you to follow me the first time."

I took a huge sigh of relief. "Thanks. Well, I appreciate you coming out there for me."

"Don't mention it, Ellie. I hate to see you panicking like that. I know it's daunting at first, but you'll get used to it." He kept his hand firmly on my shoulder, and we stood for a second looking at each other. Charlie cleared his throat and removed his hand, putting both hands awkwardly in his pockets and looking down at the floor. "Glad that's over with anyway. Just need to get this press conference over and done with now. Have you got the list of questions from my publicist?"

I smiled and sieved through the black leather file I'd carried in, pulling out a piece of A4 paper and handing it to him. We walked over to the lift doors and stood, waiting. "Ellie, you know, I've been giving Big Sur some thought, and I'd like to go now. I think it'd be good for me to spend some time up there, away from LA and this madness. It's been a pretty busy week. We'll head up Friday afternoon. Can you let Rose know too?"

I looked at him and frowned. Had he just completely disregarded our conversation in the car about Friday and my date with Ross?

"But what about my personal time Friday?"

He didn't look at me. Instead, he glued his eyes on the closed lift doors and reached over to press the buttons again. I stood watching him, waiting for him to acknowledge what I'd just asked him. "Oh, yes. Sorry, I forgot. I guess you'll have to just rearrange for another day." And that was it. I just looked at him, his hair sleeked back behind his ears, black Ray-Bans sitting on top of his head. I shook my head and looked down without saying a word.

The elevator doors pinged open, and he strode in. I watched him as he turned around and looked at me. His expression hardened. "You coming?" Saying nothing, I forced a smile and followed him in.

I knelt on my bed, staring out of the window up to the blue sky smudged with a pink and yellowy haze as the day was drawing to a close. "Rose and I have literally spent the last forty-eight hours ticking off his friggin' to-do list for this trip. I haven't even packed a pair of knickers for it yet."

Pete laughed at the other end of the line. "Sounds like you're having fun there."

"He's just so …"

"Sexy?" Pete laughed.

I rolled my eyes and sat down on the edge of my bed, pulling a packet of Reece's Pieces out of my purse and playing with the packaging. "Well, *that* obviously. But I was going to say something else."

"So, OK, you had to cancel on this Ross guy, but that can be re-arranged, right? The way I see it, you wanted to go to Big Sur, and now you can. And the best bit is you're getting paid to go, so just enjoy it."

"I guess. He just drives me nuts with his demands for this, needs for that. The world revolves around him, you know?"

"He's pretty much the hottest movie star on the planet, Ellie. The world does revolve around him. Get used to it. Deal with it and try to enjoy it." I nodded. I knew Pete was right. He was always my go-to for a good moan, and I could rely on him to tell me exactly what he thought. "I'm guessing he is as hot as ever though? Do you think he's packing 'down there'?"

I smiled, trying to hide my amusement as I spoke. "Jesus, Pete! Why do you have to turn every conversation smutty?"

"Come on, you've thought about it. Do you think he's a master between those thousand-dollar bedsheets?"

I laughed, pulling myself up off the bed and walking over to the bathroom mirror, observing my pale skin and dry lips. Remnants of the day's lipstick filled the cracks. "Stop it!" I feigned outrage, pushing my fringe away from my eyes, my reflection staring back at me. "But, you know, I have definitely observed a bulge in the relevant area, so, you know, I think he could just be."

"I knew it! So, you have thought about it, you dirty girl!"

I combed my fingers through my ponytail, twisting it round my hands. "It was pretty hard to miss, to be fair."

Pete laughed, and we giggled together. "Oh, snap!"

Still laughing, I walked back over to my bed and sat down. "He's just so hard to figure out," I told Pete. "The other night, driving back from Santa Monica, I really felt like we clicked, you know? I felt comfortable with him, as if I'd known him for years. And then the next minute, he's being ... well ... a complete dick." Pete didn't say anything. I could just hear his slow breath down the phone. "You still there, Pete?"

"Yeah, just thinking. You like him, don't you? I can tell."

I put my hand to my head, shutting my eyes. Pete had got it all wrong. "No, no, not like that at all. I mean, I like him as a person. He's a nice guy sometimes but ..."

"Ellie, be honest. You'd shag his brains out given half the chance."

We both laughed. And I had to admit it, Pete was right. "Right." I said. "Anyway, on that note, I'm going. I have some black lacy lingerie to pack before tomorrow, so I'll call you next week, okay?"

"Like, that's it? You saucy minx! Well, do let me know if you make use of the lingerie. I want a comprehensive breakdown of events as soon as you get back. Don't do anything I wouldn't."

I ended the call and stared at my overnight bag, empty and slumped in the corner of the room. *I'd better stop faffing and get some packing done.* It would be an early start tomorrow, and with Charlie all set to go, I needed as much beauty sleep as I could get.

I was feeling tetchy after a terrible night's sleep, as we drove up the sweeping driveway towards the house. I'd tossed and turned all night and had felt agitated despite being exhausted. It was one of those nights during which you lie there thinking about decisions you made two days ago and decisions you made in high school or when you were twelve. All the mistakes I'd ever made came flooding back to me—boyfriends I'd broken up with but not seen for years, dresses I'd decided to keep when they should really have been sent back, and of course, Charlie. He was there, popping in and out of my semi-lucid thoughts. I thought about what Pete had said. Sure, I wouldn't kick him out of bed given half a chance. I'd be hard pressed to find any woman who would. But, behind all the Hollywood glamour and his public image, I still couldn't figure him out as a person. I thought back to when he'd saved me at his press conference earlier in the week, and the goosebumps pricked up on my skin again. He most likely hated having to do that. He hated walking down that carpet with all the press anyway, so doing it twice with everyone wondering why he'd suddenly made a second appearance must have been worse. He could have just left me, forced me to get out the car and go solo. I was getting paid, after all.

But, then, I thought about his plans for this weekend, and his sheer couldn't-care-less attitude, not just towards me, but also towards his other staff members. It was baffling. Thinking about him had driven me bloody crazy, and not even half a bottle of Merlot had been sufficient to send me off into a blissful sleep.

Thankfully, this morning, Rose had driven most of the way since she'd been before and wasn't as overwhelmed as I was by the stunning scenery as we drove along the dusty, winding roads. The drive was stunning in every direction. The Atlantic Ocean sprawled out before us, and with every twist and turn the beauty of the ocean lured us into its beauty further. I had never been anywhere so stunning.

I took over the driving towards the last part of the journey. As we neared what Charlie had described to me his friend's cabin, I slowly drove up a winding drive towards a huge stone house. *Cabin?* I thought as I observed the sheer size of this place. *This isn't exactly how I would describe a cabin.* Brown shutters on the outside of the windows, a huge wooden front door, and two extremely expensive-looking sports cars parked outside, one being Charlie's silver Maserati which he'd driven up himself earlier this morning and a grey Aston Martin. As I got out of the car and turned my back on the house, I took in a view that was to die for—ocean that went on for miles as far as the eye could see, little plumes of white breaking the water as the waves crashed around. Trees and lush shrubs surrounded the house, and pretty pots of pink and blue flowers sat on each step leading up to the front door. It was truly beautiful, and as I shut my eyes and listened, all I could hear was the crashing of the waves against the rocks. I took a deep breath in, and my lungs felt cleaner. Charlie's voice broke my thoughts and my eyes flew open as he came bounding over to us, his brows pulled together. "I thought you guys would have been here sooner." *Oh, fucking hell, here we go.* Charlie moved to stand directly in front of me. "You okay?" His frown broke into a warm smile.

"Yeah, sorry. Just this place, it's overwhelming."

He nodded, looking past me towards the ocean. "Let's get in. Can you manage? Here, let me grab that one." I gaped at him as he pulled my overnight bag from my hands and started to walk into the house. I glanced over at Rose, who was also watching him, her eyes narrowed. She glanced at me and shrugged her shoulders. Perhaps it was the sea air that had gone to his head.

We followed him up the steps through to the impressive entrance. The walls inside were natural stone, the same as the outside. A huge sweeping staircase dominated the hallway, and a mammoth glass chandelier like nothing I had ever seen before acted as centrepiece. I looked at Rose. She'd been quiet the whole way here and didn't seem herself. I'd tried to get out of her what was wrong, but she had just said she was tired. I suspected something else was going on, but I didn't feel that I'd known her long enough to press her. I'd try speaking to her again later.

Charlie led us through to the kitchen and stopped, motioning to a short guy who appeared to be in his forties. He had a balding head and a new beard. "Ellie, this is Patrick."

Patrick took his hands out of his beige chino pockets and walked over to me, extended his arm and smiled. "Ellie, great to meet you."

"Patrick is a producer. We worked together on a mini-series a few years back."

I nodded and smiled back. "Great! Nice to meet you. What an amazing place you have here. It's just stunning," I said, looking round the entrance hall.

"Yeah, love it here. Try to get up here a couple of times a year at least. It's nice to get away from the craziness of Beverly Hills, you know?"

I nodded, and he turned his attentions to Rose, walking over to her and extending his arms as if he'd known her for twenty years. "Rose, so lovely to see you again. I am looking forward to more of your culinary delights this weekend."

Rose smiled but didn't say anything. What was with her? She was usually so warm and friendly.

"OK," Charlie interrupted. "You guys go and get settled in. Rose, I believe Jessica filled you in on the menu requests for tonight and tomorrow. I assume that's all sorted?"

Rose nodded, her eyes glistening. She looked on the verge of tears. "Sure, Mr. Robinson. No problems at all."

"OK, great. Go get settled in. See you later."

Patrick gave us directions to our guest quarters, and off we toddled. I wasn't sure about him. He was ever so friendly and polite, but I had never really been able to trust any man who wore a turtle neck, and he didn't strike me as the kind of person Charlie would hang out with. But then, Charlie was constantly surprising me.

"Hey, Rose, can I come in?" I was determined to get to the bottom of what was bothering her. I hadn't known Rose long, but she was usually such an upbeat, full-of-life kind of person, and I was worried about her recent behaviour.

"Sure, Ellie." Rose was sitting on the edge of her bed, her thick wavy dark brown hair pinned into a bun on top of her head. Her eyes looked red and puffy, and she was holding a tissue in her hand.

"Rose, there's something wrong. What's the matter?" I said down next to her.

"Ellie, please don't say anything to Mr. Robinson. I don't want to put a cloud over his weekend."

"I won't, Rose, but what is it? You're worrying me."

Rose took the tissue to her cheek, wiping away more tears. "I didn't know if you knew. I was meant to be off this weekend. I'd asked Jessica months ago. My daughter, Joy, turns sixteen tomorrow. She's having a sweet sixteen birthday party, organized by me, and obviously, I won't be there now." She looked down at the floor, scrunching the tissue in her hands. "Jessica rang me yesterday to tell me I had to come here. I explained about Joy's birthday and the party, but she was having none of it. From her tone, I swear she'd have fired me on the spot if I'd declined. She said if I valued my job and the prestigious position I was in, then I wouldn't make a fuss and would just do it. What could I do?" Rose looked at me, distraught.

I felt so angry. "The bitch!" I spewed out. Rose looked at me in shock. "Well, she is. I can't believe she's done this. Does Charlie know about the birthday party?"

"I don't think so. I requested the personal days months ago through Jessica and never told anyone what my plans were. As a rule, I keep myself to myself, and just get on with my work, Ellie. It was in the diary that I was off. Jessica knew, and that was it. I thought it would be honoured no matter what."

I shook my head in complete disbelief. I wondered if Charlie knew about this. I didn't want to believe he did. And if he didn't, I wondered how he would react? "Yeah, you'd think, wouldn't you?" I said.

Rose looked at me and put a hand on my knee. "Please don't say anything to him, Ellie. I know you're closer to him than I am, but I just want to get on with it now. I'm here. It's done."

"But your daughter's birthday—you're going to miss it!"

"I know. Occupational hazard of having such a high-profile boss, I suppose. I wouldn't get paid better anywhere else, and Joy ... she understands. Of course, she was upset. Lots of tears, you know? But she's a good girl, and she knows I'll make it up to her at some point."

I nodded, but I was still fuming inside. How could Jessica be such a heartless cow?

Rose stood up and walked towards the door, brushing down her crisp white shirt and black knee-length skirt. "I'm going to head down to the kitchen, start preparing tonight's dinner. I'll catch up with you later, OK?"

I smiled with a heavy heart. "Sure. See you later."

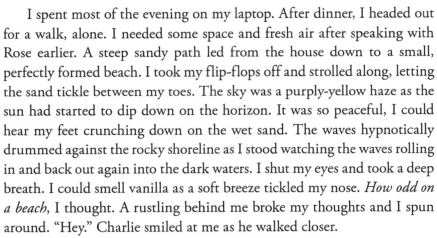

I spent most of the evening on my laptop. After dinner, I headed out for a walk, alone. I needed some space and fresh air after speaking with Rose earlier. A steep sandy path led from the house down to a small, perfectly formed beach. I took my flip-flops off and strolled along, letting the sand tickle between my toes. The sky was a purply-yellow haze as the sun had started to dip down on the horizon. It was so peaceful, I could hear my feet crunching down on the wet sand. The waves hypnotically drummed against the rocky shoreline as I stood watching the waves rolling in and back out again into the dark waters. I shut my eyes and took a deep breath. I could smell vanilla as a soft breeze tickled my nose. *How odd on a beach*, I thought. A rustling behind me broke my thoughts and I spun around. "Hey." Charlie smiled at me as he walked closer.

Why was he down here? Could I not have a peaceful minute? I was desperate to know if he knew about Rose and Joy's birthday party, but a promise was a promise. I observed him as he sauntered over. *Damn*, I thought, *he looks good tonight*. He moved closer towards me. He was wearing a white cap that covered his hair, knee-length blue denim shorts, and a black T-shirt. His deep suntan looked even more golden in the sunset. I felt myself melting inside. I put my hand to my chest. "Hey!"

"Amazing here, isn't it? You look deep in thought." He walked straight up to me, his body within inches of mine. I felt goosebumps cover my arms as I rubbed them, hoping he wouldn't notice.

I smiled. "It is. Patrick is so lucky to live here."

"He is. I've often thought I'd move out here someday, escape the city."

"Escape? You feel trapped in LA?"

Charlie nodded and sat down. I sat next to him. "Sometimes. I guess it depends what kind of day I'm having."

"Most people feel that way about work, or whatever. Not every day can be good—take the rough with the smooth and all that."

He picked up a handful of sand and passed it from one hand to another, then slowly let it flow through his fingers. "I guess so."

"It's a crazy world you live in though. Crazier than most people's. I'd say you have a lot more good days than most people." I leaned back on my arms, stretching my legs out and tucking my feet into the dry, soft sand.

Charlie lay his back on the sand, staring up towards the fading sunlight. The sky became a darker blue as the sun started to drop behind the sea. "Well, before I moved here," he said, "London was pretty crazy too. And when I got to LA, things built up over time, you know? This life—it didn't happen overnight. I worked hard, and I guess I just adjusted with each day. I never expected to end up here. I just found myself here one day. Happens to lots of people. But I have my moments when I stop and think about things." Charlie closed his eyes, took a deep breath, extended his arms in the air in front of him, and then laid them back down. He turned to look at me. "I often wonder how different my life could have been, and I guess I know how lucky I am. But I need reminding of the bigger picture sometimes—what's important in life, if you know what I mean."

I nodded, though I guessed I could never understand. His life was the exception, not the rule, and very few people would ever experience his world.

"You're doing a great job, Ellie. I want you to know that. I know you've been thrust straight into things, but you're doing good."

I didn't say anything. I just looked at him and smiled. In truth, I wasn't sure what to say. I pushed my fringe out my face and looked at him for a moment. Then I stood up and brushed sand off my denim shorts. "It's getting a little cool, so I'm gonna head back. I'll see you up there." I turned to walk back, putting my hands in my pockets.

"Ellie?" I turned back round. "Patrick and I are going to a local bar tonight. Want to join us?"

I thought about it for a moment. And since I was stuck there, I guessed I might as well see what the nightlife in Big Sur had to offer. "Sure. That would be nice," I said brightly. "Do I need to dress up?"

"Nah, you look great the way you are. Be ready in ten, okay? Patrick will drive."

"OK, I'll be ready."

"Amigos, good to see you." A hipster-looking guy with a super impressive thick beard and black-rimmed glasses beamed from behind the bar as Charlie and Patrick walked through the door. Charlie high-fived him as we sat down on wooden bar stools.

Charlie smiled and took out his wallet from his jeans pocket. "Good to see you. How's tricks?" He was looking super fit tonight, but then, this was becoming my usual description of Charlie. I doubted he'd ever walk in a room and I'd sit there thinking to myself, *He's looking rough as a bear's arse today.* And as always, he'd kept it casual—light blue baggy jeans, a white T-shirt, and white Vans trainers. His hair was pushed behind his ears, a couple of stray strands falling onto his face. I couldn't take my eyes off him, though I tried desperately to.

"Ellie, what are you drinking?" Charlie asked me.

"A Bud is fine. Thanks, Charlie." *Best keep it light,* I thought. Wine had got me into trouble too many times, and of course, once you'd had one glass, it was two, then three, and before you knew it you'd be on the top of a table, bra in hand, performing the entire dance routine for Girls Aloud's "Love Machine". Tonight was not the night for that.

The place was small and very plain—white walls, brown wooden chairs and tables, and a couple of pool tables. Two older guys were playing darts in a dark, dreary corner. It wasn't the swanky type of place I would expect Charlie and his friends to be seen in, and it was all about appearances, wasn't it? There'd be no paparazzi hanging around here, that was for sure, but then I guessed that maybe that was the whole point.

Charlie smiled and nudged me with his elbow as he passed me the bottle of Bud. "I didn't have you down as a Bud drinking girl."

"Oh? Well, actually, you'd be right. But my usual choice of wine can get me into all kinds of trouble. I think I'd better go easy tonight."

Charlie raised his eyebrows, and a smile crept onto his face. "It can? Maybe I can tempt you with a glass or two later then. See what trouble you get us into?"

I looked away, my cheeks feeling as if a nuclear bomb had just exploded all over them. He sat, observing me as I shifted in my seat. Then he jumped off his stool and headed over to one of the empty pool tables. "Right. Who's up for a game?"

Patrick sipped his Bud. "Can you play, Ellie?" he asked.

I gritted my teeth together. "Not really, but I'll give it a good go." I'd played pool about four times my whole life. The last time I remembered playing was on holiday in Ibiza with Finn. It was our first holiday together, and we'd been seeing each other for only a year or so. The bar had been empty, and he had ended up throwing me onto the pool table, hitching up my pink mini skirt, sliding my knickers to one side and fingering me, right there. Back at the hotel room, we'd had the most incredible animal-like sex on the balcony overlooking the pool. I flushed just thinking about it. There had been days when we'd wanted each other and days when we'd simply had to have each other. In the beginning, he was all I'd ever wanted, and there was nothing I wouldn't do for him. But towards the end, we couldn't even look at each other. And it was hard to ever imagine being that way with anyone again.

Charlie was standing on the opposite side the table, holding his cue, smirking at me. "Okay, Ellie, you can go first." He moved closer. As I bent down with my cue ready to break, he leaned into me, whispering in my ear, "You do know, if you lose this, your next drink is a large glass of Merlot."

Two hours later, three games of pool down and four glasses of red wine consumed, we headed back to the house. Rose had already gone to bed, and Patrick disappeared up the stairs. I wasn't drunk, but I felt tipsy—that sort of hazy lucidness. You know what's happening and where you are, but the world's just a little fuzzier, and the world is just a little bit better. I wandered into the kitchen and poured myself a glass of water as the outside veranda lights came on, illuminating the darkness. I kicked my Converse trainers off and walked over to the open French doors. The pool water rippled as I walked round it. I perched myself on a cosy sun lounger and set my glass on a nearby table. I pulled my knees up to my chest and wrapped my arms around them. I couldn't see a thing beyond the house—just blackness—but I could hear the waves crashing against the shore. I rested my chin on my knees and shut my eyes, listening to the soothing music of the ocean as a light, warm breeze brushed my face. *This place is magnificent*, I thought. *I could stay here forever.*

A sudden splash made me jump. My eyes flew open. "Fucking hell, Charlie!" I couldn't help it. He had done that deliberately.

Charlie laughed hysterically and started to swim over to me. "Sorry! The opportunity was too good to be missed." He swam to the edge of the pool and folded his arms, resting them on the stone pavers that surrounded the pool. He combed his hand through his wet hair as water dripped down his face. *OK, this must be a dream. I must have passed out in the bar from way too much Merlot, have been brought back to the house, and am now in a blissful slumber in bed. Because this, right here, right now, could not be happening to me.* His body, his shoulders, water dripping down his toned biceps. He was just so damn hot! Charlie Robinson was practically naked in front of me, and what? I'm just expected to commence normal-person conversation? My mouth was dry as I gasped for air. I felt on the table for my glass of water. My palms were sweating, and as I took hold of the glass, it slipped out my grasp and fell to the floor. I jumped up from the lounger, putting my palms to my face.

"Shit!" Charlie jumped out of the pool. He grabbed his towel from a nearby table and ran over to me. "Bloody hell, Ellie. You OK? Did you cut yourself?"

"No, I'm fine. Just watch where you're stepping. I'll get it cleaned up."

"Ellie?" Charlie wrapped the blue beach towel around his waist, his perfectly honed chest still in full tantalising view. If he knew what he was doing to me, he'd fire me, just as he had the other crazed fans Jessica had told me about. I bent down and started to pick up the biggest pieces of broken glass. What a total idiot.

"Ellie," Charlie grabbed hold of my arm, stopping me in my tracks.

"I'm fine, let me go and get a brush. Just be careful where you're walking, okay?"

I didn't look at him as I spoke. I couldn't. I walked through to the kitchen, and once I knew I was out of his view, I just stood there, motionless, heart pounding. I needed to get a grip of myself. After a few deep breaths I regained my composure and headed back to the pool, brush in hand.

Charlie had got back into the pool and was treading the water, watching me brush the glass up. "Jump in if you fancy a swim." He smiled up at me.

As I kept my head down, eyes firmly on the job in hand, I wondered, *Is this guy playing with me? Is this a test?* I was still in my one-month probation period. Jessica had reminded me about that in my first week. Maybe she'd put him up to it to try and catch me out. But I wasn't going to be caught out. I was one step ahead of Jessica's game. I knew she wanted me gone, and I wasn't about to give her any reason to fire me. If she thought she could use Charlie to entice me into being unprofessional, she was wrong. I finished brushing and stood up. "No, thank you. I'm just going to get this broken glass inside and head up to bed."

Charlie swam close to the edge again, leaning his arms on the side. "I love a late-night dip. Especially out here. It's so quiet. You can hear almost every drip and slosh of water." I nodded, looking around. "Do you like it out here?"

I looked at him, my eyes narrowed, startled that he even had to ask. "Of course! Who wouldn't? it's beautiful. I'm so lucky to be here." I looked at him, watching drops of water trickle down his nose and onto his smooth, very kissable lips.

"You're not lucky. You've worked hard. And in case I haven't said enough, thank you for the last couple of weeks. I know I can be a bit of a pain sometimes."

I rolled my eyes, smiling. "Not at all. Whatever made you think that?"

He smoothed his hair back, chuckling to himself. "You won't come in? Just for a little while? It's amazing how a bit of light exercise before bed can send you into a great night's sleep."

I was starting to walk towards the doors, but he kept his eyes on me. "I sleep okay, actually, with or without the light exercise. I'll see you in the morning, Charlie."

I sauntered back into the house, smiling to myself and feeling pretty damn impressed. *See, Charlie Robinson, you can't catch me out.*

Chapter 17

The next morning, I woke to the sound of pots and pans clanking together in the kitchen. I pulled myself out of bed and walked over to the window. The sky was filled with hazy yellow and white clouds that told me it was going to be another beautiful morning. After a few unexpected glasses of wine last night—my forfeit for loosing every game of pool—I was starving and hoped that Rose was in the kitchen whipping up some of her signature blueberry pancakes for breakfast.

I climbed into the shower and let the hot water massage my shoulders. Then I tipped my head back, washing away my stale make-up and red wine-stained lips. My mind wandered back to last night. I wondered what Charlie thought of me. Being out with him had been fun. At times, I'd forgotten Patrick was even with us. The odd time I'd caught Charlie's eye, watching me as I took another sip of my drink or lining myself up for a shot, I'd wondered what he was thinking. And I'd wondered whether his inviting me out last night was another of his tests. But, given the amount of wine I consumed, I'd held it together well.

A knock on the door jolted me out of my thoughts. I switched the shower off and listened. Was I hearing things? Another knock. *Damn it!* I switched off the shower and reached for my towel, wrapping it around my body, my soaking hair falling down my shoulders. "Yes?" I shouted. Only silence. "Rose?" Knocking again. "Oh, for God's sake," I whispered under my breath as I wrapped a towel around my head and tiptoed over to the door. OK, OK, I'm coming." I opened the door a crack and peered out into the landing. Charlie stood there, his Ray-Bans covering his eyes, beaming at me. He held up a plate of bagels. "Morning!"

I frowned and pulled my towel further up towards my shoulders. "Hey!"

He moved the plate further towards my face, clearly having made it up by himself. "I brought you some breakfast. Thought you might be feeling fuzzy headed this morning. My fault for suggesting that silly "loser drinks wine" game. I'm sorry." He dropped his bottom lip in feigned remorse. "But I honestly didn't think you'd lose as many games as you did." His lips curved into a smile, and he put his hand to his mouth in a crappy attempt to hide it.

I couldn't' help smiling as well, though. I was particularly bad at pool. "Stop it! I told you I couldn't play."

Charlie nodded, still smiling. "Tell me about it." He looked down at the plate. "You want one?"

"That would be amazing, thanks. You didn't have to. I've just jumped out the shower so—"

"It's OK. Patrick and I are heading out for a drive now. Gonna dust off my camera and try to get some nice shots. The views are stunning out here, aren't they?"

I nodded, letting my eyes linger on his chest. I could see the outline of his incredible pecks, only a tight blue T-shirt covering them. I snapped back into the conversation. "Yes, the view is stunning here." He smiled and kept his eyes on me. I readjusted the towel on my head as a sudden pang of self-consciousness overwhelmed me.

"So, I have my phone," he said. "Just ping anything super urgent over to me, but I guess most things will wait till later. Or tomorrow."

"Sure."

"Great. Erm, also, I don't know if Rose told you. A couple of Patrick's friends are coming over tonight. At eight. So, once everything's sorted—the table, drinks, food—you can do whatever tonight. You don't have to stick around."

I looked at him, but he was looking down at his Vans trainers, rubbing his neck. Why no eye contact? What was he up too? "Okay, fine. I'll help Rose out with whatever you need. I assume she has all the details?"

He lifted his head and looked at me. "Yep, she's got everything covered." I nodded, rubbing my damp face with my hand. Charlie passed

135

me the plate through my slightly open door. "OK. Here you go. I'll see you later." He winked at me and walked down the landing towards the stairs.

I shut my bedroom door, leaning against it. A night off in Big Sur. What to do? Perhaps I'd take a picnic down to the beach, relax, and watch the sun vanish for the day on the horizon. Maybe I'd call Pete. I needed to check in with him anyway. I missed him, and he was long overdue an update. Perhaps, if he wasn't too far away in Monterey, we could meet up. I threw on a pair of blue skinny jeans, a white, loose linen shirt, and pink Havaianas flip-flops before heading downstairs. Rose was in the kitchen chopping up some spring onions.

"Wow! Smells amazing. What are you making?"

"Watercress and pea soup for the starter and a langoustine ravioli for the main."

I smiled and gave a wink. "You need anyone to test it, make sure it's up to scratch?"

Rose looked up and forced a smile, though her eyes looked puffy and red. "I'll let you know."

I sat down at the breakfast bar and placed my elbows on the table, propping my head up on my hands "How are you feeling today? Have you spoken to Joy?" I knew Rose would be feeling pretty down about today, it being her daughter's sixteenth birthday, and I didn't know if I should ask or not, but I felt that it would be more awkward to say nothing. I didn't want a white elephant in the room the whole time we were away, and I still couldn't believe how Jessica had treated her.

"I have. She was crying on the phone. I felt awful." A tear streamed down Rose's cheeks, and she lifted her hand to wipe it away. "I'm sorry. I'm being silly. But my baby girl is having her sweet sixteen today, and I can't be there. I know work is work. It comes first, really. But that doesn't make it less upsetting. I guess I've got to get over it. I'll be OK. I'm staying busy." She motioned at the four huge pots covering the top of the stove.

"Work is important, Rose, but it doesn't always come first. I'm sure if Charlie knew about this weekend he wouldn't have expected you to be here."

Rose shrugged. "It's OK, Ellie. I'm here now. It's too late to change that, so I just have to get on with it."

I nodded, watching her as she concentrated her hardened stare on the chopping board, bearing down the knife on the poor dead langoustines.

They were taking the hit. She wasn't happy at all, and I understood why. "OK. Well, if you need some help setting up, or with the food, shout me. I'll serve drinks later and do some of the hosting I guess, but Charlie said once the food's been served, we can have the night off."

"Yeah, he said that. I think I'll facetime Joy, see how the party's going, have a hot bath, and get an early night."

I nodded, "Well, I'm gonna take my laptop outside and make some calls. Shout me if you need anything."

I walked out onto the veranda. The sun's bright rays bounced off the pool water as it rippled around. I perched myself on the edge of a lounger and took a deep breath in, observing the stunning view in front of me. Trees in the foreground, and then ocean for miles and miles in every direction. God knows what this place must have cost. I pulled out my iPhone and hit the dial button.

Pete laughed as he picked up the phone. "Hello, stranger! Great to hear from you."

I couldn't hide my smile. "You, too. How's things?"

"Things are great! I'm still in Monterey. Beautiful here, and I miss you as always."

"I know. I miss you too!"

"So how are things going there with Mr. International Sexpot Superstar?"

I laughed, flushing as I brushed my fringe out my eyes. "OK, I guess. It's a strange world, Pete. I wouldn't know where to begin trying to explain, but you wouldn't believe the view I have right now."

"Let me guess—you are staring right at his muscular, sweaty, throbbing abs as he sunbathes by the pool?"

I laughed. "No, that was last night, Pete."

"Oh snap! You're joking, right? You saucy minx. Tell me more."

We both laughed, and once I'd regained composure, I whispered into the phone, turning my face away from the house. "Nope, not joking. We went out for drinks, and he just jumped in the pool when we got back. Asked me to get in!"

"Tell me you did. Oh, God, it's like a Mills and Boon. What happened?"

"Nothing happened. I didn't get in."

Pete's voice was high pitched. I could tell he was outraged. "You didn't get in? And why not?"

"Well, we'd been drinking, and I didn't want to let my guard down too much I suppose. I'm not sure what he's up to. I feel like he's playing a bit of a game. Like he's testing me to see how I'll react around him and if I'll cave into his charms."

I could hear the disgust in Pete's voice as he spoke. "Is there something wrong with you?"

I shook my head, even though I knew he couldn't see me, and I wondered if there was. I started telling him about Jessica—what I'd heard her say on my first day, and the things she'd said since about how demanding the job was, trying to scare me. I told him about Charlie's red-carpet entrance earlier in the week, how Jessica had reassured me I could slip in the back entrance so I didn't need to get dressed up for the occasion, when it turned there was no back entrance at all. I told him how Charlie had had to save me at the last minute. I'd spoken to Jessica about that the next day. She'd told me she got the venue confused with somewhere different. I didn't believe her, but I'd never prove otherwise.

"Okay, so Jessica's a total two-faced bitch. We've established that. But you said Charlie rescued you from the red carpet. Would he have done that if he was trying to test you? Wouldn't he have just left you to flounder?"

"I don't know if he's in with her or not, or if he's playing a little game of his own. Trust is very important to him, and we spend a lot of time together now. I know a lot about it, and he has to know I'm trustworthy and professional."

"So, in summary, we have a bitch who's trying to oust you and a guy who has—no doubt from what you tell me—been flirting with you. And you think he's flirting to somehow lull you into ... what? Having sex with him? So that he can then sack you for partaking in something he's actively encouraged?" Pete started laughing. "I mean, sex with him—stuff of nightmares, right?"

I couldn't help laughing with him, and after a few moments, I composed myself. "I just can't help but feel there has to be something else behind his behaviour. There's has to be another explanation for it."

"Ellie, what you're saying about this plan he has—it just doesn't make sense. How about he just likes you? Maybe he just does and that's it. I mean, why wouldn't he? He'd be bloody lucky to have you."

"Pete, really, you know I hate you saying things like that." I shifted on the chair, twisting my ponytail between my fingers. "I just can't believe that, when he has the pick of the world's most beautiful women, girls throwing themselves at him from every direction, he'd have any interest in me." And it was true. I couldn't. I was Ellie, just another girl in LA to Charlie. I knew he could do a whole lot better than me.

"I think you have so little confidence in yourself, Ellie Gibson, that you've concocted some theory in your head that makes no sense to anyone other than you, and even then I think you've confused yourself by it all simply because you can't bring yourself to believe he may just like you and that's it."

I fell silent and didn't want to talk about it anymore, but Pete was right. My self-esteem had taken a hit from Finn's behaviour. It had already been running on near empty, but Finn's cheating had cleaned it out completely. I hadn't been enough for him. Nothing I could give him had kept him loyal to me. He found what he wanted elsewhere, and if I wasn't good enough for him, I wasn't going to be good enough for anyone else, certainly not Charlie. He was way out of my league, and I had to remember that. Thinking anything else was just a false hope, which would only lead to further self-destruction. I didn't want to let a silly crush get out of hand. I gathered my thoughts during a brief silence that was never awkward between Pete and me. "Pete, the one thing that's standing between me and Charlie is reality. It's something that will never be, and I can't allow myself to believe anything else." I looked back over at the kitchen. "I've gotta go. I think I can hear Rose calling me."

"Okay, Ellie. Sure."

"But I was ringing to say that Charlie has given me the night off tonight. So, I know it's short notice—he only told me this morning—but if you have no plans, how would you feel about meeting me halfway and grabbing a drink later?"

"Absolutely! That would be fabulous."

"Great. I'll text you later, once I have an indication of what time I can leave, but it shouldn't be late."

"Sure. Let me know. I can't wait to see you," Pete said before clicking his phone off.

I sat staring at the ocean's waves as they danced across the top of the water. I thought about what Pete had said. Was I completely delusional? Could it really be that Charlie did like me? My phone pinged, breaking my thoughts. "Hey! Hope the boss hasn't got you working too hard this weekend. I'm looking forward to seeing you soon, Ross. X"

I hadn't thought about Ross all weekend, and I still felt terrible for cancelling on him last minute. He knew, though, that schedule changes came with the territory in my job as Charlie's PA, and he understood. I'd promised him another night, and I'd keep my promise. For now, I had a lad's night to prepare for.

We all experience moments in life, I'm sure, when we wish the ground would open its huge mouth and swallow us whole. Now was one of those moments. It was just after seven when the bikini-clad Victoria's Secret models arrived at the house.

I stood gawking as they cat-walked into the kitchen wearing skimpy bikinis and sarongs, displaying their toned stomachs and endless, perfectly tanned legs, each carrying a bottle of expensive-looking champagne. *Thanks, Charlie*, I thought. *Just super. What happened to the casual affair? And just friends?* This wasn't a lad's night in. This was a bloody booty call for the boys. No wonder Charlie had told me to have the night off. He wanted me out the way so he could have a debauched pool orgy. Ugh! I closed my eyes in disgust, and I felt my stomach do a flip. One thing was for sure, that was Pete's "he-bloody-likes-you" theory blown out the water. I felt a twinge of upset, but I took a deep breath and reminded myself what I'd told Pete—allowing myself to believe Charlie was in the slightest bit interested in me would only lead to self-destruction. *No more now*, I thought to myself as Charlie came sauntering through the open-plan kitchen into the lounge.

"Hey guys! Good to see you," he said brightly. And he'd made an effort. The baggy jeans had been replaced by smart beige chino shorts and a short sleeved crisp white shirt that showed off his tan. Brown sunglasses sat on top of his head, holding his hair back. He looked over at me. Please ground, take me now. "Ellie, this is Anna and Chloe."

They both locked eyes with me, and each gave one of those fake, I-clearly-know-I'm-better-than-you smiles. I smiled back politely, not really taking notice of which one was which as I allowed their names to pass over me. I felt quite uninterested.

Charlie looked at me again and let out a sigh, clasping his hands together. "Drinks?"

One of the girls, who couldn't have been older than twenty-five and who had dark, mid-length, wavy hair smiled at Charlie and giggled. Her skin was perfect—not a spot or wrinkle—and the apples of her cheeks glowed with a natural dewiness. I wanted to kill her. "Open one of these. I love this champagne. It's my favourite," she shrilled, giving a little excitable jump in her pink wedges. I looked away and rolled my eyes. I'm sure they were all going to have a thrilling evening.

Charlie took the bottle from her and handed it to me. "OK, sure. Ellie, would you take this and open it up for me?"

Before I could reply, Patrick swaggered in, his arms open wide. He was wearing that bloody black turtleneck, again. What was with him and roll necks? It was, like, thirty-five degrees outside. His look was so dated, I thought. He looked like that 1980s detective, Columbo, his short brown hair gelled to one side. All he needed was a beige trench coat and his look would be complete. Not the type of guy I'd expected Charlie, with his effortlessly cool style, to be friends with.

Patrick learned over and kissed each girl on both cheeks, and I couldn't help but find him a little sleazy. The girls, on the other hand, seemed to be enjoying the fanfare, throwing their arms around him and playing with his hair. I looked at Charlie again. He was just standing there, rubbing his neck and looking out the window. He seemed a little uneasy, nervous even. What was the matter with him? He looked over at me again and caught my eye. I looked away.

"Gorgeous ladies, how are we this evening?" Patrick sang. He really was quite the entertainer when he got going.

I told myself this was always going to happen, and I was surprised it hadn't happened before now. Of course, Charlie was going to hook up with beautiful women—models, actresses. This was the very thing I'd been saying to Pete earlier. Charlie wouldn't look twice at me, not in that way, when he had girls as beautiful as this around him, and I felt a twinge of embarrassment for having entertained the notion of anything different. All I wanted to do now was get drinks on the go, get dinner served, and get the hell out of there, leaving them too it.

I took the champagne bottle from Charlie and made my way into the kitchen, leaving the four of them chatting. The smell of the food was amazing as two pots bubbled away on the stove. OK. Glasses. Where are you? I walked into the store cupboard, and the cool air hit me. I shut my eyes and leaned my hands on the fridge to steady myself as a wave of nausea engulfed me. What was wrong with me? Maybe it was just the heat, and I'd hardly eaten a thing today. Apart from breakfast, I hadn't felt like anything at all, which was very unlike me. Taking some more deep breaths, I thought again about my conversation with Pete earlier and began to feel silly, a little hurt, and angry. For just a milli-second, Pete had almost talked me into believing Charlie's flirting, if it ever even was that, was genuine and that he may have liked me despite him being who he was, and me being … well … just me. Now, I was angry at Pete for even suggesting it, and I was hurt, just a little, by Charlie. I knew all along I was right, that his behaviour towards me had just been a series of tests—getting me to go into his bedroom for lightbulbs late at night, then walking in on me in a towel. He'd known I would be in there, and he'd wanted to see how I'd react in his bedroom—with him. All the looks he'd given me while he was inviting me out for drinks last night, trying to get me drunk, and then inviting me into the pool with him. It had all been a ruse to see how I'd react, to see if I was just here to get to him rather than genuinely work for him. But he hadn't succeeded. I was still here. His plan had failed, and now I hoped he would just leave it, believe that I was here simply to do the job I'd been given, and know that I'd ignore any temptation he put my way. Charlie had no interest in me, not in that way anyway. Of course he didn't. I had been bloody stupid and naïve to even contemplate it. I was invisible to him, and I'd be making sure Pete knew it later too.

I opened my eyes and reached up to some shelves, grabbing four flute glasses. I turned around to find Charlie standing within inches of me. I put my hand to my chest, jumping back. "Jesus!"

Charlie started laughing, but quickly saw I wasn't and stopped. "Sorry! I have a bit of a habit of scaring you, don't I?"

I nodded, looking down at the glasses. "Yes, you do. You're a skulker." I held my hand to my chest and took a deep breath to get over my fright, and then it hit me. *I'm standing inches away from Charlie in a store cupboard.*

He looked down at me, and I looked down at the floor. "It's funny," he said, "if I could have one super-human power for the day, I'd be invisible. Then I wouldn't have to skulk. I could perve on whoever I wanted all day and they'd never know."

I rolled my eyes. "Well, that's creepy. What a total waste of a super power," I said.

Charlie looked at me and leaned his hand against the sideboard next to me. I could feel his breath. My face went bright red as I moved back slightly, the bottom of my back brushing the worktop behind me. The room was closing in as my breath got heavier. The room had gone from cool to boiling in a millisecond, and a bead of sweat dripped down my back. I turned around and placed the glasses on the counter top, my back to him.

"I'm only teasing you. Sorry," he said. "I just came in to see if everything was okay. You seemed a little tense there."

I cleared my throat. "Oh sure. Yes, fine. Just … erm … getting everything sorted."

"The girls, they're okay, you know? Just friends. I didn't want them over, but Patrick organized it. It's his place, you know? What could I say?"

Opening a draw under the cupboard, I pretended to be looking for something, keeping my back to him. "That's great, Charlie. It's no problem at all. It's fine. You don't have to explain yourself. You guys can do whatever you want. I'll go with the flow. It's fine. Let me bring you these drinks. Go and have fun. I'll be out with them shortly. It's fine."

"You've said 'it's fine' about twenty times there." I could hear the smile in his voice. And did he just move closer to me? I could feel the heat on my back, radiating from him. Did he not know about a thing called personal space?

Still hunting through the draw for an unknown object I muttered, "Did I? Oh, it's probably the heat. It's pretty damn hot in here, isn't it?" I pulled at the front of my white shirt several times, allowing the air to waft through to my skin, hoping to demonstrate to him the hotness of the *room*.

"It is warm, for sure. So, what are you doing tonight again?"

He moved slightly back as I turned round, still looking at the floor. "I'm meeting Pete. I told you about him, right?"

"Yeah. The guy you travelled with?"

"Yeah. He's in Monterey, so he'll be driving down here later. Just a quick catch-up while we can, you know?"

"Sounds cool. I'd like to meet him sometime."

"Sure."

I turned back round to avoid any awkward eye contact and opened another drawer. I pulled out three spoons, which I didn't need, but the action gave my hunting some purpose. I could feel my face still red raw. "Ahh, spoons, great. I need to go and get these … erm … these spoons to Rose." I turned around, focusing my eyes on the door as I nudged past him to leave." *Jesus, get me out of here.* "Shout if you need anything, Charlie." And I was free, leaving him in the store cupboard, as I closed the door behind me.

After regaining my cool, I headed out onto the veranda. The four of them were lounging round the pool, laughing and chatting, the girls having taken no time settling in. They'd thrown their sarongs over a chair and were displaying their cellulite-free, toned bodies.

"Thanks, Ellie. How is dinner coming along?" Patrick asked.

"I think it's about ready, Patrick. Rose said you can come in whenever and she'll serve it up."

Patrick stood up and started to walk round the pool and into the house. "Ladies, shall we?"

Ugh, he sounds like such a slime ball, I thought, pursing my lips together as he walked past, beaming from ear to ear, followed by the two girls. Charlie picked up his glass and followed behind, flashing me a quick smile before putting his head down and making his way in. He looked good tonight, I had to admit it. It killed me to say he looked so good tonight. He always looked good, but tonight, it was just killing me. I struggled to look at him.

I walked into the kitchen. Rose had four white bowls in front of her. She was placing sprigs of watercress on top of the green soup. "All ready to go, Ellie. You take two, and I'll follow with the other two."

The food smelled amazing as I hurried through into the smallish dining room. The room was pretty plain—white walls, white ceiling, and two floor-to-ceiling windows overlooking the gardens. No paintings, photos, or trinkets. *Very different to Charlie's house,* I thought, which exploded with personality. The four of them sat at the Ercol table. A small tealight candle burned in the centre of the table without purpose since it was still daylight, and two large cream pendent lights hung overhead. I served the two bowls

I carried, one to Charlie and one to Patrick. Rose followed behind and served the two girls. Chilled-out jazz music was playing in the background as Charlie poured more champagne into the empty flute glasses.

Patrick looked up at Rose. "Okay, thanks guys. Shut the door when you leave. I'll come out when we've finished this course."

Idiot! I thought as we hurried out, closing the white double doors behind us.

Rose was red faced back in the kitchen, dragging her thick, almost-black curly hair out of its clip, sweeping it up again with her hands, and putting the clip back in place. "One down, one to go." She smiled.

"They're not having dessert?"

"No, just the two courses. I don't exactly have the girls down as big chocolate fudge cake eaters anyway, do you?" We both chuckled, and Rose made a cup of coffee.

Before we'd even finished, Patrick was at the kitchen door. "All done, guys. Ready for our main."

Within a few minutes, without a hitch, we cleared the bowls and served the main. Back in the kitchen, we each took a deep breath. Rose wiped her brow with her apron. "Well done, Rose," I said. "That food looked delicious tonight. You've worked so hard today."

"Thanks, Ellie. I might just treat myself to a glass of wine later."

"I'd join you, but I'm meeting my friend Pete. In fact, what time is it?"

Rose looked at her watch. "Just gone eight."

I took my phone out from my jeans pocket and quickly wrote Pete a text with the bar's location. I told him I'd be an hour, tops, and I'd see him there. "I'll help you clean up, Rose, before I go. Okay?"

Rose gave a dismissive wave, pouring herself a glass of water. "Oh, don't worry, Ellie. Just get sorted and head out. Enjoy the night off while you can. I'll finish up here. There's not much to do anyway."

Just as I got to the kitchen door and was about to head upstairs, a loud voice from the dining room boomed out. "Rose!" Patrick was shouting from the dining room. What the hell? Rose looked at me, her forehead creased in sudden anxiety. Patrick called again. "Rose!"

Rose put down her glass of water, and we both scurried into the dining room. Rose stood in the doorway. Patrick stood up from his seat, holding his fork. "Yes, Patrick? Everything OK?"

The girls had stopped eating. They put their cutlery down and turned to look at us as we hastily walked in. Charlie was eating.

"Rose, I told you earlier today *not* to put any herbs into this ravioli!"

I looked from Patrick to Charlie. Charlie to Patrick. Charlie had now stopped mid chew and was looking up at him, a puzzled look crossing his face. Patrick's face was bright red and all screwed up. Jesus, it was only a few herbs.

"Erm ... no, I don't remember you saying that at all, Mr. Locke. I'm sorry I put only—"

"I told you earlier today, Rose, that I didn't want *any* herbs in the bloody ravioli. I wanted to taste the langoustine and keep it simple."

Rose's voice was quivering as she took a step further into the room. "Well ... erm ... don't you like it?"

"No, I don't fucking like it!"

Charlie's eyes looked as if they were about to bulge out of his head as he put his fork down. The girls were now staring at Patrick, who looked as if he was about to develop an embolism. Charlie put his hand out to Patrick's plate, coxing him to sit down and eat. "Patrick, dude, don't worry about it. It's delicious. I'm sure if you don't like it, you can get something later, but I think it's really nice." He nodded, looking over to Rose and smiling. Rose didn't smile back; her eyes were wide as she stared at Patrick in horror.

"You don't get paid a fucking fortune to mess things up," Patrick shouted at her. "When I ask for no herbs I mean no *fucking* herbs!"

Rose stood, frozen on the spot. I could see her hands trembling and her eyes starting to well up. What the hell did Patrick think he was doing, humiliating her like this? This was no way to speak to someone, especially someone who had been busting her arse all day to make this meal, paid or not paid. Patrick was being an absolute dick. I bit my lip and looked at Charlie, who was looking down at the table. I willed him to say something, but he didn't.

"Patrick, I'm sorry, I don't remember you saying anything about—"

Patrick put his palm up in the air, silencing Rose. He gave a dismissive hand wave towards the door, dismissing us like a pair of dogs. "Just save it and get out. Go on. You can take my plate." He sat down, wiping his brow with his napkin, and then throwing it in the bowl of uneaten ravioli.

"No!" I shouted, my fists clenched at my sides. Everyone turned to glare at me, mouths open. I side-glanced Rose, who was staring at me in disbelief.

Patrick scrunched up his face, his eyes burning into my soul. "What?"

But I'd had enough. I wasn't going to let Rose be treated like this. "Patrick, no! You can't speak to her like that!" I pointed at Rose, who looked as if she wanted the varnished parquet flooring to swallow her whole. "You can't treat people like this. Rose has spent all day grafting in the kitchen. She cancelled her weekend plans to come here, and you think you can speak to her like this?"

Rose gasped and hissed, "Ellie, no!"

But I couldn't let it go. I shook my head and my voice crackled, "No, Rose. I'm sorry! Did you know she's missing her daughter's sixteenth birthday celebration to come here this weekend?" I pursed my lips together, which I felt added weight to the situation. Patrick stared at me, but I was on a roll. "I don't know who you think you are, or what you think gives you the right to treat people like this. With your big holiday home, flashy Aston bloody whatever it's called sports car, and Victoria's Secret mannequins hanging off your arm." I glanced over at the two girls who both gasped and folded their arms as they sat back in their chairs.

"Well, Ellie, I—" Patrick began.

"No, Patrick, you don't get to treat people like shit and get away with it. I've had enough of it here. I can't work like this, around people like you. I'm going, and if Rose has any sense about her, she'll do the same. I'm not sticking around here any longer with a total arse-wipe like you. Oh, and the turtle neck? I'd lose it. You look like a total wanker."

I looked at Charlie, who was staring at me. How could he not speak up? Was he just going to let his friend treat Rose like this? Well, yes, obviously he was. I gave everyone at the table a dirty look, and then I turned on my heel and stomped out of the room, my heart racing, my face sweating. I walked fast up the stairs and into my room and slammed the door behind me. I grabbed my bag and hot-stepped it right back down the stairs and out the front door before anyone had left the table. I was sorry to leave Rose, but I was too angry to stay, and I'd already said enough. *I can't believe I just called him an arse-wipe. And why did I have to mention the turtle neck? Shit.*

I jumped into the driver's seat of the black Mercedes and looked down at my phone. A text from Pete: "At the bar. Finally found it. Jesus! Talk about tucked away. Getting a beer. See you soon."

I pulled out of the driveway as tears welled in my eyes. I knew this was it. This dream I'd been living for the past few weeks was all but over. Maybe this was the way it should be. Maybe it had run its course, and it was time for me to hit the road again. Maybe I needed to get back to reality, because this was anything but. After a few minutes, my tears dried up and my upset turned to anger again. Who the hell did these people think they were? Just because you have fame and fortune doesn't mean you can treat people like that. And if Charlie wasn't man enough to say something to Patrick, then I was.

Dusk was setting in. The sunset sat neatly on the ocean's horizon, but I couldn't enjoy the view. The thin, winding roads demanded all of my attention. I wasn't in the mood for the radio. I just wanted to get to the bar and see Pete. He'd never believe it. The Bluetooth started to ring. It was Charlie. Oh, God, he was almost certainly ringing to fire me, and I couldn't face that conversation right now. I'd have to go back to the house anyway for my things and take the car back, so I'd wait until the morning. I cancelled the call.

Within seconds, it started ringing again. Charlie. *What is up with him? Can't he just leave it for now? He has company.* I was out of the way— exactly what he'd wanted. He could go and get his blow job now, and we could deal with things tomorrow. Taking a deep breath, I cancelled the call. And then again, a few moments later, he called. *What is with this guy? Ugh!* Feeling myself getting even more angry, I grabbed my phone out of my bag and switched it off.

After a few minutes, I pulled up to the bar and climbed out, feeling flustered. Pete's car was in the carpark, and I felt a huge sense of relief. I looked at my phone. I should really turn it back on in case there was an emergency or something. I held my finger down on the power button until the screen lit up. The phone beeped. A text message from Charlie. He'd given up calling me: "Ellie, why aren't you picking up? We need to talk. At least let me know you're OK."

We need to talk. Well, that says it all. I shook my head and scurried inside the bar. Pete stood up and smiled as I walked in. "Ellie!" He threw his arms around me, and I embraced him back.

I needed this hug. I had never been so glad to see a friendly face. "Pete, I've missed you."

"Right back at you, Ell." We stood there hugging, and I felt a tear slide down my warm cheeks. I pulled away and he stood observing me. "Fucking hell, you look like shite! What's happened? You okay?

I shook my head. Tears fell down my cheeks. I sat down and hugged myself with my arms, wiping my chin as the tears started to drop to the table. Pete sat down. Placing his hand on my shoulder, he lowered his head. "Bloody hell! What's happened?" I couldn't speak. I gasped and put my head in my hands. I needed a second to calm down and collect my thoughts. "Let me get us a drink. What you having?"

I didn't look up, my voice muffled in my hands. "Vodka. Double. And Pepsi."

Pete stood up, smoothing down his black T-shirt and running his hand through his blonde hair. "I'll be right back."

I knew I wasn't meant to divulge certain things to anyone; I'd signed a confidentiality contract with Jessica the day I started. But it didn't matter now. I was being fired anyway, and I could trust Pete with anything. He knew more about me than anyone else. A few minutes later Pete arrived back, two glasses in hand—one G and T and one vodka and Pepsi. I took my drink from him and took a big swig. I needed this. Drawing in a deep breath, I relayed to Pete everything that had happened during the evening. I told him what Patrick had said, what I'd said, and what Charlie had failed to say.

Pete started laughing, holding his hand up to his mouth as if trying to stop himself. "Fucking hell, Ellie. And you called him a what?"

I shut my eyes tight and rubbed my temples to ease the stress. "A fucking arse-wipe."

Pete gave a cackling laugh and took another sip of his drink. "You never have been able to keep your mouth shut!"

I gritted my teeth. "*Ughhh!* What have I done?"

Pete nodded towards my half empty glass. "Drink!" I took another mouthful, gulping it back. "So, what will you do now?"

"Well, he's been trying to call me. I didn't answer. He's texted me to ask if I'm okay and to say that we need to talk, so I guess I'll go back tomorrow, get supremely fired, collect my stuff, and hit the road again with you."

Pete raised his eyebrows. "You don't know he is going to fire you."

"I do, Pete. I'm disposable to him. He could find another PA in a heartbeat. He doesn't need me."

"He doesn't? But he told you he picked you out of the other applicants for a reason. He likes you. He's invested in you."

"Somehow, Pete, I think you're wrong." I paused, looking down at my hands. "Like you were wrong about him being into me. You almost had me convinced he was being genuine, but all along, I knew, it was a ruse."

"And why are you so confident of that? Nothing has changed from our conversation this morning."

I sat hunched in the chair, vodka in one hand, biting the nail of every finger of the other hand.

"Of course it has. The girls, Pete. The models! If he was into me, like you said, why would he be having dinner with them tonight? I'm sure he's peeling off Chloe's size six bikini from her perfectly toned, bronzed fucking fake-boobed body as we speak." Pete sat sipping his drink, looking out safely from behind the glass. "I'll go back tomorrow, face the music, and leave. Completely unapologetically." It was getting late, and my eyes felt sore when I blinked. It had been a long day. My phone started ringing again. I took it out my bag, looking up at Pete, eyes wide. "It's Charlie again."

"Wow, he's persistent. You sure you don't want to speak to him? Would he bother calling you so late just to fire you? Obviously, Chloe fake boobs isn't with him."

I rolled my eyes. "Maybe it's Patrick using Charlie's phone to tell me I'm fired."

"I doubt it, Ellie. Why would he do that? Come on. I guess if you're not going back there tonight, you need somewhere to stay. We've an hour's drive ahead of us back to my hotel, and it's nearly eleven now. We can chat some more in the car."

I swigged back my vodka, and we headed out to Pete's car. "You sure you're not going back there?" he asked.

"No, Pete. I'm not. Let's just drive."

Chapter 18

The California sunshine peeped through the blinds of Pete's small hotel room, waking me from a fretful sleep. I squinted and turned over, but it was no use. I wasn't going to get back to sleep this morning. Charlie and the events of last night were all I could think about. My outburst replayed over and over in my head. I pulled myself up from the bed, rubbing my sore eyes. Pete was still flat out on the floor, snuggled under a sleeping bag. I'd lain awake most of the night, constructing in my head the conversation I was going to have with Charlie today. I hated confrontation, but it had to be done. The sooner I picked up my things and said goodbye to him, the sooner Pete and I could be back on the road, and I could put this whole crazy chapter behind me.

I slowly inched my way out of bed, creeping over to the bathroom. Shutting the door, I turned on the shower and stepped in, letting the warm water sooth my aching, sleep-deprived limbs. The aloe vera body wash filled my nose with the most amazing scent. I shut my eyes and took a deep, energizing breath as the comforting water drenched my face and hair. One thing I couldn't wash away, though, was the parade of thoughts that was running through my head. Even though I knew I'd been right to stick up for Rose, I couldn't shift the feeling that I'd let Charlie down. Despite Patrick being wrong, maybe I should have just kept my mouth shut. I mean, why was I getting so worked up about it all? This was, in the end, just a job with a means to an end, that end being enough money to hit the road again and stay in the US a little longer. Maybe I should have just done what everyone else seems to do, turn a blind eye to it, toughen up, and realize it was just a job and I wasn't in it forever.

I took a few deep breaths before climbing out of the shower and wiping the steam off the mirror with the palm of my hand. Observing the bags under my eyes and poking another fresh pimple on my chin, I felt a mess. *I'll need more than a dab of Touche Éclat to solve these problems today*, I thought as I wrapped a towel around my chest, water dripping down my back and onto the tiled floor. As I opened the bathroom door, the steam followed me out.

"Morning." Pete was sitting up, leaning his elbows on his knees, and rubbing his eyes.

"Hey, sorry. Did I wake you? I couldn't sleep."

"Probably. But it's fine. What time is it?"

"Just gone eight."

Pete lay back down on his sleeping bag and put his hands behind his head, exposing his skinny, hairy chest. "So, dare I ask what your plan is for today?"

Sitting on the edge of the bed, I put my head in my hands. "I guess I need to go back to the house and speak to Charlie. He'll fire me, and then I'm afraid you're stuck with me again."

"Damn it! I knew this would happen!" Pete kicked his legs in the air and rolled onto his stomach, covering his face with the sleeping bag.

I forced a laugh, though I was in no mood for jokes. "Thanks!"

"I'll get ready then," Pete said, emerging from the covers a few seconds later. "You really think he'll sack you?"

I nodded, wringing my wet hair into the towel, looking down at the floor. "I really do, Pete. I called his bestie an arse-wipe, for God's sake. Why wouldn't he?"

Pete gave a little laugh to himself. "Yep, you're fired. But you've always been the same, Ellie. Can't keep your gob shut. I know you did it for the right reasons though, so if Charlie can't see that, good riddance to him."

I nodded, putting my head in my hands. "If he was going to fire you, though, why did he keep pestering you last night on the phone? Wouldn't he have just left you to it?"

"Maybe he was ringing to fire me there and then over the phone. Maybe he doesn't even want me back later. Oh, God, he might not even let me in the house."

Pete screwed up his face and stood up, folding up his sleeping bag and throwing it on the bed. "Doubtful. Didn't he say in his text message to let him know that you were okay? Why would he be bothered about you if he was going to fire you?"

I shrugged. "Who knows what the guy is thinking? He's so hard to read. Let's just hit the road and get this over with, OK?" I stood up and started to dress, pulling on the blue jeans and T-shirt I'd worn the night before.

"Would you stay, if he doesn't?" Pete asked.

I hadn't contemplated that scenario. In my mind, I was gone, and that was it. "I honestly don't know. I enjoy it—the job. I thought Charlie and I got on okay. I enjoy being in LA, and the money is great. But I'm not irreplaceable, Pete. I felt like I was starting to find my stride, you know? Or at least I thought I was, but maybe this is just nature's way of making my inevitable departure easier, if a little premature."

Pete walked over to me and put a hand on my shoulder. "I guess it was a temporary thing, and you must have earned enough to stay here for another couple of months. Just keep all this in mind when you speak to him, okay?"

"Thanks, Pete. I will. I was just enjoying it, you know? And now, it's over."

Pete smirked and raised his eyebrows to an unnaturally high position on his forehead. "Enjoying it, or enjoying him?"

I rolled my eyes and gave him a light push. "I told you I liked him. And of course I fancy him. Who wouldn't? We get on well. He makes me smile. But as a PA, you have to get on with the person you're working so closely with. If you don't, you can't do the job." I shuddered, my skin still damp from the shower, my forearms going goosebumpy. "If you'd have seen those two models last night, you'd realize that I'm not the type of girl he'd be thinking about in any way other than professional."

"OK, Ellie, if that's what you think. I can see your own mind is stronger than anything I'm gonna tell you, so fine. Let's get this show on the road. I'll jump in the shower."

I nodded, wiping the hint of a tear from my eye. "Pete, if I didn't say it last night, thanks for meeting me, letting me stay here, and sleeping on the floor. Just, thank you for everything."

Pete stood in the doorway and pouted "Don't thank me. You just owe me mojitos on tap for the next, like, forty years. That should cover it."

As we pulled in, Patrick's silver car wasn't parked up, but Charlie's black Aston Martin was still in the drive, exactly where it had been last night. I'd secretly hoped he'd gone out so I could inconspicuously grab my things, pen a quick letter of resignation, and leave. But it didn't look as if I was going to get off the hook quite so easily. I pulled the visor up and observed the house, looking for signs of life. I parked Charlie's Mercedes and walked over to Pete's car. "Pete, I think it's best you just stay out here. I won't be long. Fifteen at most, okay?"

"Sure. Whatever, Ellie. But holler if you need me."

I hesitantly walked up the stone steps to the heavy brown wooden door and pulled down the wrought iron handle. Unlocked. Someone was in. The smell of coffee flooded the hallway, and I could hear the bubbling and hissing of the coffee maker. "Hello?" I called out, slowly making my way through the hallway into the kitchen.

"Ellie! Hi!" I froze. Charlie stood with two blue mugs in hand, smiling at me. Two mugs. Had one of the girls stayed overnight? Was he making her a romantic breakfast in bed? "I'm just making coffee for Rose and me. Would you like a cup?"

Oh, the relief! "Erm ... no. Thank you." Charlie turned away from me. He placed the mugs on the counter and walked over to the fridge. This felt so awkward. He was acting as if nothing had happened. I walked over to the breakfast bar and placed the palms of my hands firmly down on the black marble countertop. "Charlie, I'm sorry about last night. I'm sorry if I embarrassed you, and I'm sorry if I offended Patrick and those girls. Please just accept my resignation as of today, and I'll be out your hair straight away."

Charlie opened the fridge door. He took out the milk and turned to me as he closed the door. "Ellie, why are you resigning?" he said calmly

"Because of last night. And what happened. It saves you having to fire me."

"Ellie, I'm not going to fire you. Why would you think that?"

"I just thought—" I continued, but Charlie me off.

"Look, Patrick can be a dick sometimes. He's my friend, but he can be a total dick. He loses all sense of reality and speaks without thinking. Last night ... well, that was just an example of his total 'dickness'!" Charlie smiled. He walked over to me and placed the palm of his hand over one of mine, which remained firmly pressed against the counter top. My whole body quivered. Here we go again. The Charlie effect. I doubted this would ever stop happening. "You stood up for Rose, and I totally agree with what you said to him. Well, I mean the arse-wipe thing was pretty cutting." He laughed, and I put my free hand over my eyes. "But he needed telling, and I told him again after you left."

I looked at him and raised my eyebrows. "You did?"

"Yep. I told him what a complete wanker he was for speaking to Rose like that, especially in front of guests. We argued, the girls went home, and I went to bed, worried about you, hoping you were okay. Did you not see my calls?"

My heart started to beat faster, my breath quickened, and my mouth was dry as I tried to gulp down my nerves. This wasn't the way I was expecting this conversation to go. And he was worried about me? Charlie Robinson was worried about me? I felt my face flushing.

He moved his head closer to mine, but I kept my gaze firmly set on the kitchen worktop.

"I don't want you to resign. If you feel you have to, then do, but I have no intention of firing you, and I want you to stay."

I looked up at him, but I couldn't keep his stare. He pulled his hand away from mine and strolled over to the coffee machine. To avoid any more eye contact, I walked over to the open French doors leading to the pool and looked out. I took a huge breath and shut my eyes. Of course I wanted to stay, more than anything. I was enjoying being in LA, being part of Charlie's life, even if it was only a small piece of it. "OK. Well, as long as you're sure?"

"I wasn't expecting anything else," he said. "I just thought you headed off last night to let go of some steam, that's all. It's business as usual here. Where did you go anyway?" his eyes narrowed.

I turned now to face him, hands clasped in front of me. He was at the coffee machine, trying to froth the milk in a metal jug. The hissing sound was loud. I raised my voice, so he would hear me. "I met Pete in that bar we went to the other night. Then we drove up to Monterey. He's been there a few days in a hotel, so he let me stay over." He didn't say anything, his expression giving nothing away as he continued to fiddle about with

155

the machine, pressing buttons which didn't need to be pressed. "Where's Rose? Is she upset with me?" I continued.

"She was a little shocked. We all were." He gritted his teeth together. "She's upstairs, I think, packing her things. I'd like to start heading back within the next hour or so. We've got a busy week ahead, and I've given Rose the next few days off. I've spoken to a friend at the Hill's Spa and Hotel up on Rodeo and managed to get Rose and her daughter in for a couple of nights with a few treatments thrown in. You ladies like that sort of thing, right? Pedicures and massages?" He flashed a cheeky grin as he moved closer to me. I felt my heart melt and my face turn crimson again. "I think Patrick could be a little wounded though. After you left, he asked me to give him my 'genuine' opinion on his turtlenecks."

We both burst out laughing, "Oh no," I said, spluttering, trying to hold back my delight. To avoid any eye contact, I moved over to the counter and grabbed the milk. I opened the fridge door and placed it on the door shelf, but it was no use. He stalked me round the kitchen until I stopped by the door. We stood there. "But, Charlie, doing that for Rose— that's so nice of you."

"I genuinely didn't know about her daughter's birthday, you know? If I had done, I wouldn't have expected her to come. I'm surprised Jessica didn't mention it. Rose said she'd put a personal time request in."

"Are you surprised?"

Charlie's eyes bore down on me. "Well, what do you mean?"

I shook my head, internally reminding myself I would not tell Charlie about Jessica. Not yet anyway. "Nothing. I'm just glad she has a few days off now. I'm sure she'll appreciate it."

He looked down at me. I blew my fringe out my eyes and then pushed it away with my hand. I looked up, and he was still staring. "I didn't do it for Rose and her daughter. I did it for you. I know how strongly you felt about the whole thing, I didn't want you upset."

"Hey." Charlie looked up, and I spun round to see Rose standing in the doorway with her overnight bag in hand, smiling. "Glad to see you back safely, Ellie. Anyone want a coffee?" Rose put her bag down and walked over to the coffee machine.

I turned back round to face Charlie, my face burning, I needed a breather from him. "Okay, well, let me go and speak with Pete first. He's outside."

"Your getaway vehicle?" Charlie smiled.

"Something like that."

I bounded out the house and onto the driveway. Pete was leaning against his car, legs crossed, looking down at his phone. He turned his head, hearing me coming up behind him. "Well?"

I settled down next to him, smiling from ear to ear. "Well, he didn't sack me, and I didn't resign!"

Pete rolled his eyes and smiled. "How did I know this?"

"He said he agreed with me. He and Patrick had a bust-up when I left, and he had no intention of sacking me. He wants us back in LA by early this afternoon."

"Well, fuck me, Ellie."

"Pete, I'm sorry to—"

"Ellie, don't apologize! It's fine! I'm glad this has worked out. Just get back to it, and I'll see you soon, I guess."

"You don't hate me?"

"What the hell would I hate you for?"

"Messing you around?"

"I couldn't hate you if I tried. Now go. And remember to keep me updated on all major developments—please." We stood up, and Pete reached out his arms, pulling me in for a hug. The stubble on his face scratched my cheek as I pulled him closer to me placed my head on his shoulder. I felt warm tears pool in the corner of my eyes. I really would miss him, but I knew my time in LA had a shelf life and I'd be seeing him again soon. "Thanks, Pete. I'll see you soon." He climbed into his car and drove back out down the slight hill, winding down his window and waving until he was out of sight.

I turned and looked at the house. In the downstairs lounge window, movement caught my eye. Someone moved out of sight from behind the cream shutters. Was that Charlie? The person was too tall to be Rose. Perhaps the lack of sleep last night was causing me to hallucinate. I took a deep breath and headed back through the open front door.

Chapter 19

It was Tuesday, and Charlie was having his weekly rendezvous with Jo in DeLatte. I walked over to the counter. Ross stood with his arms folded, smiling at me. "Hey you!"

"Hey, you too." I smiled back. He was cute, and I was ready to rearrange our cancelled date night.

"So, how was your weekend in Big Sur with the big star?" He looked over at Charlie who was animatedly chatting to Jo.

"Mixed. Let's put it that way."

"Oh, really? You can fill me in over our belated dinner date then, if you still want to join me that is?"

"Of course! I was planning on asking you, but you've beaten me to it."

"How's this Friday? I could pick you up at, say, seven o'clock?"

I dug out my iPhone and clicked into the calendar app. No appointments, no meetings, no shopping planned for Charlie's auntie's friends' shih-tzu. It was a date. That was, as long as Charlie had no more surprises for me. But I was confident that, after the weekend, he'd cut me some slack. "Friday looks good to me."

Ross smiled widely. "Great! I'm looking forward to it."

"Ellie!" I spun round. Charlie was staring at me from his booth. "Coffees? We don't have too long," he shouted over

What was with him this morning? He was being super tetchy today, and I had a feeling the day was going to be a long one. "Sure. Sorry." I turned back to Ross.

Ross rolled his eyes and walked over to the huge black coffee machine. "The usual?"

"Of course. Mind if I come through to the back again? I have about a thousand emails to sieve through."

"Of course. Go through. I'll bring you an espresso."

I pulled up the countertop door and heaved my laptop bag through. As I pushed the door back down, I felt eyes on me. I looked up to see that Charlie was still staring over. Jesus, he was so impatient. I motioned to him that Ross was on his way, but he didn't respond and just kept staring at me as I cumbersomely went through into the back. Had I done something wrong? I didn't know.

A couple of minutes later, Ross came in, a tea towel slung over his shoulder. As he sat down, I noticed that he looked tired. There were shadows under his eyes "Did you get up to much at the weekend?" I offered, sipping my piping hot espresso.

"I have drama class every Saturday morning, so I was kinda busy with that, and then I just met some friends for drinks. The usual."

"I didn't know you were into acting. Is that something you want to do, like professionally? You're in the right place, that's for sure."

"I'd love to. Who wouldn't? It's just getting that break, you know? It's been a passion of mine for years. My parents started taking me to the classes when I was just a kid. I'm twenty-seven now, and there's no sign of my break yet." He looked down into his coffee. "Who knows though? Hey—never say never."

I smiled at him and nodded. He didn't seem himself today, but we all had off days. It dawned on me that I didn't know much about him at all, so I was looking forward to getting to know him better on our Friday date.

And half an hour later, Charlie and I were back on the road, on our way to meet with Charlie's press agent. As we drove along the highway, Charlie leaned his head against the car seat, his black sunglasses concealing his eyes. "Charlie, this Friday night, I was wondering if I could get some time off. A few hours if you don't have anything you need me for?" He was silent, hiding behind the lenses.

I felt the material under my arms sticking to my skin as I started to sweat. "What have you got planned?" he asked abruptly.

"Well, just trying to rearrange my dinner date with Ross. We were meant to meet up last weekend, remember? But I cancelled with him to come with you to Big Sur." I was treading lightly. He'd been in a strange, grouchy mood all morning, but it was now or never, and I had to ask. Anyway, it really was about time I had a few hours to myself.

Silence. Charlie kept his head casually leaning against the seat as I kept my eyes forward on the road. "That OK?" I persisted.

He didn't look at me. "Sure, Ellie. Go and enjoy the evening. I have nothing urgent happening."

"Thanks. That's great!" I stared down at the road, a smile creeping over my lips. I was looking forward to getting dressed up for Friday night—throwing a dress on, some heels, and a dash of lippy. It had been a while, and now not even Charlie was in the way.

The week had been never ending as Friday crept up at a snail's pace, but it was finally here, and of course, that meant date night with Ross. Jessica, much to my relief, had left for the day, and I had the run of the house whilst Charlie was out at rehearsals and wouldn't be back until late. Enjoying the free time, I'd spent a whole half hour in a warm, rose-scented bubble bath, exfoliating and conducting the mandatory de-fuzz of all body hair. I'd filed my nails and splattered a thick, gloppy, green detoxifying face mask on, which promised to give me an "instant glow".

And now, cooling off on the bed, wrapped in fresh towels, I sipped my third cold glass of Pinot Grigio as I listened to some random house music on the radio and psyching myself up to get dressed. The week had been so hectic and full of surprises. I could hardly believe what happened on Thursday when I was opening Charlie's fan mail. In a brown mailer bag I'd found a pair of black thongs wrapped round a life-size dildo. A picture of Charlie's face was stuck to the front of the thongs. I'd laughed to myself. *Why anyone would do this?* I'd wondered.

I felt good tonight whilst sipping my wine and pondering what to wear. I'd meant to pick up something new, but shopping for me this week had been nothing but a pipe dream. My little black dress and red high heels would have to do. Meghan Trainor's "I'm All About that Bass" started playing and, of course, my instant reaction was to get up and dance. I threw the now-warm cucumbers off my eyes and jumped onto the bed, swinging my hips from side to side, using my wine glass as a microphone. I shut my eyes, living the moment.

"Ellie?"

My eyes flew open and I fell down onto the bed, dropping my wine glass and its contents onto my sheets. "Shit!" I put my hand to my chest and looked up to find Charlie standing in my doorway, smirking at me. "What the hell, Charlie! You scared me to death? Don't you knock?"

"Ellie, sorry! I knocked, but the music … you didn't hear me." He pursed his lips together, trying desperately not to laugh, but his attempts weren't working.

I pulled my towel up towards my shoulders and covered my thighs. "Charlie, I'm just, I'm … you really ought to stop creeping up on me. What are you doing here, anyway?"

"The meeting wasn't as long as I thought it was going to be, so I got a lift back."

"OK, well, you know I'm out tonight, right? So, I—"

"Sure, that's why I didn't call you for a lift. I thought you'd be getting ready. Didn't want to interrupt important preparations." He smirked, being facetious. "What time are you heading out? You want me to drive you?" he continued.

"In about an hour." I grabbed my phone and touched the screen. "Actually, in about half an hour. Shit! I really better finish getting ready. Sorry, can I just … erm … sorry, what did you want anyway?"

He shook his head, backing out of the room. "No, nothing. Was just letting you know I was back. I'll let you get dressed. Did you want that lift?"

"Oh gosh! No. No, it's fine. Ross is picking me up."

"Okay, have a good night!" Charlie wasn't wearing his usual smile as he turned to walk out the room, and then he stopped, looking down at the floor. "You wearing those tonight?" he asked, pointing down at my red heels next to the door.

"Yeah, why?"

"Nice. I bet you look—can I say 'sexy' to an employee?"

Oh, my God. I felt mortified. Everything went hot. Charlie had just called an item of my clothing sexy. I didn't reply. I couldn't.

He shrugged, and then winked at me. "Well, I like them. I'm sure you'll look lovely. Have fun."

He stood for a second looking at his hands before he walked out and closed the door.

I arrived back at Charlie's just after eleven. Considering it was still pretty early, I was surprised to find the house in complete darkness, apart from a small bluish light flickering in the lounge. I figured Charlie must be home, but I was surprised he didn't have something more exciting to do on a Friday night than sit alone watching TV. Or maybe he wasn't alone. It was strange how we'd never talked about relationships—his exes or rumoured love interests. The subject had just never come up. I didn't like to ask outright, and he'd never volunteered the information. Though I had to say, I was intrigued to find out.

My date with Ross had been lovely. He'd been a perfect gentleman all evening: attentive, chatty, funny, and smart. He was exactly the kind of guy I saw myself with. He'd turned up looking super cute in a pair of blue skinny jeans, a black loose-fit shirt, and black suede brogues. His long dark hair was tucked behind his ears, topped with a pair of aviator glasses balanced on his head. He was just the right side of being grunge without looking too grungy. After he picked me up, we drove to a little American diner on Wiltshire Boulevard, and after dinner, we took a stroll down Rodeo Drive, stopping in at a trendy bar, the Cuba Room, for a cocktail. Wine and cocktails flowed, and everything about the date was pleasant. Ross couldn't have been nicer, but there was something niggling at me. I wanted us to have that "spark", and I'd been searching for it between us all night. I liked him. He said all the right things, and we had a surprising number of things in common like music and movies and travel, so why wasn't I feeling that spark? Theoretically, I should have wanted to rip his clothes off and jump straight in between the sheets, but I didn't, and I didn't know why.

I unlocked the huge wooden door, pushing it open with both hands, and placed my black leather shoulder bag on the hall table. Kicking off my red heels, I looked at my reflection in the imposing wooden mirror hanging on the wall at the bottom of the stairs. My black mascara had started to smudge around my eyes, and only traces of red lipstick in the cracks of my dry lips remained. I combed my fingers through my hair and ran my index finger along my eyebrows. I looked tired, and I was ready for bed. As I walked on the tiled floor through the hall and into the lounge, my feet didn't make a sound. I peeked in around the half-open door. Charlie was alone, lying on his back, remote control resting on his stomach, engrossed in *The Terminator*.

"Hey!" I said brightly, trying to not let the exhaustion show in my voice. Charlie turned his head to look at me. He turned down the volume of the film. I smiled. "Great choice. I love these films."

He leaned up, propping himself up on his elbows. "Hey, I wasn't expecting you back so early. And, yeah, me too. Absolute classics."

"I didn't have you down for a Terminator fan actually," I teased.

"Well, likewise. I thought you were more a *Sound of Music* kinda girl."

We both laughed. Oh dear, the cocktails. I was having a sudden head rush of alcohol, and I found myself *flirting*. Or at least attempting to. "I've been known to watch that on occasion," I teased back. "Have you not been out tonight?" I walked over to the empty couch opposite Charlie and rested my hip on the back of it. I pulled my tummy in and pushed my boobs out.

"No, I just felt like having a quiet one tonight, you know? My head is pretty mashed after spending most of the day in the studio." I nodded, glancing over at the flickering TV. My eyes strained in the darkness. "How was the date with Mr. DeLatte, anyway?"

I shrugged, not wanting to give too much away. "Fine. Nice."

Charlie raised a brow. "Fine? Nice?"

"Yeah, you know, just getting to know him."

"Well, I sure hope that, if I were ever to take you on a date, you wouldn't describe it as 'fine and nice'."

I flushed, and now was grateful for the darkness. "Well, it's a good job you won't be taking me out then, isn't it?"

He lay back down. He pressed the mute button and placed his hands behind his head. The room was plunged into silence. "You seeing him again?"

"I don't know, maybe. Who knows? Anyway, I'd better get to bed. It's late."

"Sit for a bit if you want. We can watch this together? I wouldn't mind the company. Plus there's popcorn." Charlie picked up a pink plastic bowl from the wooden coffee table and shook it, rustling the contents.

I glanced at the clock as if I had somewhere to be. Only my bed socks and my empty bed called. Fifteen minutes wouldn't hurt. "OK. Sure." I smiled and walked round to the empty couch opposite Charlie's.

The lights from the TV flickered in the darkness sending shadows across the walls. I pointed to the TV and smiled. "You gonna put the sound on?" I slouched back into the brown leather sofa, trying to look relaxed. I felt anything but. The cocktails had taken some of the edge off, but sitting there, in his presence, was something I still wasn't used to. I glanced over at him, his blonde hair falling over one eye as he lay in his favourite white T-shirt and grey joggers. He looked so sexy, my stomach ached for him.

"Oh, yes! Sorry."

"We should watch one of your films," I teased.

"Oh, God, no! I would be mortified to sit here watching them with you."

"It would be just a tad weird, I have to admit. I saw a billboard with your face on it yesterday. That was pretty surreal." I squinted at the screen as a loud explosion caught our attention. Arnold Schwarzenegger was blowing up yet another car that had dared to cross his path.

Charlie put his head in his hands. "I know. It's pretty hard to get used to. Imagine how I feel when I see my huge ugly mug staring back at me! It's like looking at a different person—someone who looks like me, but isn't."

I nodded, grabbing the bowl of popcorn. Charlie muted the film again and rested on his elbows. "But it's, like, you live and work in one world, in Hollywood, and people see you as this shiny, perfect person they see in the movies and on TV. It's my face they're looking at, and people assume I'm that person. But then there's the real me, in my world—just plain old me. And sometimes people don't get that." He paused, staring off into space. "I don't know. I feel like a bit of a let-down in real life. I don't think I'll ever get used to it."

I sat up, my eyes boring into him. "Charlie, you're not a let-down! I can't even believe you would think that. You're an amazing person—talented, kind, thoughtful. You shouldn't think that way about yourself. If you were a let-down, would you be where you are now?" Charlie looked back at me as I placed the bowl of popcorn back on the coffee table. I continued, "I get it. Really I do. I've been here for only a few weeks, looking into your life from behind the spotlight, and it's crazy. I've seen billboard pictures of you. I've seen random people walk up to you to take selfies and say hi. I've seen people taking pictures of you just taking a stroll on the beach or in your car. One of them even managed to get me in shot last week, and it was creepy. Hey, did I tell you some girl from Atlanta sent you her worn black thongs and a dildo this week?" Charlie's lips curved into a smile. "Don't worry. I quickly disposed of them."

Charlie clicked his fingers, feigning disappointment. "Damn it, you've thrown them? I would have taken them with me to bed and slept with them under my pillow." We both giggled. I fell back into the couch, pulling my legs up and hugging them with my arms.

"I've a friend back home," I told him. "We've known each other since we were kids. You could see the actress in her even during our primary school days. She loved drama class and was always first to volunteer for lead roles in the school plays and nativities. She went on to drama school, of course. She works in H&M now as a store manager." Charlie cleared his throat, and I continued. "I guess my point is, you're one in a million—a billion—to make it. Your career is off the scale. You have the most amazing home and a pretty nice life, to be fair, living here in LA with the sunshine and the beaches. I'd be willing to bet there are loads of aspiring actors out there who would trade places with you in a heartbeat."

Charlie laughed. "So, basically, stop moaning, get over yourself, and be grateful."

"I couldn't have said it better myself." We both laughed again.

"Ellie, I love how you speak your mind and tell it like it is. People, especially in this town, need that sometimes, me included. And I know you're right. I completely agree, and believe me, I lie in bed at night staring at the ceiling, amazed that I ever got here and scared at the same time that it's all going to end. Every day I think to myself, how did I ever make it here? I know I'm lucky."

I fidgeted in the chair, fiddling with my leaf stud earing. "But with any job," I said, "you know there will always be things to moan about. I used to moan all the time about my office job in the mortgage department at the bank. Then I'd remind myself, at least I had a job and could work.

And then, I'd moan some more." We both laughed. Charlie combed his hair and pushed it back behind his ears. "Since the day I got here, and every day since," I confided, "I've wondered how I got here too. Just sitting here with you now ... this is an extraordinary world I've found myself in. I honestly don't know how I got here. So I feel pretty lucky too, though it's not on your scale of lucky."

Charlie didn't give anything away as he sat staring at me. I shifted in my seat. Perhaps I had said too much. The mojitos must have gone to my head. Peeling myself off the couch, I stood up, taking in a deep breath. "Anyway, I guess it's time for bed. I'm gonna head up."

"OK, Ellie. Thanks for the chat. Thanks for being honest. I needed it." I nodded and turned to walk out the room, but he stopped me my tracks. "Ellie?" I turned around. Charlie was sitting up off the sofa, his beautiful big blue eyes staring up at me. "You said before that you don't know why you got this job. You know, I saw you walk into the building on the day of the interview. I was sitting by the entrance. I had my sunglasses on—you know, that foolproof disguise of mine?" I smiled, taking a step towards him. "I heard you say your name to the receptionist, and out of all the people that came for an interview that day, you stood out to me. Just something about you. I thought you were really pretty and had the loveliest smile. And I liked your red high heels of course." He laughed, but It wasn't his usual carefree laugh. This was an awkward—even nervous— laugh. Was I making Charlie uncomfortable? Had the blue glow of the TV screen concealed his blushing? "I knew there was something about you. You interested me. You seemed real, unpretentious, and I wanted to get to know you. I wanted someone like you in my life. So I chose you, and I want you to know that."

I felt a lump in my throat, and I didn't know what to say. I inched forward a little more. "Wow, I didn't know. I only hope I haven't disappointed you."

"Quite the opposite."

I just stood there in the darkened room, looking at him as he looked back at me without saying a word. Finally I spoke. "Okay, well, I'd better get to bed. I'll see you in the morning." I didn't give Charlie a chance to respond. I just turned and left the room.

Chapter 20

The buzzing of my alarm woke me from a fretful sleep. I'd struggled, despite being exhausted, to drift off, tossing and turning most of the night. Charlie's admission of how he felt about me swirled in my mind. He thought I was pretty? I had the loveliest smile? And after hearing what he'd told me about choosing me after he saw me on the day of the interview, I was stunned. Charlie Robinson had said those things to me. I didn't know what to think. I couldn't believe he was still testing me. Who would be that cruel? I covered my face with my hands, shaking my head. How much had he drunk last night? Maybe it had been the alcohol talking. I wondered how he'd be today. My eyes were sore. Feeling groggy, I pulled myself up and jumped into the shower before making my way downstairs and into the kitchen. The house was quiet as I turned on the coffee machine and stood watching the water bubbling as it boiled. I wondered what Charlie had in store for me today. It was Sunday, but if there was one thing I'd learnt about this job, there was never a day off.

I felt a vibration from my jeans pocket as my phone bleeped, intruding my thoughts. It was a text from Charlie. Who else? "Hey. Early start for me, and I'm out tonight. I need the jacket I've left on my bed dry-cleaned. I'll be back before 6 to pick it up. And can you call Jo? Let him know I'll be at the club by 11."

Another bleep: "Can you drop me at Franco's Restaurant. It's on Wilshire. I need to be there for 8. And I may need picking up later. I'll call if I do."

Another beep: "Oh, and I'm gonna need a decent bottle of champagne for a friend. It's her birthday. Can you pick that up, put it in one of those bottle gift bags? Thanks, C."

I read the text messages over, sighed, and poured a cup of coffee—black, no sugar.

It was just after ten in the evening when I sat down. It had been a long day, and I was drained. The house was my own after a whirlwind hour of Charlie getting ready for his night out. Jessica, Rose, and Noah had gone home for the evening, and so I found myself sat eating nachos and guacamole alone in the kitchen, streaming classic FM on my laptop.

I headed into the lounge with a glass of Merlot and collapsed onto the soft brown leather sofa. Grabbing the remote, I switched on Netflix, searching for a classic chick flick. *When Harry Met Sally*. Perfect. Sinking back, I hit play. I'd been waiting for this quiet moment all day and intended to savour it.

Ten minutes into the movie, just as Meg Ryan was about to do her cringy fake organism scene, I heard a key in the front door lock. The door opened and then slammed shut. I bolted upright. Silence. Had Jessica or Rose forgotten something? I sat, staring at the door waiting for someone to appear, but after a few seconds, no one came in. I paused the film and stood up, placing my glass of wine on the table. "Jessica?" I called out.

I took a few steps towards the doorway, but before I could get out to the hall, Charlie emerged from the shadows, making me jump. I threw my hand to my mouth and jumped back, startled. "Charlie! Bloody hell, you scared me."

He laughed. "Hey, sorry!" He stood smiling at me, looking casual in black jeans, a white T-shirt, and the grey blazer I'd had dry-cleaned earlier in the day. His hair was falling over his face, and he hadn't shaved today. There was a light stubble growing on his chin. "How's your night going?" he asked, walking past me into the lounge.

"Well, fine, until you scared me half to death. I didn't expect you back till the early hours. What's up?"

He leaned a hand against the doorframe. "I just didn't feel like it tonight. I got there, and—you know—I couldn't be bothered."

"Wasn't it your friend's birthday?"

"Yeah, but I just didn't feel like a club tonight. I wanted to get home."

I stood looking at him, perplexed. Had he been drinking? I couldn't tell.

He walked over to the couch, taking his blazer off, folding it and hanging it over the back of the sofa. "What you watching?" He peered over at the paused screen. "Oh, I love Billy Crystal."

I nodded, walking over to him. "Yeah, it's one of my favourites."

"Can I join you?"

"Sure."

I walked back over to the sofa and sat down. Charlie sat next to me. We sat in silence. Though we'd spoken on the phone several times today, I hadn't seen him since last night. Perhaps he had forgotten what he'd said. He'd definitely had a few drinks. Maybe it had been the alcohol talking. The sound from the TV masked the awkwardness, but he was so close I could feel the heat from his body. I looked at his hands as they rested on his lap. He looked good tonight. But then, he always looked good.

He spoke suddenly "Do you want a drink?" I turned to him, but he was already looking at me staring at my lips and then looking back up to meet my eyes. "Is everything—"

And then he kissed me. And it felt so good that I kissed him back without giving it a second thought. His lips felt soft as he sunk deeper onto mine, his tongue moving into my mouth. Putting his hands on either side of my face, he kissed faster, harder, moving his hands through my hair, smoothing it away from my face. Desperately, he pulled my head closer to his, his stubble scratching my face. I could smell his familiar vanilla aftershave, and I wanted to consume more of it as I found myself completely under his spell. He pulled my hair tighter. Placing his knees on the couch, he leaned over me, pressing his body against mine, sinking me back into the sofa. I could feel him growing against my leg, getting harder. He pushed himself onto me more, making sure I could feel how much he wanted me.

I felt his chest thumping as he pressed his whole body closer against mine, holding my arms above my head and then moving his hands down to my top, then to my pink pyjama bottoms, pulling them down. My breath was fast. Butterflies swirled in my tummy. I couldn't believe this

169

was happening but, as if I was watching a movie, I just let it run. I let his body take over mine, and I let him do whatever he wanted to do. He kissed my stomach, moving down to my thighs. I was tingling, getting hot and wet as he moved his mouth down further. As he held the small of my back with his hands, I convulsed with pleasure as his tongue moved around me, inside me. I wrapped my legs around his shoulders as he went deeper with his tongue. I was dripping all over the sofa as I pressed his head harder against me. The rough stubble on his face tickled me. I grabbed his hair and pulled it, twirling it around my fingers as the pleasure started to build. And then it came. I shut my eyes and cried out, arching my back, and allowing myself to enjoy it. Charlie licked me harder, more ferociously, until I fell silent and opened my eyes. He looked up from in between my legs, his face dripping wet. He smiled, licking his lips.

I smiled back, my breath slowing down. What the hell had just happened? "You taste how I thought you would, Ellie. Divine."

Then he stood up and started to undo his jeans, shaking them off. He peeled off his shirt. He wiped his mouth and lay on me, kissing my lips hard again. I was so wet, and I needed him in me as he pulled my hair back again, this time harder, kissing my neck. And I didn't have to crave it any longer. Within seconds he was in me. I felt tight as he pushed in. I pushed my waist towards him, tightening myself around him, as he moved harder and faster.

I pulled his hand to my mouth and sucked on two fingers inside, biting them lightly as he closed his eyes. Faster and harder. This felt so good. Sweat from his chest dripped onto me. He leaned down and kissed me again. His lips tasted salty as he bit my lip. He opened his eyes and stared straight into mine. I'd never wanted anyone as much.

He started to gasp and moan as he went faster. I tightened myself around him as he pulled at my hair, the sweat from his brow dripping onto my cheeks. He arched his back and groaned before resting his head on my chest.

We lay there, silent. Charlie's breath slowing down as he took hold of my hand and kissed it.

I shut my eyes and kissed his head, I didn't know how to begin processing this. After a few minutes, Charlie opened his eyes and looked up at me, resting his arms on either side of me. I suddenly felt exposed.

Vulnerable. He smiled and lightly kissed my lips. "Wow! I've been thinking about doing that since the day we met."

"What?"

"You didn't see it? The night I asked you to sort the lightbulb, I so desperately wanted you right there on my bed. And the night we went for a drink, at the pool?" He kissed my lips again. "But you were having none of it." I smiled, shaking my head, and thinking back to that night. I put my hands to my face. I honestly had no words for this moment. So there was no point even trying to speak. "Will you stay with me tonight?" His eyes sparkled in a way I hadn't seen before, and he was very sweaty. "Don't think, Ellie. Just say you will."

"You mean with you, in your bed?"

"No, I was thinking I would go in my bed, you can go in my bathtub." He rolled his eyes and we laughed. "Of course, in my bed. I want to be with you all night."

I couldn't hide my smile. I felt like a school girl again, beyond chuffed with myself. "Sure, I'd like that too."

Charlie stood up, his naked body fully in front of me. Unsure of where to put my eyes I sat up and picked my pyjama bottoms up off the floor.

"Leave those there. You won't be needing them." He grabbed my hand and led me up the stairs.

Chapter 21

The shifting in the bed woke me. Charlie sat up, leaning against the grey padded headboard. He looked down at me as I raised my eyes to him and smiled. I smoothed the hair away from my face and wiped my eyes with my fingers. I must have looked a mess—my hair all over the place—though I hadn't cared about that last night. I hadn't cared about anything except him. The thought of him being all over me, on top of me, working my body next to his, made me tingle all over, and I wanted to do it again. The warmth of him next to me … that familiar vanilla scent … his sweat dripping on me. I wanted more of him.

"Morning! How are you feeling?"

I nodded, turning onto my stomach, propped myself up on my elbows, and cleared my croaky throat. "Fine! Good." I smiled up at him.

He stroked my hair, pushing my fringe away from my eyes. I closed them.

"You don't regret last night?" He looked down at me.

"No, not at all. I hope you don't."

"You hope I don't?" He smiled, sweeping his hair back off his face, his broad shoulders leaning towards me. He whispered in my ear, "Let me show you how much I regret last night." He rolled on top of me, rolling me over and holding my arms above my head, his eyes wide, and before I could reply he was kissing my neck. And then he stopped, held my chin with his finger, and looked at me, smiling. "It turns out, I like you a lot more than I'd originally planned. Is that okay?"

I climbed into the hot shower and let the steam envelope me. I could still taste Charlie as I ran my tongue along my lips. I smiled to myself, my mind whirling with thoughts of last night. I didn't want to wash his smell off me as I massaged coconut-scented shampoo into my hair.

After I dried off, I threw myself on the bed. My body was aching with satisfaction as I touched my stomach and shut my eyes. I wanted him on me again, in me, all over me. But would it ever happen again? I was confused. Should I go downstairs as if nothing had happened? Wait for him to make the first move? Would Rose and Jessica get onto it?

I threw on my black jeans, blue denim shirt, and white Converse trainers. Then I dried my hair and pulled it up into a high ponytail. After I applied a slick of mascara I headed downstairs. I guessed I would just have to let Charlie take the lead. I could smell bacon as I walked into the kitchen. Rose was at the hob tossing about a frying pan, and Jessica was sitting with her daily newspaper at the breakfast bar, a cup of steaming black coffee in hand.

I felt my face explode into a flush as both of them looked up at me. Was I being paranoid or was last night written all over my face?

"Morning." Jessica looked over the top of her black rimmed glasses

I tried to sound breezy "Hey, what's happening?"

Jessica observed me from behind her glasses. "Busy morning, Ellie. Charlie has that press thing in an hour, but ..." She nodded over to the French doors leading out to the pool. "We can't get him out the damn pool. Been over to him three times, and he hasn't even looked at me."

I glanced out. Charlie was at one end of the pool, his arms crossed, leaning against the side, looking out over the hills. "Oh," I said.

"You wanna go and speak to him? We need him dressed now and in the car like, fifteen minutes' ago."

Jessica threw her hands up in the air. "I don't know what has gotten into that guy this morning," Jessica continued as she shook her head, looking back down at her newspaper, her long blonde hair brushing against the pages.

"Sure, I'll go and speak to him." I took a deep breath and started to walk towards the French doors. Rose turned to me. "Hey, Ellie?" She nodded towards Jessica.

I turned around. Jessica was placing her glasses on top of her head, and in the other hand she was holding up my pink pyjama bottoms. Her eyes narrowed, and her lips curved into a smile.

Shit.

"You left these in the lounge last night, they were next to the sofa. Charlie left his grey blazer in there too. Let him know I've popped it in the dry-cleaning pile will you?" She walked over to me and stopped within inches, handing them over. My face was burning, and my mouth went dry. I gulped in an attempt to get some words out. Jessica drew her brows together and pouted. She'd definitely had those lips done. "Are you OK, Ellie? You've gone all red faced."

I took the evidence from her. "Fine. Thanks, Jessica."

"No problem. Strange, you stripping off down here before heading to bed last night."

"Oh, I was ... um ... it was just so warm."

She pursed her lips together and forced a smile. "Sure, honey."

I paused, not sure what to say. Jessica placed her glasses back on and sauntered back over to the bar stool. She knew. She bloody knew. It was written all over my face, and I was a terrible liar. I turned and walked outside, letting the cool morning breeze extinguish my burning cheeks. Charlie hadn't heard me come out. He was still perched up against the edge of the pool. Was he thinking about us? Last night? This morning? Maybe he was regretting it now, figuring out a way to get rid of me. Pete would scold me if he knew I was being so negative and down on myself, but let's face it, no one would ever have expected last night to happen, least of all me. I inhaled, preparing myself for whatever was to come. "Hey," I said.

Charlie looked round and smiled, running his fingers through his dripping wet hair. "Hey!"

I smiled back, crouching down next to him at the edge of the pool. "You OK?" I asked, splashing my fingers in the water.

"I'm more than OK. I think you know that."

I shook my head, looking down at my hands, pushing my cuticles in on my thumb. "Charlie, last night, this morning ... I don't know what to think about it. You're my boss. I want you to know I don't make a habit of, well, sleeping with bosses, you know?"

He laughed, touching my leg with his hand. "I'm glad about that."

"So, yeah, I don't know …" I said, unsure what else to say.

Charlie pushed himself away from the side of the pool with his feet, sending ripples of water over his broad, muscular shoulders. I watched him treading the water. He was the most beautiful man I'd ever seen. After a few seconds, he broke the silence. "How do you feel about me, Ellie?"

I was taken aback. None of my boyfriends in the past had been so forthright. I didn't know how to answer.

"It's not a trick question, and I don't do games. Really, how do you feel, about me?"

"I—I like you, of course. We get on well. You're a great boss. I enjoy my job and—"

"Stop. Forget work. Forget me being your boss. Last night, this morning. I think you enjoyed it as much as I did. Am I right?"

I stood up, crossing my arms, my heart beating harder than ever. He swam back over to the edge and placed his arms on the stone pavers, looking up at me, water dripping down his face. I crouched down again next to him. "Ellie, the truth from me is that I like you. A lot. You make me happy, and you make me laugh. You're smart and different and a little bit crazy and awkward and silly. But your smile alone makes my day. I like talking to you. I like spending time with you. And you have no idea how much I want to just pull you into this pool right now and kiss the hell out of you." He reached his hand out and touched my ankle. I felt a shiver up my back, and an urge came over me again. I was completely blown away by his words. He'd made explaining his feelings seem so easy. But everything he'd said—the way he felt—I felt the same. "Let me take you out tonight, or tomorrow. Whenever. Check my diary—when am I free?" We both laughed. "Let's go and have a date. Let me hold your hand and kiss you. And then when we get home, let me let me throw you up against the wall and show you how much I think about you."

I sat staring at him as he ran his hand further up my leg. "I would like that." I cleared my throat but only a whisper came out. I leaned forward and combed his hair back with my fingers. He shut his eyes and let me. My heart felt as if it was going to explode in my chest it was beating so hard. I couldn't ever remember a time I had wanted someone so much, even when Finn and I had first met, no moment had ever felt like the way it did with Charlie right now. His smile, his eyes, the way he talked, the way he laughed. I could stare at him forever. What was happening to me?

He pulled my whole body towards him, pushing his head between my legs. "Whoa, Charlie, wait! You have a press conference in an hour, not to mention the fact that Jessica and Rose are in the kitchen!"

He stopped and looked towards the house. "I know! I know! I'll jump out."

"Okay, you have zero minutes to get ready to go. Now! I'll see you in the car."

He nodded as I untangled my fingers from his hair and stood up. I started to walk back to the kitchen entrance and froze. Jessica stood in the doorway, staring at me. She'd been watching. Forcing a smile, she turned and headed back into the house. I followed. "Jessica, I—"

She gave a dismissive wave of her hand. "It's OK, Ellie. Really none of my business. I'm just the housekeeper. Now, is he getting ready? He should be there already" Her floral perfume wafted across the room as she picked up her black patent handbag and swept out of the room without looking back at me.

"Right, OK." That's all I could muster. I was expecting a lot worse than that. But then I couldn't shake the feeling that she was plotting something. Maybe I was just overthinking it. She was right after all. It was none of her business. Why would she care? Charlie could do what he wanted in his own home, with anyone he wanted.

I stood watching Charlie jump out of the pool and wrap a towel around his waist, his bronzed, toned body glistening in the sunshine. In that very moment, I'd never felt happier.

"So, how was your weekend?" Ross looked up at me from the coffee machine.

I gave a sideways glance over at Charlie, who was staring over at me. I turned away. "Great! Busy."

It was Tuesday morning, and Charlie's weekly meet with Jo at the coffee shop. I felt an awkwardness between Ross and me, or maybe all the awkwardness was just oozing from me. I liked Ross, but after our date on Saturday, it was clear—to me, anyway—that something was missing.

There was no sparkle with him, no real connection, and I hadn't thought about him at all since our date. The guy I couldn't get out of my mind was sitting right behind me, staring in my direction. I didn't know where I stood with him, or what I really meant to him. All I did know was that, every time I thought of him, I wanted to be with him, kissing him, touching him.

My phone bleeped. I pulled it out my bag. A text from Charlie. I looked over. He was chatting away to Jo. "Your pants are bothering me. Can you take them off? C X" I couldn't stop smiling. As I glanced over again, Charlie was still talking.

"Is everything OK between you and him today?" Ross said.

I felt a sudden flush. "Yes. Why?"

"Well, it's just from the moment you walked in here he's been staring over at us. At you. I'm guessing you told him we went out Friday?"

"Yes, of course. But he's been in a funny mood all morning. Don't worry about it." I waved my hand in the air flippantly. I wanted to get off the subject of us. I gave an awkward laugh as I picked up the tray of coffees. "I'll take them over, Ross. You're busy." Before he could answer, I walked over to the table, Charlie glaring at me.

"Ellie, we can't stay long here this morning. I'll be a few minutes then we need to get going."

I frowned, unsure what the sudden urgency was. I walked back over to Ross. "We're leaving soon, so I'm not going to bother getting a drink. I'll head to the car."

"Oh, OK, Ellie. Can I text you? I had a great time Friday. Want to do it again sometime?"

"Oh, I had a great time too, thanks so much,"

"Why do I sense a huge but?" Ross frowned.

I didn't want to lead Ross on. We'd had fun Friday night, but I just wanted to be friends.

"Ross, I told you about Finn, back home. I'm just not ready to start anything else with anyone right now." I lied. I wanted to start everything with Charlie, right now. But I wasn't about to start shouting that about. "I don't want to lead you on or mess you around."

Ross nodded, twirling a tea towel around in his hands. "Can we still be friends?"

"I would love that. I really would! I'll see you next Tuesday?"

"OK, Ellie. Take it easy."

I smiled and walked out the door, Charlie followed a couple of minutes later, and we drove in silence along the highway, Charlie leaning his head back on the leather car seat, sunglasses covering his eyes. He could be pretty damn moody sometimes. "So, what's up?" I asked

"Nothing. I just wasn't in the mood this morning."

I scrunched up my face. "You weren't in the mood for coffee?"

He pulled his glasses off his eyes and sat up straight in the chair, looking right at me. We stopped at some lights, and I looked right back at him. "You and him, what's up there?" he asked.

"Excuse me? Me and who?"

Charlie motioned in the direction of the café, now long down the road.

"DeLatte guy. What's happening there?"

I turned my head to look at him. He was jealous—actually jealous—of me talking to Ross. This was insane. I pulled over and stopped the car, Charlie still looking at me. I leaned into him and kissed him hard, grabbing his face and pushing myself as close to him as I could. I grabbed his hand and placed it at the top of my jeans. He got the message, unfastening my zip. I lifted my bottom up, allowing him inside my jeans and then my knickers. I could feel myself dripping all over him as he went deeper with his fingers and we kissed harder. It felt so good, I needed more.

Charlie pulled his lips away from mine but stayed close to my face, whispering to me. "Let's go home."

"Ellie, I have somewhere I need to go today." Charlie walked over to the kitchen table and sat down next to me.

"OK. Sounds ominous." I stopped typing and took a sip of my black coffee.

He sat down next to me, playing with his thumb ring. "A friend of mine—it's been just over three years now—was involved in a car crash on Pacific Coast Highway. He was in a coma for months, but sadly, he passed on."

"Oh, I'm so sorry." I reached out for his hand and he took mine.

"I want to go and visit the cemetery today. It'll be his birthday tomorrow; he'd be thirty-one."

I looked down at the table, unsure what else to say. "Of course. Whatever you need. What was his name?"

"Johnny Webster, but we all called him Webby." He smiled, clearly remembering him fondly. "He was a film producer, well respected in the industry." I nodded. "At the time, the press got hold of it and it was all over the papers, the news. There was speculation that he'd been drinking and doing drugs before the accident, all the usual press crap. The autopsy after his death came back clear—nothing in his system at all. But there was a lot of hate towards the papers, you know? For trying to damage his hard-earned rep, especially after his awful death. His family members were so angry, so upset, as you can imagine. He was their boy."

I gasped, putting my hand to my mouth. "Jesus, that's awful."

"But, Ellie, the paps, they've been following me a little bit more recently. I think with the publicity for the film, speculation about my love life ..." He smiled and rolled his eyes, squeezing my hand. "I just gotta keep this one under wraps. No press, no photographers. His family wouldn't thank me if his place of rest became a hotspot for journalists."

"No, of course. I understand."

"I'll sneak out incognito and take your car. If they're hanging around they hopefully won't see me slip out. Don't mention it to anyone other than Jessica. She knows too. She was working here when it all happened."

I nodded, and I stroked his head, pushing his hair behind his ears. "Of course, Charlie. You can trust me."

"Thanks." Charlie lifted his hand and placed it on my cheek. I shut my eyes and nestled into it, kissing his palm.

I wanted so much to ask him what this was between us, what we were doing and where it was going, but he looked drained today, and it just wasn't the right time or place. The conversation could wait. It needed to be done over wine later.

"I'm gonna hit the gym now, and I'll leave here at two for the cemetery on Santa Monica Boulevard. I've got my phone if you need me." He leaned forward and kissed my forehead, standing up and sleeking back the hair that had fallen over his face. "I'll see you later."

I nodded, watching him walk out of the kitchen, his blue jeans framing his tight buttocks. I turned back to my laptop and opened it. Time to check some of my own emails and check in with Pete. I hadn't spoken to him for a few days. I wondered where he was and what on earth he was up too.

When I logged into my Hotmail account, I saw a message from Mum marked with a red exclamation mark but no subject. Why was Mum emailing me so urgently? Confused, I clicked into the message: "Ellie, your dad is in hospital. The doctors think he's had a heart attack. I've tried calling your phone, but it's not connecting, and I don't think my texts are getting through to you. I know you'll check this soon. Please call. Love, Mum."

I read the words over and over and looked down at my phone. Nothing. Without hesitation I hit the speed dial.

"Ellie! Thank goodness."

"Mum, I'm so sorry. My phone hasn't rung or pinged at all with a message. What's happening? How's Dad?"

"He's stable. The doctors are keeping him under observation and doing some more tests. They're keeping him in overnight at the very least. I've told him over and over about all the bacon, sausages, and butter, but he wouldn't listen."

Mum was rambling, so I interrupted. "Mum, will he be OK? Have you spoken to him?"

"No, Ellie. He's been out of it since they brought him in this morning. Thank God I was home. I don't want you to worry, but I had to tell you."

I put my head in my hands, tears welling up in my eyes. "Of course, Mum. I'm glad you've told me. I can't believe it. I'll come home. I'll sort a flight tonight, for the morning."

Mum's voice became frantic. "No! No, Ellie. Please! You don't have to. You have your work and stuff there."

"Mum, this is Dad we're talking about. Nothing is more important to me than the two of you. I'm coming home. Charlie will understand. He'll have to do without me for a few days."

"Ellie, really I—"

"Mum, please! I'm coming home. I'd never forgive myself if anything happened to Dad and I wasn't there."

"OK, Ellie. OK. As long as you're sure. But speak with Charlie first and make sure it's OK with him. Let me know. OK?

"OK, Mum. I'll text you later. Keep me updated on Dad. I'm so worried."

"He's in amazing hands here. They're looking after him. Try not to worry too much."

"OK, Mum. Love you. Speak soon."

I sat motionless and felt freezing cold. Goosebumps prickled up on my arms and neck as I wrapped my arms around myself. I didn't want to disturb Charlie now. I'd have to just tell him later. He would understand, and if he didn't … well, he'd have no choice anyway. I was going. If this wasn't good use of personal time, I didn't know what was, but one way or another, I was getting on a flight home. Suddenly I felt panicked. Logging onto the Delta Air Lines website, I searched for London flights. Tomorrow morning from LAX to Gatwick 6.40 a.m. Several clicks, a credit card number, and it was booked. I felt halfway home already as I leaned my elbows on the kitchen table. It would be only for a few days, hopefully, and then I'd be back once Dad was out of hospital, or at least out the woods.

I struggled to get through the rest of the day, sluggishly shopping for a pair of blue Levi jeans Charlie had requested and visiting a posh Hollywood clinic to book in a few months' worth of his weekly acupuncture sessions. I had no motivation, and at six o'clock, feeling drained from the LA sunshine, I closed my laptop, put my car keys in the cupboard, and headed upstairs for a shower.

As the hot soothing water ran over my face, I closed my eyes. My mind was spinning with things I needed to do before leaving tomorrow: pack my bags, call Pete, and of course, break the news to Charlie.

A loud banging noise on my bedroom door broke my thoughts. What the hell? I turned the shower off and grabbed a huge white bath towel, wrapping it around me. Stepping out, I tip-toed over to the bathroom door, leaning out to the bedroom.

"I'm just in the shower. What's up?" I shouted.

Charlie's voice boomed through the door. "Ellie, it's me. I need to speak to you."

Charlie? What could be so urgent? Tip-toeing over to the door and securing my towel around my chest, I opened the door a crack, peering out. "Hey, what's up? I'm just—"

"*What* is this?" Charlie's face was full of anger and drained of all colour. He thrust a yellow stickie note covered in glittery pink writing into my face.

"Erm … I'm gonna go out on a limb here and say a stickie note?"

"Don't joke, Ellie. I just found this on your desk in your office."

I opened the door further and reached for the note. "Two p.m. Santa Monica Cemetery. Josh at National Enquirer."

Charlie crossed his arms, his face still contorted in anger. "It's funny, you know. Despite the fact that I used a different car today and saw no one follow me from the house, I get to the cemetery and two guys on motorbikes are there, cameras in my face. I assumed they just got lucky until I got back here. When I came looking for you, I found this!" He didn't look as he spat out his words.

I shook my head. "Charlie, this isn't my note. I didn't write this. Why do you think I would do that?"

"Why, Ellie? Because I've lived and worked in this town long enough to know that rarely can you ever trust anyone. I thought you were different. I thought you and I—" His voice cracked. Then he stopped and just looked at me, the corners of his eyes glistening.

I stepped forward to touch his arm, but he backed away. "Charlie, I'm telling you, I didn't write this. I promise you. Think about it. What possible reason could I have for doing this to you?"

Charlie just stood, shaking his head, looking down at the floor. After a few seconds, he took a deep breath, his chest heaving in anger. He looked at me, straight in the eyes. "Money. That's what you're here for, isn't it? It's amazing how money motivates people to do all sorts of things. How much did they pay you for the tip?"

I didn't know what to say. I couldn't speak. Warm tears started to slide down my cheeks. I wiped them away. How could he think for a second that I'd do something like tip off paparazzi? I snapped back into fighting mode. I wasn't going to let this happen. "It has to be Jessica. You told me she's the only other person who knew. She's wanted me gone since the moment I stepped in here." Charlie shook his head, his eyes wide. I continued, "On my very first day here, I overheard her talking to someone on the phone. She was saying I wouldn't last. Something to do with—I don't know—someone else getting this job. She never wanted me here, Charlie."

"Jess has only ever spoke highly of you, Ellie. She's worked with me for years now. I know I can trust her."

"Just as much as you know you can't trust me?"

Silence. Charlie looked down at his hand, continuing to twist round his thumb ring.

"You know, Charlie, I know we haven't really had chance to talk about things—what has been happening here between us—but I want you to know that I really like you. I'd never breach your confidence in this way—in any way." I gulped back tears as he continued to stare down at his hands. "If you don't believe me about Jessica, that's fine. I understand. You believe what you want, but I think she's a game player, and it has to have been her, because I know for damn certain it wasn't me."

But he still couldn't bring himself to look at me. My heart ached at the thought of him thinking I'd do this to him. It ached even more because he still stood here and didn't seem to believe a word I was saying. I watched him for a few seconds, my upset quickly turning to anger. "I have a flight booked for London tomorrow," I told him. "I was going to tell you this evening. My dad has taken ill. He's in hospital, so I need to go and be with him." Charlie finally looked up at me. "I was going to just take some personal days and be back by next week, but I think since there's clearly no trust between us, it's time for me to move on anyway. I'll leave first thing in the morning." Suddenly conscious that I was standing there covered only by a towel, I felt vulnerable and just wanted him to go. He'd said everything he needed to, and so had I.

"I'm sorry, about your dad. I hope he's okay."

I couldn't bring myself to reply. I bit my lip and closed my eyes. I wanted him to say, "Don't resign, I believe you. Jessica can be a bitch, I'll go sack her." But instead he simply said, "Okay. I'll leave you to get dressed." And he turned and walked away. I closed the door behind him, leaning my back against it to steady myself as tears streamed down my face.

Just like that, he was gone.

Charlie had left the house straight after our argument, and he hadn't returned all night. I'd lain awake thinking about him, about us, and about how he'd changed my life without even trying. I wanted to tell him how much he meant to me, how I couldn't imagine what my life would be like right now if he wasn't in it. I'd spent most of the night writing out text messages to him, my finger hovering over the send button every time but never pressing it. I realized after my fifth draft that no words I could put in a message would ever say how I felt, so I didn't text at all.

In the morning, I woke, dressed, grabbed my cases, and didn't look behind me as I closed the door to my room. I wandered past Jessica's office. The door stood ajar. A buzzing made me stop in my tracks outside the door, and I peered in. Jessica's work phone was lying next to her computer keyboard. She must have forgotten it yesterday. I walked over to it and looked at the illuminated screen: "Ross Wadey."

I stared at his name flashing across the screen, and then it stopped buzzing and his name vanished. Ross? From the coffee shop? Why was he ringing Jessica? I wasn't aware they even knew each other. I'd mentioned Jessica to Ross on our date Friday, and he'd never given any indication that he knew her. My mind was whirling, and a wave of nausea engulfed me. All I wanted to do now was get on that plane and get home.

Chapter 22

It had been four months since I had left LA. My dad was on the mend, and I was back in London, having found a flat share with a girl called Amaya. She had a habit of leaving her tweezers, nail clippers, and emery boards all over the house, which annoyed the hell out of me, but other than that, she was okay. Christmas and the New Year had come and gone—a blur of family meals, mulled wine, mince pies, and the Hanson Christmas album. I'd found a job as an admin assistant for the council, which was pretty dire to say the least, and Pete had returned home a month ago and was working as a waiter at a bar in Clapham. He'd travelled all the way up to Redwood National Park in the end and met a guy called Justin, a park ranger. It was only a fling, of course, and he hadn't spoken to him since returning home, though I think they were still friends on Facebook. Carla and I had stayed friends, and she was in a current state of euphoria after Tom proposed "quite unexpectedly" on the London Eye on Christmas Eve. Finn, I believed, was now shacked up with his now girlfriend slash homewrecking slut Louise. I hope she kept in mind the saying, a leopard never changes its spots.

I'd had an email, shortly after I left, from Rose, enquiring after my dad and wishing me all the best. She never mentioned Charlie, and I never heard from her after that. I heard nothing from Jessica.

Several days after arriving home, I texted Ross. His name flashing up on Jessica's work phone had played on my mind the whole way home. I didn't want either him or Jessica knowing I'd seen the call, so I sent a breezy 'How are you?' text message, just to open up some sort of conversation in the hope of getting to the bottom of the call at some point, but he never replied back.

And, of course, I thought about Charlie. A lot. It was impossible not to. When other relationships had come to an end and I wanted to forget, I'd just delete the person from my Facebook and Instagram and told my friends to never mention his name again. But with Charlie, the reminders were constant. I saw posters of his face stuck to the sides of bus stops, and I'd watched him being interviewed on *The Graham Norton Show*. He was in London, promoting his new film. It was difficult living with the daily torture of him on my mind when I knew deep down that he probably hadn't thought much about me at all.

I tortured myself about not saying enough to him before I left, not confronting him and convincing him I'd had nothing to do with the press showing up at the cemetery. I wished I had fought harder for him, told him how much I was going to miss him and how much I was starting to believe that he was possibly the greatest thing that had ever happened to me. But I hadn't. I had slipped away under the veil of an LA sunrise and hadn't looked back.

He'd text me once, a few days after I left LA, asking about my dad. I'd kept it brief, to the point, and hadn't heard from him since.

The premier for this new film had shown in the West End a few days back, and for a fleeting moment I'd considered going. I thought about standing with the crowds at the red carpet, hoping I might catch his eye, but I decided not to. It would just have looked really desperate and sad, and besides, what would I say to him anyway? On the phone to Pete, a couple of nights ago, he'd asked me if I missed Charlie. Tears had streamed down my cheeks. I think Pete could tell; he was quiet, easier on me than usual. And as the tears fell I'd told him I did miss him, I missed talking to him, but I knew I had to move on, because missing him was pointless. And I had resigned myself to doing just that, moving on. How, I wasn't so sure, but I knew I had too. It had been months now and, like a dream, it had ended, more abruptly than I'd ever wanted. Unlike a dream though, the memories of it were yet to fade.

And so here I was in my new office, filing papers, photocopying memos, filling in spreadsheets, and contemplating what the hell I was going to do with this life of mine. I looked down at my red heels, still going strong. I'd promised myself that, on my return home, I'd treat myself to a new pair, but I couldn't bring myself to do it. Charlie had told me he liked these shoes. He'd seen me in them. I couldn't let them go.

My new colleagues had asked me about my road trip—how long I'd been in California, what LA was like, and had I managed to get any selfies with celebrities? I told them no. Who would believe me? And, besides, the fewer people who knew, the more sacred my memories were.

My phone dinged. It was a text from Pete: "Hey. Happy birthday. What are we doing tonight? Drinks?"

I replied: "Family meal this year, Pete. I'm low on cash, and Mum feels sorry for me. We're going to that posh new Italian restaurant in the West End. Been booked for weeks."

"Okay, babe. Cocktails soon. Call me."

I put my phone down and leaned my head on my palm. I checked the clock; it was time to pack up. Throwing on my beige trench coat and navy scarf, I headed out into the cold London evening.

I was standing outside Viva, a new Italian restaurant in the West End. My fingers were turning blue from the cold, and I tucked them under my arms for warmth and danced on the spot to stop my toes from dropping off. Damn it, Mother! You could be on time for my bloody birthday, at least, I scolded to myself. I wasn't particularly bothered about the meal tonight. Sure, it was my birthday, but I wasn't in a celebratory mood. I'd thought about Charlie a lot today. During lunch in the canteen, two girls I didn't know from another department sat next to me. One of them was reading a copy of *Celebrity* magazine. I'd side-glanced the front page, and there he was, his beautiful, familiar face all over the front cover. I hadn't been able to see the storyline. I'd turned away without getting that far, despite my intrigue.

So, I just didn't want a fuss tonight. If Mum hadn't involved herself in today's plans, I'd be at home now, drinking a large glass of red wine in a hot bath. Instead, here I was, freezing, waiting for Mum and Dad to arrive.

Throngs of people whizzed past me, all probably off to have a hot bath and a glass of red while I was tucking myself into the entrance of the restaurant, hunching my shoulders in, and trying to shield myself from the biting wind. The restaurant didn't look open. The black velvet curtains were closed on both the windows and the door. Oh, God, I hoped Mum hadn't got the venue wrong. I had wondered when she told me a table was booked here, how she'd managed it at such short notice. It was on London's hottest list of new restaurants to visit and places to be seen in. I'd been dying to go for weeks and had tried booking in with Carla to celebrate her engagement news, but I'd given up.

After a few more minutes, I decided to call them. I fished my phone out of my pocket, and pulled my brown leather glove off to dial. Mum's perky voice answered. "Hey, honey."

"Mum? Can you hear me? Where are you? I don't think this place is even open!"

My phone crackled, and I could barely hear anything. Mum's voice was nearly drowned out by the bustling traffic behind me. "Darling, it's open. It might not look it, but it is. Just knock on the door. Somebody will be there."

I looked up, brushing strands of hair out my face. "Okay. Are you sure? Where are you, anyway?"

"Close. Just go inside and get seated." Mum clicked off the call before I had time to reply. Great, Mum! Short and sweet.

I looked up again and, with in trepidation, walked up the steps towards the door. A bell was lit up at the side, so I pushed it. Tucking my chin into my scarf for warmth, I stood waiting. Finally, I heard the click of a key in the door and it opened. A blonde-haired, tall, pretty girl wearing black trousers, black shirt, and a white apron answered the door. She looked at me and smiled warmly.

"Hi, sorry," I said, shivering. "Are you open tonight? My mum said she booked a meal here for six o'clock?"

"What name was it?"

"Gibson. The booking should be under Anna Gibson. My name's Ellie."

"Sure. Come in. We do have a table under that name." The girl smiled and stepped to the side, holding the door open for me as I hurried in, fixing my fringe back into position with my fingers. I could have done with applying a fresh dab of lippy, but I'd wait till Mum arrived. As I stood in the reception, the place seemed empty—quiet. It certainly was not the bustling restaurant I'd expected given that no one could get a reservation in this place for months.

"Can I take your coat?"

"Erm … yeah. Thanks." I pulled off my trench and handed it to her. I hoped I wasn't underdressed. I'd hurriedly changed at work in the loo before leaving, pulling on my black shift dress and tights, and keeping my red heels on for ease.

Please, go through. Your table's ready for you."

I threw my black tote bag over my shoulder and pulled the black velvet curtain that hung across the door. A glow of candles illuminated every corner of the room, creating shadows that danced around as the flames burned. They were on every table. They covered the bar. Then I froze. All the tables were empty—all of them except one. Tucked away in the far right corner of the room, there he stood. Charlie. And he was looking at me, his eyes wide. He looked nervous, shifting around and smoothing the front of his floral-print shirt.

I gasped and put my hand to my mouth as I stared at him. My knees felt wobbly as I reached out and took hold of the nearest chair for stability. He walked out of the shadowy corner, a small smile curving on his perfect, soft lips. He cleared his throat. "Ellie, happy birthday. You look beautiful." I felt a warm tear trickle down my face. I still couldn't move my mouth to speak. I tried, but my lips were stuck together. Charlie continued to step closer to me until he was inches away. "I've missed you so much, Ellie. You really have no idea." He gulped and licked his lips. I hadn't seen him nervous like this before. "I think about you so much—all the time actually. First thing in the morning and just before I go to sleep at night. In the middle of the day. I can't stop thinking about you, and I don't want too."

He stepped even closer. I could feel his body heat now, see his chest moving up and down. And I could smell that lovely familiar vanilla scent. He reached out and placed his hand on my cheek, wiping away the tears under my eyes with his thumb. "I had to see you. And I need you to know that I'm so sorry."

"I don't … I don't … I thought you'd have forgotten all about me." I tried but failed to muster any kind of sentence.

He combed his hair back, tucking it behind his ears. His eyes bored into me as a smile formed across his face. "You're not that easy to forget."

189

He stepped closer, placing his hands on my waist. My insides felt warm and tingly. He was all I wanted too. "I need you, Ellie. Not many people have taken my breath away, but you seem to do it without even trying to, and that scares the hell out of me." He placed his finger under my chin and lightly pushed my head up, forcing my eyes to his. "The way I behaved, the way I acted over the Jessica thing was ... disgusting." He wiped more tears from my cheeks, "Not believing you about her and that coffee shop guy, and then just letting you leave—I should never have let you go like that. But then the days went on, and it got harder to call. But I just felt so miserable. I just had to come and find you."

My eyes widened, and a twinge of anger rose in me. What did he just say? Not believing me about Jessica and the coffee shop guy? I stood up straight and took a deep breath "What do you mean, Jessica and Ross? What has Ross got to do with anything?"

Charlies eyes widened, and he shook his head. "You didn't know?"

"Know what?"

"Jessica and Ross had been dating for about eighteen months. He has some ailing acting career, obviously, being stuck at the coffee shop, and she wanted to help him. She thought that, if she got him a job working for me, he'd be meeting people in the industry. He'd make contacts that could boost his career."

I was speechless. I stood staring at Charlie's face, my heart about to explode in my chest. How could Ross do that? Why ask me to go out on a date? Why show any interest in me at all? It seemed either Charlie knew me too well or it was written all over my face what I was thinking, as he continued, "I didn't tell Jessica I was advertising for a new PA when Sarah left. I had some contacts, and I wanted someone fresh and new, someone who wasn't blinded by LA and—I dunno—was just a breath of fresh air. So, I put my feelers out, and you came along." He smiled, running his hand down my hair, making my entire body ache for him. "When Jessica found out, she was furious. She had been hoping to put Ross forward for the job when the time came, but obviously, she never got the chance. She wanted you out and him in."

I was in complete shock, my mind spinning. Had I passed out on the street? Had someone at work slipped drugs into my coffee this afternoon, and I was having some kind of delayed hallucinations? "How do you know all this? What about the press tip off?" I managed to splutter

"After you left, I went into her office to speak to her about everything, to confront her. She'd left her laptop on. There was an open email on the screen from Ross. I recognized the name because you'd mentioned it to me. Basically he was telling her that, now you were gone, she needed to put his name forward. He said that the cemetery tip-off had been a great idea. He signed the email off 'See you later, Juicy.' Charlie rolled his eyes and stuck out his tongue. "I confronted her. She confessed, and I fired her immediately. I believe Ross got her a job at DeLatte."

I couldn't help but let out a laugh. And then, there we both were, laughing. Charlie clasped my hands in his. "What I have with you, Ellie, I don't want with anyone else. I just want you. Today, tomorrow, next week, next year. Forever. I want all my LA sunset's to be with you."

More tears fell down my cheeks, and then he kissed me, fast and hard, holding the sides of my head, pushing my face closer to his. I felt so much in that moment, and yet I barely knew how I felt at all. After a few moments I pulled away. "I assume my mum and dad were in on all this?" I smiled, pointing towards the glowing candles covering the bar.

Charlie gazed down at my lips, running his index finger along them. "Oh, totally in on it. Your mum was amazing on the phone. I went around to their house a few days ago, and we planned tonight. Your mum is very good at plotting." He chuckled.

I panicked. "You went around to my house? You've met my mum?"

He nodded, placing a hand on my shoulder. "So, I take it you'll stay for dinner?" He gestured over at the table. "Oh, and I brought you this." He winked at me and reached into his pocket. "I think I owe you one of these?" He raised his eyebrows. "Perhaps you could have it for desert?" A smiled beamed across his face as I stared down at the Cadbury Freddo he held before me. A lump formed in my throat, and I gulped it down, tears welling in the corners of my eyes. "It's you, Ellie. You make me happy, and that's it."

I nodded, searching for words but finding none. I opened my mouth expecting at least some formation of a sentence to come out. Nothing. I needed a glass of wine, or vodka, or anything with alcohol content right now. I couldn't believe this was happening, and I could barely catch my breath let along think straight. All I knew in that moment was that he was *the one*. I guess I'd known from the start, but then, who wouldn't fancy the pants off her rich, talented, gorgeous, international movie star boss? It had become more than that, though. I'd just been blinded to it by my own lack of self-worth. But, hey, as it turned out, Charlie Robinson did actually like me—*like me!*

Charlie took my hand and escorted me over to the table. I sat down, my legs feeling weak. He sat opposite me and reached down, pulling a good-size box from underneath the table. "For you."

"What?" My eye glistened, and I was suddenly grateful for the soft candlelight. My face must have looked a state after all the tears.

"It's your birthday, right?" He looked down at the box. "Now, open."

I picked it up and shook it, but heard nothing. Charlie tutted, hurrying me up. I pulled the end of the pink ribbon that was wrapped around the centre and tied in a neat bow. I pulled off the lid and peeled back white tissue paper. There they were—a pair of brand-new, red, Christian Louboutin high-heel shoes. The exact ones I'd seen whilst we had been window shopping on Rodeo Drive. I sat staring at them, running my fingers down their side. "Oh my, Charlie. They're beautiful! I love them!"

"I love your old red heels, Ellie, but I figured a new chapter needs a new pair, right?"

"A new chapter?"

"Ellie, you and me—us together in LA. That's all I want. Please come back. I need you. I got so used to you being around. Everything feels weird without you."

"I ... erm ... Charlie, wow. This is a lot to—"

He looked at me, reached across the table, and put a finger to my mouth. "This life—the celebrity, the fame—it's not real. None of it is. It's like a dream, and every day I feel as if I'm waiting for it to all implode. When you came into my life, that changed. Things felt real again. I felt normal and alive for the first time in a long time. Everything will be the same as before, only maybe you could move bedrooms."

I dipped my eyebrows, confused, "Move bedrooms?"

"Well, as long as you don't mind sleeping on the right. You see, I have to have the left side." He smiled, running his hand down my cheek. Before I could say anything, Charlie took hold of my black dress and pulled me towards him, leaning his face towards mine, looking down at my lips again. "Will you come?" He smiled.

It really was a no brainer, and I knew it. I nodded and smiled back at him, running my fingers through his soft hair. Pulling away, I looked down at the Louboutin's. Kicking off my old red heels, I slipped into these new, shiny ones. "Well?" I smiled, extending my leg mischievously so he could see. "What do you think?"

"Wow!" He smiled back, taking my hand, and squeezing it tight. "They really suit you."

I looked down at them all shiny and glossy, no scuffs or scrapes. They had no stories to tell. Yet.

Charlie stroked my head, and I looked up. "You look deep in thought. What are you thinking?"

I placed my hand on his cheek and leaned over, kissing him on the forehead. "Just admiring these amazing shoes and wondering where they'll take me."

Charlie smiled. "Anywhere, as long as I'm with you."

About The Author

Laura Mullally now lives in Crosby after spending seven years in her beloved university city of Leeds where she studied for degrees in law and journalism. A former editorial assistant, journalist, and creative writer for a women's lifestyle magazine, she is now mummy to two young boys. When Laura isn't acting as referee to her children, she can be found daydreaming; writing about sex, love, and relationships; blogging about random life events; and eating fajitas. Follow her on Instagram @laura_e_mullally and visit www.lauraemullally.co.uk for her latest blogs. Just a Girl in LA is Laura's debut chick–lit novel.

Lightning Source UK Ltd.
Milton Keynes UK
UKHW01f1956241018
331132UK00001B/11/P